THE SPELLBINDER'S GIFT

The

SPELLBINDER'S

GIFT

OG MANDINO

Fawcett Columbine
New York

A Fawcett Columbine Book
Published by The Ballantine Publishing Group

Copyright © 1995 by Og Mandino

All rights reserved under International and Pan-American Copyright
Conventions. Published in the United States by The Ballantine
Publishing Group, a division of Random House, Inc., New York, and
simultaneously in Canada by Random House of Canada Limited,
Toronto.

http://www.randomhouse.com/BB/

Library of Congress Catalog Card Number: 98-96733

ISBN: 0-449-00577-1

Manufactured in the United States of America

Cover design by Michelle T. Gengaro
Cover painting by Bryant Eastman
Cover printed in USA

First Ballantine Books Hardcover Edition: January 1995
First Ballantine Books Mass Market Edition: December 1995
First Ballantine Books Trade Paperback Edition: August 1996

10 9 8 7 6 5 4 3 2 1

For my grandson . . .

WILLIAM AUGUSTINE MANDINO

. . . another spellbinder

He ended, and a kind of spell
Upon the silent listeners fell,
His solemn manner and his words
Had touched the deep, mysterious chords,
That vibrate in each human breast alike.

—Henry Wadsworth Longfellow,
Tales of a Wayside Inn

THE SPELLBINDER'S GIFT

It was truly a relaxed and wonderful evening and well past midnight when Mary and I finally arrived home. As we were both undressing, I asked, "Well, hon, what do you think of the man?"

"Bart, he is as impressive and charming up close as he was onstage. There is a special magnetism, an aura of some sort surrounding him that's hard to explain. He's appealing and attractive and yet I caught myself lowering my voice a couple of times when I was answering his questions . . . as a child might do when speaking to an adult who represented authority. And with that handsome face and beard he reminds me of some of the figures in religious paintings in our church when I was little. He almost looks as if he should be wearing a halo."

"Mary, what are you saying?"

"Bart, I'm sorry. I'm not really sure what I'm saying."

I

🌿

For more than forty years, going back to the days when our young American boys were dying in a mysterious far-off place called Korea, *Guys and Dolls* was lighting up Broadway, cold sufferers were learning to love antihistamines, Dr. Kinsey had most of us talking openly about sex, Brando was flexing his muscles in *A Streetcar Named Desire* and we finally ended our Berlin airlift after almost 300,000 flights of mercy . . . for four memorable decades from a small second-story walk-up office not far from Times Square I had served as exclusive booking agent to many of the most famous and dynamic motivational speakers in the entire world.

And then, with little advance warning, the entire roster of uniquely talented individuals that I had developed and represented loyally for so long vanished in less than twelve months! My three oldest professional speakers decided that they had endured enough plane flights and hotel meals and would stay home, live off their fat mutual-fund portfolios and write their memoirs, another developed cancer of the throat, one had a stroke that paralyzed most of his left side and my four most in-demand and highest-priced speakers, all close friends of mine, passed away.

On that very sad and bleak February morning, after I had served as a pallbearer for the fourth time in seven months, I returned to my office both physically and emotionally drained, gathered up my most important papers and files and locked the door behind me, quite certain that my business and professional future had been buried along with the bodies of my friends. I was sixty-eight.

A year or so later I was still trying very hard to enjoy many of the activities that retirees who can afford it are usually doing to fill their hours and enrich their so-called golden years. Mary and I joined a Manhattan bridge club, played golf often during the week and even began attending movie matinees. My helpmate, bless her heart, did more than her share to make retirement for us the heaven on earth that so many dream about. We traveled, we competed in slot-machine tournaments in Reno and Atlantic City, fished in the blue waters off Bermuda, ate peanuts and drank beer at Yankee Stadium, visited scores of museums and cheered the horses and greyhounds in Florida. Still, every now and then, in the midst of some activity, the lady I had been married to for almost forty-five years would cup my face in the palms of her two tiny hands, cock her pretty head and say, "You're bored, aren't you?"

I would always shake my head, kiss her on the forehead and reply, "Of course not," but after two people have loved each other as long as we have, there's not much sense in trying to lie.

There was one activity from my pre-retirement days that I still continued to enjoy and probably needed a lot more since becoming an unemployed "couch potato," and that was jogging. Every morning at dawn, for more than thirty years, if I was in town and the weather allowed, I had always followed the same routine. I'd ease myself out of bed slowly so that I wouldn't wake Mary, climb into one of my many warm-up suits, consume a large glass of orange juice, cereal and a single cup of black coffee, make certain I had my keys, and close the door quietly as I departed.

Central Park was only two blocks west of our Park Avenue apartment, and through the years I had probably jogged over every foot of its roads, trails and pathways, alternating my course from time to time so that I could enjoy all the park's wonders from Cleopatra's Needle to Strawberry Fields, from the Belvedere Castle to Shakespeare Garden, from the Pond to the Great Lawn.

The park's eight-hundred-plus acres, set in the heart of the busiest and noisiest metropolis in the western world, was my heaven on earth, my constant refuge from all the pressures and cares of life and business. Through the years I habitually timed my run to last just about an hour, usually emerging through the Artists' Gate on Central Park South. I would then turn left, pass through the cool green area known as Grand Army Plaza, cross Fifth Avenue when the traffic lights allowed and continue jogging east for two more blocks before turning north on Park Avenue, gradually slowing my pace until I finally arrived at our apartment building.

Mary was always up by the time I returned each morning, and after I had showered, shaved and dressed, I would spend some time with her and another cup of coffee before either walking or taking a cab to my office on West 44th Street, depending on what was on tap for the day. Since my retirement, however, I would usually just crawl into my blue jeans and a sports shirt, after showering and shaving, and together we would watch the morning news and "The Today Show." However, being a witness to the world in action on television while I sat passively on my duff and struggled with the morning's crossword puzzle in *The New York Times* was just not my idea of what I should be doing with the rest of my days.

And then, on a hot and humid early June morning that I shall never forget, my life suddenly took an unexpected turn. I'm not sure I understand what happened, even to this day. Someone once wrote that God seems to play chess with all of us from time to time. He will make moves on our personal chessboard of life and then sit back, waiting to see if we react, how we react and what our next move will be, if any.

"Use it while you have it!"

"Tomorrow is found only on the calendars of fools!"

"It's a lot later than you think!"

He was wearing a tattered red T-shirt and stained blue jeans and his right foot, sockless, protruded through a gash in a grimy, untied sneaker. Unkempt hair, dingy gray and streaked with yellow, hung limply below his shoulders. His large and sallow face was etched with heavy dark lines, scarred by several blotches of purple and his deep-set eyes, beneath bushy eyebrows, were bloodshot, but the voice screeching out those old maxims was strong and commanding. He was sitting in a wheelchair, dangerously close to the curb, on the sidewalk at the corner of Central Park South and Fifth Avenue. As I completed my morning in the park, saluted the statue of Simón Bolívar and turned east toward Fifth Avenue on my way home, he was directly in my path.

Central Park South and Fifth is a busy corner at almost any hour of the day, but in this morning rush period the wide sidewalk is always packed with a constant parade of briefcase-carrying men and women, one horde heading north and the other south, eyes staring straight ahead as if they were all hypnotized, pushing and scurrying as they dodge the smaller group of marchers moving east and west . . . all heading toward their own little high-rise cubicles of aggravation. As I drew closer to the noisy and frightening apparition coiled in his wheelchair, I could see that he was holding a small, tattered Bible in one gnarled fist and a metal cup in the other. To my amazement, instead of working the commuter crowd in general, he was directing his hoarse words and gestures solely toward me! Hesitantly I slowed my pace as I approached and he raised his old Bible, aimed it right at my head as if it were a weapon and shouted, "Do it now! You! You! Do it now!"

He was directly in my path as I neared my Fifth Avenue crosswalk, waving toward me—me!—with both hands and yelling, "You! You must pick them today! You must pick them today! They will not be blooming tomorrow! They never bloom tomorrow!" Even a few sophisticated commuters were now beginning to slow down and stare.

Rarely in my life, if ever, have I tried to avoid confrontations of any sort. But this time, instead of jogging right past my frightening wheelchair counselor and continuing on home for a nice warm shower, I made a sudden right turn when I was only a few yards in front of him, dashed across Central Park

South with the rushing crowd and the green light and continued jogging south on Fifth Avenue's busy sidewalk—away
from the wheelchair—and very definitely in the opposite direction from my northern route home!

I still don't understand what happened that morning but
not once . . . not once in the next twenty minutes or so, as I
continued on my southerly course, did I ask myself what the
hell I was doing or where I thought I was going or why I wasn't
heading north instead of south. I just kept jogging along, at my
usual Central Park pace, like some sort of puppet on a string as
I moved past old familiar landmarks—Bergdorf Goodman,
Tiffany, I. Miller, the Crown Building, Corning Glass, the
brownstone Fifth Avenue Presbyterian Church, Gucci's, the
St. Regis Hotel, Cartier and St. Patrick's Cathedral.

Finally I slowed to a walk, turned right off Fifth Avenue and
continued west for another two blocks before pausing, slightly
out of breath, to lean against a rusted green lightpost and stare
down West 44th Street's final dingy block before it emptied
into Times Square, the very same block where for four decades
I had presided over one of the most profitable and unusual talent agencies in the world.

Now I was walking west toward Times Square . . . slowly,
very slowly, almost as if I were in some sort of trance. I moved
carefully over the cracked, pitted and litter-strewn sidewalk
while two snarling lanes of one-way traffic, primarily cabs and
delivery trucks spewing foul-smelling fumes, roared eastward
as their drivers leaned on their horns, causing crescendoes of
frightening sound to wash off the old stone buildings in wave
after wave.

Halfway down the street I stopped and turned until I was

facing the buildings on the north side of the noisy and busy thoroughfare. I stared to my left at the old, mottled Savoy marquee and the nearby garish yellow sign above a store entrance proclaiming DELI GROCERY in bright red. Then there was the Cafe Un Deux Trois with its red awning extending almost to the curb, a cozy spot where I had dined with clients, talent and friends for so many years. Adjoining the restaurant was the famed Belasco Theatre, built by David Belasco in 1907 and the home of countless unforgettable theater experiences for New Yorkers and the world through so many seasons. Now signs that were stained and dingy hung from the once-famous marquee of the empty theater, suggesting that one should see a Broadway show "just for the fun of it" and displaying a telephone number that one could call for tickets. How sad.

At last I finally summoned up enough courage to turn my head to the left of the Belasco and ran my eyes along the second-story row of windows until I saw it—and to me it looked as good as any painting of Raphael's! On one window, in gold leaf and still very legible, were the words MOTIVATORS UNLIMITED and painted on the window to its right was my name, also in caps, BART MANNING, PRES. On the bottom portion of the first window was an air conditioner but on the other, also in gold leaf, were the words WE MOVE THE WORLD WITH THE SPOKEN WORD!

As I stared up at those grimy pieces of framed glass, the center of my universe for so long, my vision suddenly became very blurred. I reached down, tapped the pocket of my warm-up suit, felt my keys and, as soon as there was a break in the traffic, dashed across the street to an old, familiar street-level metal door almost blocked from view by carts and dollies filled with boxes of all sizes that were being unloaded from a huge red truck. I inserted my key in the lock, as I had done thousands of times over the years, and leaned against the gray, pitted frame until it finally swung inward with a loud groan. I raced up the stairway.

What was I doing here? Instead of being in our cozy apartment, watching the morning news with Mary, why had I returned, after more than a year, to the familiar scene of so much personal success and triumph when I had already closed the book on those chapters of my life? Had God made a move on *my* chessboard of life this morning? That screaming ruffian in his wheelchair, blocking my path home, was he part of some design far beyond my comprehension that had forced me to turn south on Fifth Avenue? Or was I now about to open the door to my old office simply because I had been dreaming about a return visit for many months? Had God really made a move? If so, I had absolutely no idea what I was supposed to do about it.

Still . . . it was *my* move now.

II

I sat tensely in the familiar old and worn leather-covered armchair for probably thirty minutes, trying to gather my thoughts, elbows resting on the faded burgundy blotter that lay on top of my dusty, oversized oak desk. Finally, after taking several deep breaths, I reached hesitantly for the telephone, removed the receiver from its cradle and hit the buttons seven times.

Almost instantly I heard Mary's voice . . . "Hello?"

"Hi . . . it's me."

Her words were clipped and icy. "Where are you?"

"I'm . . . I'm at the old office, sitting at that great desk you gave me for my fortieth birthday. Remember? Seems like only yesterday to me."

Now I could hear her sobbing. "What the hell is wrong with you, Bart? When did we start having secrets from each other? Why didn't you tell me, for God's sake, that you weren't planning to come right home today, as you always do, after your run in the park? I've been sitting here, next to the phone, saying every prayer I know and imagining all sorts of terrible things like you in some emergency room with a heart attack. And where are you . . . ?"

"I told you. I'm at the office."

"Wrong. You don't have an office anymore, dear husband of mine. Don't you remember? You retired more than a year ago! You're even collecting social security checks now!"

I hesitated. "Sorry, hon. Truly I am. I don't know what to say. Mary, you must believe me, I don't understand what happened and I surer than hell had no secret plans to come here today, either when I left our apartment or after I finished my jog through the park. And I have no idea what I'm supposed to be doing here . . . now that I'm here. Maybe I'm starting to lose it. Maybe the old mind is finally beginning to go."

"Bart, please . . . this is your wife you're talking to. I've watched that wonderful head of yours function efficiently and successfully for a lot of years. It seemed to be running just fine yesterday when you were going over our investments with me. Now—now you'd like me to believe that you have no explanation for how or why you traveled all the way . . . all the way . . . from Central Park to West Forty-fourth . . . seventeen or eighteen blocks in the opposite direction from our apartment . . . when all the time you had been planning to come directly home to me? Please! Please, dear, why not just face the truth and admit it . . . at least to me and especially to yourself . . . that it was only a question of time before you returned to your old bookie joint?"

"Bookie joint" was Mary's pet name for my office, since it was from there, she had very proudly told a *Variety* reporter long ago, that her husband booked the thoroughbreds of the speaking profession and then cashed in on their winning performances, day after day, year after year.

"Husband of mine," Mary continued in a voice one would use to talk to a young child, "how long has it been since you functioned in your professional capacity as an agent from that address?"

"Fourteen months or so, I guess."

"How about the rent? You're not occupying those quarters any longer but are we still paying the rent on that place?"

"Mary," I sighed, feeling very foolish, "you know we are. You write all the checks, as you've always done. You also know that we've still got several large file cabinets here, filled with a lot of important papers. There are also six or seven big cardboard cartons of memorabilia piled up in these two rooms plus scores of framed autographed photos that we just haven't been able to find a decent place to store."

"Face it, Bart. We never looked very long or very hard. There are plenty of safe self-storage facilities right here in Manhattan and you know it. Now, how about that telephone you're holding right now to talk with me. Must be quite dusty. Until today, it probably hasn't been used since you closed up shop but we're still sending a check to NYNEX every month, are we not?"

"Yes."

"Is that big brass lamp still sitting on your desk?"

"It's still here. On the far left corner, where it's always been."

I turned the switch above its base and the room was filled with warm light.

"Is the lamp turned on, Bart?"

"It is now. Working fine."

"It had better be, because I've also been mailing Con Edison a check every month without fail, just as you asked me to do. Remember?"

I was beginning to feel very foolish and could think of nothing to say that made any sense at all. My old celebrity friends, in their framed black-and-white glossy photographs autographed to me, hanging on the wall to the left of my desk, all seemed to be staring directly at me now. Spencer Tracy, Adlai Stevenson, Napoleon Hill, Billy Rose, Edward R. Murrow, Dale Carnegie, Judy Garland, Norman Vincent Peale, Elsa Maxwell, Elmer Wheeler, Cavett Robert, Fritz Kreisler, Bruce Barton, Jackie Gleason—all of them, even those who were smiling, appeared to be watching me with anxiety and, yes, a touch of pity.

"Bart?" Her voice had lost its frigid edge.

"Yes, hon?"

"Since your retirement, have you been in that office even once before today?"

"I swear . . . I have not."

I heard the sigh. "I believe you. Now, please listen to me. Stay there awhile and do some thinking . . . about yourself . . . about us . . . about the rest of your life. Maybe you should even think about getting back into the business. I've always felt that you were one of those Type A characters who are never happy unless they're always busy. Look at our old friend, Dr. Peale. He's over ninety but he's still flying around the country giving several speeches a month and loving it. Remember at that cocktail party for the governor, when I asked Norman why he was still making speeches and writing books instead of just taking life easy with Ruth at their farm? He said that although he had written more than forty books on positive thinking he was afraid there were still a few negative thinkers in our country and so he still had some unfinished work. If he can continue doing his thing at his age, I guess there's no reason, if you really want to, why you can't return to your desk with that phone to your ear and do exactly what you've done so well in the past—book speakers."

"Have you forgotten, lady? I don't have any speakers to book anymore. They're all either retired or dead."

"Okay, so sit back now, at that old desk, relax and think about all of this. Bart, you know you haven't been happy, really happy, since the day you locked that office door and walked away. You're not the same man I was married to for so long, and I'd kinda like to have that other guy back in my life, even if it means that he has to unretire himself and get back in the rat race, so that I have to start sharing him again with the gang at Lindy's. If that will make you happy, then I'll be happy!"

"And the talent? Where do I find them?"

"As if you don't know. First, there's the Rostrum Professionals of America that you only helped to found and organize more than thirty years ago. I'm pretty sure I sent a check, at your request, renewing your membership for another year, back in the spring. It seems to me that we received a large packet from them, in just the last week or so, announcing details of this year's annual convention in Washington, D.C., sometime in July, as I recall. Wow, I can just imagine the mob scenes if word ever got around, at the convention, that the legendary agent, Bart Manning, was present and scouting for new talent to handle. I'd have to come with you just to be your bodyguard, like the old days, remember?"

"Sure do. We had a lot of fun, didn't we? Of course, finding a few new good speakers, as damn hard as that would be, is only half the challenge. Then we'd have to keep them happy by booking enough speaking dates for each of them which would take a lot of time and effort and I haven't even talked with a single meeting planner for over a year. I don't know. . . ."

"Bart, just a phone call from you to let them know you're back in business would be all that is necessary, and you know it."

"I love you!"

"And I love you. Call me before you leave the office, please."

"You mean . . . like always?"

"Like always."

I placed the receiver gently back on its cradle, rose and walked over to the grimy window looking out on West Forty-fourth. How many times, through the years, had I stood in this same spot, turning some business problem over in my mind, while every conceivable classification of human being and vehicle passed before me on the street below?

I turned, stepped around two large, bulging cartons and walked into the smaller anteroom. There were still several sheets of correspondence in Grace Samuels's in-basket, but her typewriter was covered and all her pens and pencils were neatly stacked in a square holder along with pads of Post-it notes. "Amazing Grace" I had always called her, and I meant it; no one had ever been blessed with a better assistant. She had gone through a terrible time trying to deal with my closing the agency. I wondered how she was doing. Last time we had spoken, on the telephone months ago, she said that she still hadn't taken on a steady job since she hadn't been able to find another boss like me. Bless her.

I walked around to the back of Grace's desk and stood close to what she had always referred to as our altar, photographs of many of the speakers we had represented in the past. At the very center, in a heavy gold frame, was a sepia-tinted print of Eric Champion, that very special man who had changed my life forever. After playing very tiny roles in several Broadway productions following my discharge from the service in 1945, I had finally grown tired of going hungry and landed a regular-paying job in the offices of the William Morris Agency. In a little more than a year they had managed to knock enough of the rough edges off me so that I was beginning to deal with some of the lower-priced talent they represented as well as meeting planners and nightclub and hotel people.

I worked long hours and loved it. One evening, late in January, I didn't leave the office until well past nine. The Manhattan streets were almost deserted. Two blocks from my apartment, as I turned a corner, I came upon the first mugging of my life. The victim was sprawled on the snowy sidewalk, his body twisting violently as his assailant lifted some sort of club over his head. I leapt on the attacker's back without even thinking. We rolled over together twice on the cold cement before he pulled loose from my grasp, struggled to his feet and ran off into the darkness. Within minutes two police cruisers appeared and the well-dressed man with white hair who had been attacked had staggered to his feet, his head bleeding badly as he repeated to me, again and again, "Thank you, son . . . thank you, son. God bless you! God bless you! Thank you."

I gave the police my name and address and after I assured them that I needed no medical attention I continued on my way home, hearing the sound of an approaching ambulance's siren just as I unlocked my front apartment door.

I had almost forgotten the incident until, two weeks later, the phone rang in my little office. When I lifted the receiver I heard Lucy, our receptionist, telling me that a Mr. Eric Champion wanted to see me. I started to tell her that I didn't know any Eric Champion, when she said, "He says you saved his life on the streets a couple of weeks ago. Did you, Bart?"

"I don't know. Okay, send him on back."

Tom Murphy, another William Morris trainee sharing the small room with me, leaned across his desk, frowning, and asked, "Did I hear you say Eric Champion?"

I nodded.

"Don't you know who Eric Champion is, Bart?"

"Never heard of him."

Tom shook his head in mock wonder at my ignorance. "Eric Champion, my friend, is probably one of the highest, if not the highest-paid inspirational and motivational speaker—I guess that's what they're called—in the country! Here at William Morris we concentrate most of our efforts on show business talent, but I've got to tell you, I heard this man speak at the Garden about a year ago and the place was packed. He's really something! In his own category of talent I'll bet he's as big as Crosby and Gable are in theirs."

My impeccably dressed visitor was already removing his light cashmere overcoat and dark blue scarf as he walked down the narrow hall toward me, smiling and extending his hand as he drew closer. "The police were kind enough to give me your address, Mr. Manning, and then your landlady told me where you worked. I just wanted to stop by and thank you again for what you did to save me from that monster. Who knows, I may even owe you my life."

"I'm just glad I happened to come along when I did, sir. You feeling okay, now?"

"Feel just fine, thank you. Had to cancel only one speaking engagement, and the nasty gash on my head is already starting to heal. Tell me, how long have you been with William Morris?"

"A little more than a year. I've still got an awful lot to learn."

"Do you enjoy the work?"

"Hate all the paper shuffling and the legal stuff involved with contracts and bookings but I love working with clients and trying to provide them with the right kind of talent for their club or hotel or convention. I think I'm going to be good at it if the big boys are patient with me."

"I'm sure they will be. They're a fine organization. They've wanted to handle my bookings for the past several years, but my wife, Martha, was attending to all of that and she was very competent. Plus she loved the work. She . . . she . . . passed away just before Christmas."

"I'm so sorry, sir."

He raised his hand and closed his eyes. "Life goes on. I just had to thank you, once again, for being my savior in the dark.

I'll never forget it. Let's have dinner some night. It's the very least I can do to show my gratitude. I'll call you. What's your home phone number?"

Our first dinner together led to another and then another and gradually we grew very close. Although Eric Champion was old enough to be my father, our friendship ripened until one day, at lunch, he made me a proposal that I could not possibly refuse. He offered to lend me ten thousand dollars, interest free, that I could pay back whenever I was able. With that money I was to open my own agency, hire a secretary, rent office space and commence booking all of his speeches. He would give me his files and contracts involving future engagements already booked as well as names of his clients and companies to whom he had given speeches in the past. I was to receive a commission of twenty-five percent of his speaking fee for every booking I made which, forty years ago, in his special case, was a rare but very firm $2,000. News that I was handling Mr. Champion, he assured me, would spread quickly throughout the speakers "grapevine" and I undoubtedly would receive many queries from other speakers regarding the possibility of my representing them. Also, as time passed, Champion promised, most of the corporate meeting planners would learn of his new affiliation and they would be contacting me, especially after we did a mailing to everyone. We sealed our deal with a handshake. And so, Motivators Unlimited, in the spring of 1950, opened its tiny and unpretentious office on West 44th Street and the rest, as they are always saying, is history.

Now I reached for Eric's framed photograph, hanging on the wall of many, and placed the palm of my hand gently and lovingly over his classic face. For more than thirty wonderful years I had booked every one of his speeches until, one night, in the summer of 1984, he dropped dead at the lectern while waving and bowing to a standing ovation, after addressing a large group of Texas cattle ranchers in a Dallas hotel ball-room. "How appropriate," sobbed Grace when we received the shocking news, "that he should die in Texas with his boots on."

During my career as an agent, I never booked an actor, ac-tress, singer, musician or music group of any sort. I purposely limited myself to handling only that rare and hard-to-define individual who had both the reputation and the rare ability to deliver a stirring motivational and inspirational speech filled with facts and observations from his or her own personal expe-riences. My clients were usually leading corporations who were seeking that special person to give their annual conven-tion some additional luster as well as a much-needed positive and dynamic keynote address.

Through the years, many talented individuals joined Eric and myself to make Motivators Unlimited the great success that it was, and most of their photos surrounded his on that special wall of personalities that Grace had assembled so lov-ingly. Now I stepped back, turning slowly—and sadly—away from the photographs. What a great group! We had all worked so well together and had been, in the best of terms, family.

I lowered myself into the chair behind Grace's desk, picked up her phone and dialed her number.

"Hello . . ."

"Hello, you . . ."

"Bart? Bart, is that you?"

"Guilty. Guess where I am, lady."

"Oh, God, I don't know. Are you all right?"

"I'm fine . . . and I'm sitting in your seat . . . at your desk."

"In our office?" she screamed.

"You've got it."

"Bart, what are you up to?"

"How would you like to come back to work?"

There was no reply. I waited. Finally I said, "Grace, are you still there?"

"I'm here. My heart was beating too damn fast to talk. Are you serious? I don't know what's happening and I don't care, but I'd love to come back. When shall I start?"

"Still have your office key?"

"Of course."

"Okay . . . your first two assignments—"

"Shoot!"

"Please call one of your old friends at our esteemed Rostrum Professionals of America, find out when and where their national convention is and make all the necessary reservations for both Mary and myself, convention, hotel and airlines, okay?"

"No problem. I've done that a few times in my career. What else?"

"See if you can get someone to come in here to vacuum, clean and dust and make sure they do the windows. They're filthy."

"How soon?"

Grace's apartment was on West 48th Street, only ten minutes away, and so I knew it wouldn't take her very long to get into action. "As soon as possible," I replied.

"And when do you want me to start?"

"You already have, special lady."

After hanging up I just sat there, the fingers of both hands clasped tightly together, my eyes closed. I was trembling.

"Well, God," I whispered softly, "now it's your move again."

III

Our scowling long-haired cabbie in his frayed New York Mets T-shirt with his impossible-to-pronounce Middle Eastern name glaring back at us from his dash-mounted taxi permit did his valiant best to get us to LaGuardia Airport in time for our flight despite a steady downpour that made Manhattan's morning traffic just a little better than complete gridlock. We had just ten minutes to spare when we finally boarded Delta's Flight 1747 which took off exactly at 9:30 A.M. bound for Washington's National Airport. As always, Mary held my hand tightly during takeoff, and at last we were on our way to the nation's capital to attend our first speakers convention in five years.

"The Omni Shoreham Hotel," she sighed wistfully as the plane continued its noisy climb. "Remember that special night there, Bart?"

I squeezed her hand gently. "It already seems like a lifetime ago, hon . . . 1961 . . . JFK's inaugural ball."

Mary nodded and smiled. "There we were, all decked out in tux and evening gown, nervously pacing the lobby of our Georgetown hotel along with several other couples who were also heading for the ball while the wet snow, already more than a foot deep outside, continued to fall. The hotel people kept telling us that Washington was almost completely shut down and all streets were impassable."

"What made it so frustrating," I said, "was that the Omni was only a mile or so away and yet we might as well have been in Los Angeles for all the good it did us."

"I remember, hon, that after a couple of agonizing hours of waiting in vain for a cab we finally went back upstairs to our room and I just threw myself on the bed and began to bawl in frustration."

"That didn't last long. After ten minutes or so, as I remember, you jumped up, wiped away your tears, went into the bathroom, freshened up . . . and then we went back down to the lobby to try again, reasoning that if we were being marooned by the snow, everyone else trying to get to the inaugural ball probably had the same problem."

"Bart, I'll never forget the look on your face when, after another hour or so of agonized waiting, the hotel doorman finally produced a cab for us and two other couples and the driver announced, when we were all crowded into the taxi, that the fare would be a hundred dollars per couple—for the one-mile trip. You never even uttered a single cuss word, just nodded. I was very proud of you."

"I was very proud of me, too. But it was all worth it. When we finally checked our coats and edged our way into that packed Regency Ballroom and saw our new president and his pretty young wife on the ballroom floor alone, dancing cheek to cheek . . ."

". . . to 'Moon River.' "

"You even remember the song they were playing?"

She nodded proudly. "It was very precious and at least for a few hours we were all a tiny part of Camelot. What a nice memory."

I reached down for my scuffed and scratched old Samsonite black leather attaché case which I had placed, for takeoff, under the seat in front of me.

"The great Bart Manning's security blanket," Mary sighed as she reached over and caressed the faded leather.

"You're right. I would never go on a business trip or even to a meeting in the city without this."

"And where has it been stashed for the past year or so?"

"It was in the old office, on the floor next to my desk, right where I had left it, waiting to be lured out of retirement."

"Maybe it's time you got yourself a nice new one if you plan to do much traveling."

"Never! When the time comes, you can bury us together."

I snapped open the frayed case and removed several colorful promotional pieces that Grace had just received from our speakers association headquarters in Denver. They described in glowing terms the seemingly endless array of lectures, celebrity speakers and mini-seminars covering just about every facet of the speaking profession that would be available to attendees during the coming four full days and evenings of the thirty-fourth annual convention of the Rostrum Professionals of America. I handed a program to Mary, who frowned and asked, "What am I supposed to do with this?"

"Help me . . . as you did in the old days. Look through the pages and see if any of the speakers making presentations might be someone I'd be interested in. You know my kind of speaker. I don't care about any of the so-called experts on sales or time management or negotiating or whatever is hot this season. I want someone with charisma and that special ability to walk up to a lectern and grab any audience until you can't hear a sound in the auditorium except breathing."

"Okay, fella, I'll do it providing you don't ask me to sit with you and rate these people in person like we used to do. I'm planning to get in some real serious shopping once we're settled in at the Omni. Was hoping that a few of our old friends would be at the convention and while you guys attended the sessions, we gals could take off and spend some of your money like the old days."

After a silent quarter hour or so, Mary closed her convention program and tapped me on the knee with it. "Bart, this speakers contest sounds intriguing," she said as she removed a single glossy white sheet from her program. "Something new and different. Can't remember anything like this ever being done before. Years ago the board wouldn't even have considered such a thing."

I had no idea what she was talking about. "Mary, I don't have that page in my program. Tell me about it."

"You've heard of Ted & Margaret's Frozen Dinners?"

"Of course."

"What's their motto?"

I didn't even hesitate. "Our taste speaks for itself."

"Very good. Well, apparently the people in Ted & Margaret's marketing department decided that, after so many

years, just having the taste of their product speak for itself was
not enough in a field that now has so much competition. Bor-
rowing from the theme of their motto, they have now decided
to have the finest orator they can find speak for the taste of
their product, so they are conducting a contest at our convention to discover a World Champion of the Lectern. Apparently each of our association's six regions has been having
elimination contests to select the finest speaker in its area,
and these six will compete on the last afternoon of our convention to determine the nation's best. Each speech is to be
no more than twenty minutes in length on any subject, and
the contestants will be judged by a panel of impartial judges
selected by the corporation."

"And the winner gets . . . ?"

"A large trophy proclaiming that he or she is this year's
World Champion of the Lectern as well as being honored by
the association. He or she, of course, will also have a picnic
preparing new promotion material informing prospective
clients that now they can book the very best, if they wish.
There's more. . . ."

"Shoot!"

"The winner will get to do nine television commercials, one
of which will be run nationally each month, beginning in September. For that little chore, he or she will receive a quarter of
a million dollars. What seems so strange to me, Bart," she said
as she handed me the speakers contest page, "is that all six finalists are completely unfamiliar to me. And to think that
there was a time when we knew just about everyone by name
who attended these conventions. I guess we've been away too
long. Take a look."

I studied the photos and brief bios of each contestant and shook my head. "Me too. Don't recognize anyone. But then, let's face it, we don't even recognize very many of the new breed of movie stars. Our old world keeps changing, but it doesn't seem to be making much progress. I can't believe that we'll never again see a Sears catalogue or that IBM is struggling or that we still have ten million unemployed or that we're now giving out condoms in high school. No wonder the Eric Champions we knew have all left us for a better place."

Mary patted my knee gently. "Tell you what, husband. On Thursday I won't shop. We'll go to the speakers contest together to check out those six finalists. Okay?"

"You've got a date!"

IV

Through the years, Eric Champion and several of my other speakers had frequently addressed large groups and conventions at the Omni Shoreham in our nation's capital. Few hotels could even come close to matching the lustrous history of the sixty-year-old Omni, and as Mary and I sat in our suite, after a light room-service lunch, we both became fascinated by the material about the hotel's past that we found on one of the large mahogany dressers. I'm sure that we acted and sounded more like awe-struck teenagers than experienced travelers as we began to share interesting tidbits of information about the hotel with each other.

"Did you know, hon," Mary exclaimed, "that every president since Franklin Roosevelt has held an inaugural ball here?"

"I did, because I remember Eric telling me that the hotel had offered to build a special ramp and elevator for Mr. Roosevelt and his wheelchair after he won his first election and that established a precedent that's still alive. Inaugural balls are now always held in the Omni's Regency Ballroom. I can still remember how excited Eric was when he was booked by the American Medical Association to speak in that same room for the first time."

"Bart, listen to this," she said, waving one of the hotel's brochures. "Would you believe that Harry Truman had private poker games here while he was president? Room D-106 was the favorite room where he and his buddies gathered while his limousine was always parked just outside to rush him back to the Oval Office."

"Anything there about the old Blue Room?"

"I was just coming to it. Says that in the thirties and forties the hotel's Blue Room featured some of the greatest figures in the entertainment world. Now hear this! For the grand opening of the hotel in 1930, Rudy Vallee, then America's number-one crooner, flew from New York with his orchestra for the opening in an Amelia Earhart tri-motored airplane! Judy Garland, Maurice Chevalier, Marlene Dietrich, Frank Sinatra, Lena Horne and Bob Hope were only a few of the big names who performed in that room, and there is a large metal plaque just outside its doors with the name of every celebrity who has appeared there, from Edie Adams to Gretchen Wyler. It says here that the hotel liked to boast that the Blue Room converted Washington from 'a strictly Saturday-night town' to a place where dinner, dancing and entertainment were popular every evening. I've got to see that room, Bart!"

"I think it's just a large and lovely meeting room now."

"I don't care. I still want to see it. Apparently when JFK was courting Jacqueline he often took her there. What a very special hotel, Bart! I can't believe that in all our travels you and I have never come here before. Listen to this . . . just before his inaugural in January 1969, President Nixon made history here by introducing his entire cabinet-to-be over network television at a special dinner in the Diplomat Room."

"Mary, I can remember Eric telling me that during World War II, this hotel bought the entire stock of a Scottish distillery, so they were one of the few hotels serving good scotch all during the war. He also told me that they converted their riding stable into a chicken ranch, as a wartime measure, and raised thousands of broilers for their restaurants' tables."

"Tell you what, Bart. Why don't you muscle our suitcases up onto our bed and I'll unpack us as usual while you go down to the lobby and sign us in for the convention or whatever you have to do. Knowing you, I'm pretty sure you'll get involved in lots of chats and hugs as you renew old friendships—but just do me a favor and don't forget you've got a wife up here. Come back and get me in an hour or so and we can explore the hotel together. That will still give us enough time to get out of these jeans and into something a little more presentable for the opening reception."

"When does that start?"

Mary opened her convention program. "Six-thirty. There's nothing scheduled after that tonight. Maybe we'll get lucky and find some of the old gang. Then we can all go to the Garden Court, which sounds pretty nice, have a couple of drinks and tell lies like the old days."

Registration took only a few minutes. Beneath a bright yellow banner reading ROSTRUM PROFESSIONALS OF AMERICA, several young ladies were sitting primly, pen in hand, waiting. I approached the petite blonde who was sitting behind the G to M sign. She gave me her best welcome smile and I said, "Manning . . . Bart Manning and Mary."

The young lady said, "Welcome to the convention, sir." Then she ran her tiny hand down her list and nodded, handing me a registration form and ballpoint pen.

When I returned the completed registration blank to her, she handed me two large white envelopes. "One for you and one for Mrs. Manning, sir. In there you'll find all the convention information you'll need to have a great four days. And here are the nameplates for both you and your wife."

As she was handing me the small red-bordered, rectangular metal plates, she did a double take, frowned and looked closer at the top plate. Beneath my name was a brief line that read MEMBER, 35 YEARS.

"You've belonged to this association for thirty-five years, sir? Good Lord!"

I grinned and nodded. "Yes, I helped to found it. Long before you were born. How many do we have registered, do you know?"

"I heard someone say nearly two thousand."

"Well, counting our spouses, there were only twenty-six of us at the Brown Palace in Denver for our very first convention. I guess we've grown quite a bit since then, wouldn't you say?"

The young lady, now very wide-eyed, merely nodded.

"Bart! Bart Manning, is it really you? God, what a surprise!"

I spun around, recognized him immediately, inhaled deeply and yelled, "Jay! Old buddy! Boy is it good to see you!"

No handshake. Just big hugs. Then I stepped back to take a

good look at Jay Bridges, an old friend whom I hadn't seen since my last convention. Standing very erect in his tailored houndstooth checked suit with vest, every silver hair perfectly in place crowning a well-tanned and almost wrinkle-free face, he looked exactly as I remembered him.

"You old rascal," I shouted. "How marvelous you look and still so damn young. Have you discovered the fountain of youth? Wow!"

He cocked his head. "You were always a great BS man, Bart Manning. You look wonderful, too, but what the hell are you doing here? I heard you were out of the business."

"I was. Retired over a year ago but I'm thinking seriously about unretiring myself. I've missed all the aggravation and pressure. Just here to do a little talent scouting. How about you? Still charming all those ladies at their cosmetic conventions?"

He nodded. "I'm still having too much fun to quit, Bart. We've sure missed you, guy. How long has it been?"

"Haven't come for five years. Last one was in Vegas, remember?"

"I certainly do. You and I stayed up all night at Caesars, playing baccarat. We both lost a ton. And how's Mary?"

"Great. She's up in our room putting our clothes away. Jay, she'll be so damn happy to see you. You were always one of her favorite people and she kept hoping and hoping that someday I'd be your agent. How's Phyllis?"

"I buried Phyllis three years ago, Bart. Cancer."

"Jay, I'm so sorry. I didn't—"

He nodded and asked, "Hey, have you got any time?"

"Mary gave me an hour of freedom."

He took my arm. "Well, let's you and I go have a drink for old time's sake."

During most of the sixties, Jay Bridges was one of the most popular news commentators on New York radio before he wrote a hilariously funny book called *Sex à La Carte* which was considered shocking back then but wouldn't even raise an eyebrow on anyone's maiden aunt today. When the book, to everyone's surprise including the publisher's, became a smash best seller, Jay began accepting invitations to speak, first solely around Manhattan but soon before groups across the country. He made so much money that he finally resigned his position at the radio station. He never wrote another book but did manage to earn a fine living for himself for the past thirty years or so, delivering a hilarious talk on the never completely understood and constantly changing relationship between men and women. Early in his speaking career I had tried to sign him, especially after hearing him almost destroy a huge audience at the Hotel Astor, but the very capable agent who had represented him in his radio years continued to handle him very well during his platform career.

Now Jay guided me through the crowded main lobby, down into the Garden Court Lounge, through the lounge and veranda to the outside terrace with its tables shaded by huge umbrellas. We sat and ordered drinks. Behind us, hidden by a tall, trimmed hedge, we could hear laughter, shouts and splashes from the hotel's two swimming pools while the repeating sound of tennis balls crashing against racquets came from tennis courts to our left.

Jay pointed to the center of the cement courtyard area, where a large section, almost in the shape of a full circle, was painted green. "There was a huge hydraulic stage right there, Bart, and it was used to raise those big bands of our era such as Dorsey and Miller and Goodman so that the musicians played above the crowds while they danced under the stars. Funny isn't it, that with all this hotel has to offer, we have never before held our convention here."

I nodded but said nothing, feeling completely relaxed and at peace with the world as I took a long sip from my Cutty and water. Jay pushed his glass to the side, cocked his head in my direction and said, "Now tell me the truth, my dear friend of so many years, what the hell are you doing here?"

Knowing he would not be satisfied with any flip, hasty, off-the-cuff reply, I slowly and painfully gave Jay all the details of how my agency, in a year or so, lost every one of its speakers to death or retirement.

"There was no one left to book, Jay, and since I hadn't devoted the time and effort I should have in constantly looking for new talent to replace any loss of the old boys, I paid the price. Agency out of business. As you know, I had even stopped coming to our own convention to scout out the new bunch."

He smiled. "So what happened? Mary get tired of telling you that while she married you for better or worse she didn't marry you for twenty-four hours a day under her feet? What are you doing back here? God knows you don't need the money."

I was so tempted to tell him about that strange chain of events that had commenced with my morning jog out of Central Park and my confrontation with that curious, ranting soul in his wheelchair, followed by my mysterious jog south to my old office, but I couldn't, I just couldn't.

"Jay, I'm too young and healthy to waste my years sitting at home with a television remote control in my hand while I flip from "Barnaby Jones" reruns to "Days of Our Lives." I always felt that I was contributing a little something to make our world a better place when I sent a great motivational speaker to address a group and help them to realize what great miracles they really are. You were the only person I ever tried to sign up who didn't do a motivational or inspirational talk."

"You know, Bart," Jay sighed, studying the palms of his hands, "I've often wondered how well you and I would have done together."

"We'd have made a lot of money, that's for sure. Who's doing your bookings now?"

"No change. Sam Rapkin and I have now been together for almost thirty-two years. He's a good man."

I nodded in agreement. "Well, I'm going to scout around for four days and see what I can find. Wouldn't mind if I just handled one or two speakers to start over with and then I'd see how it went."

Three times, as Jay and I sat and talked, we were interrupted by individuals wearing convention badges. Each time they knew my name and who I was and said they just wanted to say hello and were honored to meet me. Feeling a little embarrassed, I would then introduce the stranger to Jay.

"Bart," Jay said, "you are without a doubt the most admired and respected agent in this whole damn business. Almost every speaker at this convention would just about kill to be handled by you. Your problem is going to be keeping a low enough profile so that you can check the performers out without being constantly hounded. How would you like me to run interference for you during the next couple of days?"

"I'd love it. Are you sure you want to do it?"

"It'd be a ball and I'd get to spend all that precious time with the great and famous Bart Manning."

I grasped his hand. "Thank you!"

He grinned. "Don't thank me. I'll be having all the fun just being your guide and bodyguard. However, there's one thing I must tell you right now, even before the hunt begins."

"What's that?"

"I don't believe you will discover anyone here as good as your Eric Champion."

I nodded and shook his hand again. "See you at the opening reception tonight, buddy?"

He shrugged his shoulders. "Where else would I go . . . without Phyllis?"

V

Still sitting at the linen-covered circular table on which room service had delivered our breakfast, I was turning the pages of USA Today when Mary said softly, "It was so good to see Jay and the Johnsons and the Robertsons and Anna Hubbard. Didn't realize how much I've missed the old gang."

I folded the newspaper and tossed it on the sofa. "Did you have fun?"

"I think it was a wonderful reception. Everyone, especially the hotel people, did a great job and I'm so glad it was held in the Blue Room. The three harpists scattered around the room added a nice touch, and from what I saw I do believe you really will need a bodyguard while you're here. I kept expecting someone to kneel and kiss your ring."

"Hon, I love what you said as we walked into the Blue Room last night."

"What?"

"You said, 'Bart, I'm positive we're in the right place. As

usual, whenever speakers gather, everyone is talking and no one is listening.' So, tell me, are you all set to go shopping?"

"I am. Meeting Anna Hubbard and Kay Johnson in the lobby at ten o'clock. Susie Robertson promised John she'd keep him company today, but she said she'd love to join us tomorrow if we have any money left. We told her not to worry, that we both had three Gold cards. How about you? All set?"

"I think so. Jay said he'd phone me here at nine-fifteen to find out where I'd meet him in time for the first session at nine-thirty. There are three programs going on every ninety minutes throughout the day, and Jay is letting me call my shots so that I can check out the speakers with the most potential."

"So, have you made your choice for the first one?"

I shook my head, stood, walked over to the dresser where all the convention material was stacked and picked up a program. Back at the table I opened the pages of the first day's activities and handed it to Mary. "Here, you get me started on the right foot. Maybe one of the first three caught your eye when you were looking them over on our flight. Where should I go first?"

"Okay, 'How to Tame a Tough Audience.' Presenter is John Felch from Michigan. He's one of those I did check off, come to think of it, when we were on the plane. According to this copy, his specialty is motivational and keynote speeches. He's making his presentation in the Hampton Room," she said, returning the program to me just as the phone began ringing. It was Jay.

"Break a leg!" Mary shouted as I headed for the door.

Dressed in a bright scarlet silk shirt above contrasting black pants and shoes, Jay was standing next to the Hampton Room's entrance, smiling, nodding and shaking hands as if he were running for office. "What made you select this one?" he asked, pointing toward the crowded open doorway with his thumb.

"I didn't. Mary picked it for me."

He nodded understandingly, turned and entered the noisy room. I followed. We had just located two empty seats, when a voice over the speaker system greeted us. "Ladies and gentlemen, the Rostrum Professionals of America is very proud to introduce to you one of its most dynamic and sought-after speakers discussing a subject on which he has had much experience through the years, How to Tame a Tough Audience. Let's have a warm welcome for John Felch!"

He was forty or so, and he leapt agilely up the steps of the podium despite a large, rotund body, smiling and waving until he was standing at the lectern. He pushed back a lock of black hair that had fallen across his forehead, suddenly ceased smiling and assumed an unmistakable look of fear. He cleared his throat several times and said hoarsely, "I'm very, very honored to appear before all of you today, but I realize that I am violating one of the three pieces of immortal advice given to us by Winston Churchill, who said, 'Never try to walk up a wall that's leaning towards you. Never try to kiss a person who is leaning away from you. And never speak to a group that knows more about a subject than you do.' "

Felch waited for the laughter to subside, nodding his head in appreciation, and then said, "Before I came in here this morning, my wife, Amy, and I had breakfast in that lovely Garden Court Lounge. As we were leaving she had some wise advice for me, when she saw that I was a little nervous about appearing before so many other speakers. She said, 'John, don't try to be charming, witty or intellectual. Just be yourself.'

"How do we tame a tough audience? I'll share several methods that have worked well for me, through the years, but please don't ever forget that magic ingredient called laughter as one of the best possible potions for the grouchiest grouch. Friendship and laughter are closely related. Make friends with that sea of frowning faces sitting in front of you by getting them to smile, and you will probably come away from any speech a success."

Felch paused, looking up toward the ceiling, then chuckled as if he had just thought of something funny and said, "During a recent expedition into the wildest part of darkest Africa, a group of explorers came upon a village of primitive savages. In an attempt to make friends of this very, very tough audience watching the explorers' every move, the leader of the group tried to tell the natives what it was like in the civilized, outside world.

" 'Out there,' he said, 'we love our fellow men.'

"To this the natives gave a ringing cry of 'Huzzanga!'

"Encouraged by this, the explorer continued. 'We treat others as we would want them to treat us!'

" 'Huzzanga!' exclaimed the natives with much enthusiasm.

" 'We are peaceful!' said the explorer.

" 'Huzzanga!' cried the natives.

"With a tear running down his cheek, the explorer ended

his fine speech. 'We come to you as friends, as brothers. So trust us. Open your arms to us, your homes, your hearts. What do you say?'

"The air shook with one long, mighty 'Huzzanga!'

"Greatly pleased by the reception, the leader of the explorers then began talking with the natives' chief.

" 'I see that you have cattle here,' he said. 'They are a species with which I am unfamiliar. May I inspect them?'

" 'Certainly, certainly, come right this way,' said the chief. 'But be very careful as you walk that you don't step in the huzzanga!' "

Felch nodded at the loud laughter and applause. When it had finally subsided he said, "Okay, enough of the huzzanga. Now let's zero in on some of the conditions that produce a tough audience and what we can do to make them pushovers."

On one or two occasions during the next hour I felt Jay looking at me, and when I turned he would ask softly, "Had enough?"

Each time I just shook my head. I was enjoying Felch. He had excellent platform presence, superb timing and he delivered a well-constructed talk with plenty of meat to it, without referring to a single note. Both Jay and I were among those who gave him a standing ovation when he finished.

The remainder of the morning was all downhill. One of the sessions featured a smooth-talking hustler telling us how to make a fortune on infomercials by selling packages of tapes and videos through an 800 number to lonely people sitting at home by the telephone. The other was a presentation by a heavily made-up thin woman with lavender hair extolling the virtues of publishing one's own book so that the speakers could also claim the status of an author in their promotional material . . . even a "best-selling" author, she hinted slyly. After no more than twenty minutes I nudged Jay and we retreated as quietly as we could out the door and into the Garden Court Lounge which was beginning to feel like home. We sat at the bar and ordered drinks.

"Are we having fun yet, daddy?" Jay asked after he had taken a long sip of his scotch.

"Well, we've made a start. That Felch guy from the first session has possibilities."

"Shall we continue on our talent hunt?" Jay asked.

"Oh, yes! I'm positive that somewhere among the two thousand members attending this convention I'll find one or two of my kind of speaker, the old-fashioned kind who reaches for the audiences' soul, not their wallets."

"Mr. Manning, sir . . . ?"

He was standing to my right, at the bar.

"Yes?"

"Sir, my name is Patrick Donne," he said in a deep, commanding voice as he extended a large hand toward me. "This is my first convention and when I saw you standing here I couldn't resist the temptation to at least say hello. I've admired you for many years."

"Hello," I said, shaking his hand. "Glad to meet you . . . and welcome. This is Jay Bridges, one of our very best old pros."

As they were shaking hands I couldn't help notice that three women who were sitting across the bar from us were now all staring in our direction and certainly not at Jay or me. Besides that almost hypnotic basso-profundo voice, Patrick Donne was considerably over six feet tall with wide shoulders, a sharply pointed chin covered with a light brown beard, huge brown eyes and brown hair a little too long for my taste but thankfully not long enough to be classified a ponytail.

Jay greeted the newcomer warmly, asking, "Where are you from, Patrick?"

"I'm from a little town in Montana," he grinned, "called Blessings, population less than four hundred."

"Don't imagine there's much call for public speakers in Blessings, is there?"

"No, sir," he said, smiling and shaking his head. "But there's always Billings and Bozeman and Great Falls and Helena. Actually I can get anywhere in the Northwest pretty fast in my Beechcraft."

"Oh? You fly your own plane?"

"Yes, sir. Been flying for ten years or so."

"What do you do, Pat, or is speaking full-time with you?"

"I've been speaking for about six years, Mr. Manning. I did own a pretty good size cattle ranch back there in Blessings, but this speaking began taking so much of my time, and I love it, so I decided to sell the ranch to my foreman and become full-time two years ago. Gave forty-three speeches last year, even as far away as St. Louis."

"Do you have an agent?" Jay asked casually.

"No, sir, I do it all myself."

"What do you talk on?"

"Well," he said tentatively, "the talk has been kind of changing and evolving over the years, but I'm pretty comfortable with it now. I just give my audience some rules and suggestions that have been around forever but will help anyone live a happier and more productive life. These ideas that I share with them are so obvious that the greatest mystery of all is why everyone doesn't recognize and follow them . . . so now I call my talk 'The Greatest Mystery in the World.' "

"Sounds very interesting," I replied, not quite certain what else to say. "Well, it was good to meet you. Tell me, are you enjoying your first convention?"

His large eyes opened even wider and he said, "There's almost too much to absorb. So much to take in, to learn, to remember."

I nodded. "There are some fine sessions scheduled for the next couple of days and you'll want to be sure to sit in on that very special speakers contest during the last day. You'll probably learn plenty from those six top professionals of our association when they fight it out at the lectern for a quarter of a million dollars and the world championship of our speakers profession. Don't miss that!"

Patrick Donne smiled sheepishly and stared down at the bar. "Mr. Manning, sir, I won't miss it. I'm one of the six finalists."

VI

The ballroom was crowded for the association luncheon but Jay and I finally found two empty adjoining seats at a table with four speakers who I gathered were relatively new in the business. Our presence must have intimidated them a little, because, compared to the noisy tables around us, there was not much chatter as we ate until a very pretty redhead sitting directly across from me said, "Mr. Manning, I'm sure you've witnessed a long parade of professionals doing their thing through the years. Tell us who, in your opinion, were some of the very best."

Everyone at our table looked up from their plates and waited, including Jay. "That's a tough question. If by 'the very best' you mean who were masters at holding an audience in the palm of their hands, I guess I would select Rich DeVos, Amway's co-founder, Bishop Fulton J. Sheen, Bill Gove, Norman Vincent Peale, Cavett Robert, and, of course, my own very special friend, the late Eric Champion."

The redhead winced. "No women?"

"Well, you must remember that it has been only in the last ten or fifteen years that women have finally worked their way into what was pretty much an all-male profession. Now, from all I hear, there are plenty of very talented women flying around the country and appearing before huge audiences. However, I'm sorry to say that I've just never heard any of them on the platform although I'm pleased to see that this group has honored many in the past few years."

Following lunch, David Starr, a tall and handsome young man who was this year's chairman of the special awards committee, rose to explain how strict and eminently fair the process was of selecting the association's ten top professionals of the year. These speakers would join their predecessors in a very exclusive and elite group and henceforth could identify themselves on their business cards, stationery and all promotional materials as one of the very best in the business, a "Master of the Lectern."

"This year," Starr continued, "the climax to this great convention, our Thursday evening achievement dinner, will be a very memorable occasion for all of us because, for the very first time, we have an added five-star feature, approved by our officers and board of directors. Besides honoring ten new "Masters," we will also be privileged to see one of our own members crowned World Champion of the Lectern. Considering the several other fine speakers associations in this country, I need not remind you what a great honor this is for us. It will all take place right here, in this very special Regency Ballroom. Don't any of you dare miss it."

The afternoon sessions we attended produced no likely

prospects for me. We looked in on three, one titled "Who Dresses You?", another "How to Mold a New Presentation" and the third, "How to Survive a Hundred Hotels," all presented by mediocre speakers whose nervousness in front of their peers was obvious.

I've never been very good at hiding my feelings and I probably was showing my disappointment and frustration as we emerged from the Empire Room and walked through the crowded lobby. Jay slowed his pace and gripped my arm lightly. "And now, Mr. Manning, Dr. Bridges is about to give you a prescription that must be filled this evening. If anybody ever needed a change of scenery, and fast, it's you. I want you to take your lovely wife and get out of here, away from all of this. I happen to remember how much the both of you love Spanish food, so here's what I want you to do. There is a fabulous restaurant on I street called Taberna del Alabardero. Here, I'll write it down for you," he said as he scribbled on his program.

"Now, be sure to order yourself a plate of paella. It's a delicious special dish of Spanish rice. Then try the roasted duck in blueberry sauce. Go, please. Neither of you will regret it, I promise. Okay?"

I just nodded.

"Bart, what about tomorrow? Do you want to keep on with this scouting expedition?"

"Jay, I can't stop now. I've got to find what I'm looking for no matter how long it takes, and I still need your advice. I can't tell you how much your help and counsel have meant to me."

"Okay, let's meet right here by the elevator at nine-fifteen tomorrow."

I had already showered and was sitting in my robe, watching the early news on television, when Mary returned from her day at the malls, arms loaded with shopping bags. Looking very weary, she didn't accept my announcement that I was taking her out to dinner with much enthusiasm, but the day still had a happy ending. The Taberna del Alabardero was everything Jay said it was and then some, and its elegant decor was a perfect setting for one of the most delicious meals either one of us ever ate, although I passed on the roasted duck and ordered their paella de langosta, which was literally covered with lobster.

As we were entering our cab for the ride back to the Omni, I handed our young cabbie a fifty-dollar bill and asked if he would please give us a thirty-minute tour of a few Washington landmarks. He smiled and nodded, and as Mary and I held hands, in complete silence we rode slowly along the Potomac River, past the illuminated Lincoln Memorial, then the Vietnam Veterans Memorial, the Tidal Basin, serving as a perfect setting for the Jefferson Memorial, past the Washington Monument, the White House and then down Pennsylvania Avenue to the Capitol building. It is impossible for any citizen to take that ride, especially when the moon is shining down as it was, without feeling very proud to be an American.

There were tears in Mary's eyes when she stepped from the cab at the hotel. As the taxi was pulling away, she hugged me tightly and said, "Thank you, dear. That was one of the loveliest nights of my life."

"Well," I said, returning her hug, "I sure hope God lets me hang around long enough to give you a few more of them."

. . .

Wednesday's talent hunt produced no better results. After Mary and her friends headed for the shops and restaurants of Georgetown Park, Jay and I continued our search. The morning program had commenced with a general session in the Regency Ballroom featuring a presentation by an old pro, Edgar Hubbard, whom both Jay and I had known for many years. Hubbard, according to his introducer, had delivered more than three thousand speeches in the past thirty years and had received just about every honor the speaking profession could bestow. Listening to him again, after a span of many years, I remembered why I had never tried to sign him to an exclusive contract. His stage presence was magnificent, as were his gestures and delivery with a fine voice but . . . he didn't say anything! If one were just listening to any of his speeches on tape instead of enjoying his choreographic movements on the platform, one would have been bored to death. The other featured speaker was a young man in knickers, à la Payne Stewart, who walked out on the stage carrying a huge leather bag of golf clubs and proceeded to relate each club in his bag to a stage of one's life. Cute idea that might work in front of an audience of male golfers, but I wasn't so sure that a group of Mary Kay ladies would appreciate some of his humor.

Following the general session, Jay and I spent some time in two of the three concurrent presentations that followed. Nothing, not even a "maybe."

We ate most of our lunch with little talk, in the Monique Cafe. Over coffee, Jay opened his program, forced a smile and said, "Looks like some good potential prospects this afternoon, old buddy. Boy, I hope so. If we don't get lucky in the next few hours, there ain't nothing left except the speakers championship tomorrow afternoon."

During an afternoon that seemed longer than eternity, Jay and I checked out seven of the nine speakers who were being featured. We both agreed that most of them were good examples of a truly professional speaker and undoubtedly could come away from addressing most corporate gatherings with a good rating. However, I wasn't looking for just "good" speakers, I was scouting for a motivational master with stage presence, courage, charisma and a message. No one that I saw and heard even came close to fitting those tough requirements.

Mary was already back in our suite, and I guess that when I unlocked our door, I awoke her. Her shoes were off and her stockinged feet were resting on the marble coffee table. She opened her eyes as I approached and asked in a half-whisper, "Any luck, hon?"

"None. I must be getting too fussy in my old age. We just didn't see anyone that I could admire enough to want to pitch to clients. Mary, you know I can't sell them unless I really believe they're great."

"So what now?"

"Well, there is still the speaking championship tomorrow afternoon. Six of our best will each have twenty minutes in the spotlight and you promised you'd come with me, remember?"

"Bart, I wouldn't miss it for anything."

"Hon, are you okay? You look a little strange."

"I'm fine, fine . . . and I sure hope that dream I just had while I was sitting here waiting for you comes true."

"Want to tell me?"

"Sure. I must have dozed off while reading this little hotel brochure about the jogging and exercise trail in Rock Creek

Park, which I guess is just over the hill behind the Omni. Anyway, I dreamed I was jogging along, on the trail, enjoying the lush green landscape, when I suddenly noticed a small white cloud floating directly over my head, following me. Then I heard a soft voice that seemed to be coming from the cloud, saying, 'Tomorrow is the day. The heavens are about to smile on you. Do not lose hope.' Then I guess I heard you opening the door, and when I opened my eyes, you were standing there."

"What do you suppose all that means?"

"I wish I knew."

VII

The Regency Ballroom was filled to capacity when association president Dick Cobden stepped from behind a golden curtain promptly at one o'clock and approached the lectern, smiling and waving. Looking from one side of the huge room to the other, he waited in silence, after raising the lectern microphone slightly, until the noisy chatter subsided.

Mary and I had wisely decided to come early and we were no more than six or seven rows from the podium, dead center. In both aisles, to our left and right but a little closer to the podium than we were, television crews fiddled with their unwieldy cameras and rolling tripods. On one camera were the initials NBC, while ABC was on the other. Mary nudged me, obviously impressed.

"Ladies and gentlemen," our association president began, "I welcome you to what I am certain will be a milestone day in the history of the Rostrum Professionals of America. The film industry has its Oscar Awards, television has its Emmys, the recording people have their Grammys and the very best writers receive Pulitzer prizes. Now, at long last, our profession is about to pay tribute to its top talent. In cooperation with Ted & Margaret's Frozen Dinners, before this day has ended we will crown the World Champion of the Lectern."

Cobden paused, nodding and smiling until the applause stopped. "Each of the six regional associations which together comprise the Rostrum Professionals of America have, during the past several months, conducted a series of contests to select the very best speaker in their region and all six winners are here today to compete in this premiere championship. Each will speak for twenty minutes, with a two-minute margin either way, on any subject of their choice. There will be a five-minute break between the first, second and third speaker, then a twenty-minute intermission followed by the final three speakers, who will be on the same time schedule—twenty minutes each, plus or minus two minutes, with a five-minute break between the fourth, fifth and sixth speaker. Four eminent individuals, selected by the marketing department of Ted & Margaret's, will be the judges. They are already seated, scattered throughout this room, and their identity is known only to the people of the corporation so no undue pressure or influence can possibly be exerted on them by any of our more zealous association members. The judges will meet in private, following the contest, to make their selection and tonight, at our closing Night of Achievement dinner, we will crown one special person World Champion of the Lectern, the very best in our profession. The corporation's co-founders, Ted and Margaret Clark, will then present that fortunate individual with a check in the amount of a quarter of a million dollars as an advance fee for nine television commercials that will be aired nationally featuring the speaker promoting their excellent products."

Cobden looked around the huge room once again, grinned and shuffled several sheets of paper. "Well," he shouted, "are we ready?"

"Yes!" the crowd roared.

"Okay. In accordance with the rules established by our officers and board of directors and the management of Ted & Margaret's Frozen Dinners, there will be no long and flowery introductions of our contestants to influence you or the judges in any way. And now, without further ado, I am most proud to present our first contestant, from Providence, Rhode Island, representing Region One . . . Sandra Bane!"

She was tall, blond and wore a pinstripe double-breasted camel-color suit. She strolled effortlessly to the lectern, acknowledging the loud applause with a warm smile and wave. Lovely woman, thirtyish, perhaps. Her smile gradually faded as she looked down at the audience and delivered none of the typical opening remarks one hears so often.

"I was a United Airlines pilot for six wonderful and exciting years and then, four years ago, following my promotion to captain, I flunked my physical. My examination disclosed that I had cancer in my right breast and so, for the following month or two, I had a new co-pilot. His name was death. We got to be pretty good friends as the days passed, and he taught me many things as I lay in my hospital bed filled with self-pity. Above all, he helped me to appreciate the special gift of each new day and to never again take that gift for granted as I had done in the past.

"Fortunately for me, the cancer had been discovered in time and two operations removed it all. After savoring the good news for a few weeks, I had to make a decision about my future. What did I really want to do with the rest of my life? Did I want to get back in the big birds? Flying was a wonderful career with a promising future and all the excitement anyone could possibly want, but the decision I finally made was the toughest I had ever made in my life . . . to come down out of the heavens and to alert others, who were probably no more grateful for the gift of each day than I had been, that the clock was ticking, and that they should seize each day, even each moment, with love and gusto and gratitude because they might not get another chance.

"And so, after many agonizing days and weeks of indecision, I hung my pilot's jacket, complete with shiny wings, in my closet, put on a business suit, wrote my first speech and, frightened to death, ventured out into the business world. I started at first just around Providence, waving my lantern and warning any group willing to listen that fulfilling their dreams and goals wasn't something that could wait for tomorrow because they had no guarantee it would ever arrive. . . ."

I turned slightly toward Mary. She never even looked at me but pushed on the tiny ballpoint pen she was holding and wrote "8" on the top of her program. I nodded in agreement.

Miss Bane's entire speech was powerful, inspirational and uplifting, and when she closed she did so on a high note of hope. The applause was long and accompanied by plenty of cheers when she finally bowed and walked off the stage.

"She's going to be tough to beat!" Mary said admiringly

when the clamor finally subsided and our association president returned to the lectern.

"Ladies and gentlemen, those talented six who are now competing for the title of World Champion of the Lectern attended a private breakfast this morning with our board, our officers and the marketing people from Ted & Margaret's Frozen Dinners, and a drawing was conducted to determine the order of our speakers' appearances this afternoon, in fairness to all of them. And so, according to the luck of the draw, the second speaker I am honored to present to all of you is from Phoenix, Arizona, representing the Southwest, Region Five . . . Jo Jo Smith!"

He looked more like a dapper Washington lobbyist, away from his Town Car, than a distinguished corporate keynote speaker in his dark blue blazer, maroon and blue striped tie and gray slacks. There was just a hint of silver in his black hair that framed a well-tanned face. He took only a few steps onto the stage, bowed and waved at his audience with a hand that seemed to be holding several large file cards and following a dramatic pause of thirty seconds or so, he turned and continued toward the lectern. After only another step or two he suddenly lost his footing on the hardwood floor and fell facedown on the stage with a loud crash while his file cards seemed to fly in every direction accompanied by several gasps from the audience. He rolled over, seemingly in pain, staggered awkwardly to his feet and proceeded to pick up the scattered cards as he hurriedly brushed himself off, all the while casting embarrassed glances at those in the front rows, who all seemed to be holding their breath in pained sympathy.

Finally he arrived at the lectern, placed both hands firmly on the poised microphone and just as he said, "Good afternoon, ladies and gentlemen," the cards flew out of his hand again. Now, with sheer panic and terror distorting his handsome face he raced around to the front of the lectern and began, once more, to pick up his scattered cards. He had only retrieved three or four, when loud and shrill female screams erupted simultaneously from several sections of the audience because, as he was in the process of leaning over and reaching for the cards, with his fanny to the audience, his pants slid slowly from beneath his jacket and fell to the floor, revealing bright turquoise lycra bike pants with yellow lettering proclaiming "Vote for Jo-Jo!"

Accompanied by both applause and cheers, Jo Jo Smith pulled up his pants, buckled and zipped them, then walked around the lectern grinning until he was facing his audience once again and said, "Gotcha! I sure did! Fellow speakers, hello! In my first year of public speaking, a long time ago it seems, I learned that before any audience will listen attentively, one must somehow get their attention and now, look at all of you . . . sitting up, watching and waiting for the next embarrassing or dumb stunt I might pull, aren't you? Well, that's okay because we're all partners in this special profession of ours even though we don't share the same ideas. You all know that old fable about the hen and the pig, don't you? The two of them were just gabbing and strolling down the road together, when they came to an old-fashioned diner displaying a bright sign that read HAM AND EGGS. The old hen stopped walking, nodded toward the sign and said, 'See, old buddy, you and I are partners.' 'The hell we are,' snorted the large pig. 'It's just a day's work for you but for me it's a real sacrifice!' "

Each of the speakers had a tiny high-fidelity microphone clipped to some part of their upper clothing so they could move away from the stationary lectern, if they wished, and still communicate with their audience. Jo Jo Smith took full advantage of his freedom and in the following fifteen minutes or so brilliantly imitated the voices, gestures and mannerisms of not only many of our better-known association speakers but others in the public eye from Richard Nixon to Bill Clinton, from Tony Bennett to Hammer, from Jimmy Stewart to Bart Simpson. Mary gave him a "7" and I nodded, having enjoyed him very much, although he wasn't the kind of speaker I was seeking.

The third contestant, according to his introduction, was Charles Ethan Gant, from St. Paul, Minnesota, representing Region Three. Unfortunately for Mr. Gant, there are days in all our lives when, no matter how professional and dynamic and impressive our past record and performances may be, it would have been better to have remained in bed. All of us, even the most powerful, have off days, and this was Mr. Gant's. He was a tall, handsome guy with a great smile and a smoothly shaven head which, Mary told me, detracted not one iota from his sex appeal, but he was obviously nervous and, even worse, was unable to hide it. More than once he seemed to search for his place as he shuffled his notes and what had commenced as a fine, strong voice seemed to lose its appealing timbre as the moments crawled slowly by. Every speaker in our audience, at least every authentic working professional, was able to relate, I'm certain, to this poor, un-fortunate guy's situation and because they understood his predicament so well, it probably seemed even more painful to them than it would have been to a typical convention audience. At last, to everyone's relief, including Gant's, I'm certain, he finished his remarks, bowed once stiffly and hurried offstage. Instead of writing down a rating number on her program, this time Mary drew a question mark and turned toward me, eyebrows raised. I shrugged. Gant's Region Three included the Chicago area with scores of very fine speakers, most of which he must have defeated in the preliminary rounds, though he certainly didn't beat them with the kind of performance he delivered today. However, it happens to the best. I once saw Ted Williams strike out three times in a single game, years ago, when his Red Sox were playing the Yankees in the stadium.

As had been announced, there was a twenty-minute intermission following the third speaker. At least half the audience was now on its feet and filing toward the ballroom's doors. "If you've got to go to the men's room, hon, turn right when you get outside and you'll find the men's lounge down one level," Mary said. "I'll keep our seats."

"No, I'm fine. Gonna stay put."

"You look a little down, Bart. You okay?"

I nodded. "Yes, but it's beginning to look like a lost cause. Am I just getting harder to please with old age, or what? The first speaker, that blond ex-pilot. She was very good . . . damn good, but somehow, I don't know, hon, I want someone even better. Is it me?"

"No, because unless I've just been with you too many years, I happen to feel the same way. Nobody said this would be easy. If your old friend Napoleon Hill were here, he would say, 'We shall continue to persist until we succeed.' So let us persist . . .

and have faith. Don't forget that strange dream of mine and that voice promising that tomorrow would be the day. Well, this is tomorrow . . . and it's not over yet!"

The first speaker following the intermission was a tiny little guy introduced as Leo Samuels representing Region Two and he was from Jupiter, Florida. He was wearing a white, bulky wool sweater several sizes too large for him, and he pushed the heavy knitted material halfway up both arms before he tilted the microphone downward and smiled at us. My first impression was that he looked as if he would be more at home as an opening act at some comedy club than one of the six finalists in a contest to select the very best professional speaker in the world. I was wrong. The little guy was very good and he held our attention from his opening remarks when he said, "Ladies and gentlemen. Several years after the Second World War, Winston Churchill was speaking to a group of London business people who were seated in a room much smaller than this one. The person who introduced him smilingly made a good-natured reference to Churchill's well-known fondness for alcoholic beverages.

"He said, 'If all the spirits that Sir Winston has consumed were poured into this room, they'd reach up to about here'— and he drew an imaginary line on the wall with his hand, some six or seven feet from the floor. When Churchill reached the podium, he looked at the imaginary line and then raised his head up to the ceiling, sighing, 'Ah, so much to be done and so little time in which to do it!' "

Samuels smiled, nodded appreciatively at the loud laughter and said, "I, too, have so little time and so much to do. . . ."

The speech was excellent and delivered by a real professional who described many of the ways we waste time each day and how to correct those faults. Even his oversized sweater which seemed so much "out of uniform" to this old fuddy-dud had quickly blended right into our total impression of a charming guy giving a very good talk by the time he had finished, to long applause. I glanced over at Mary as she was printing "8" on the margin of her program. I nodded. Then, underneath the "8" she printed "but not for you." I nodded again, feeling more and more as if we were on a lost cause.

"Ladies and gentlemen," Dick Cobden said, waiting until the buzzing and chatter had ended, "our next contestant, representing Region Six, is from Blessings, Montana . . . yes, I said Blessings, Montana! How about a warm welcome for Patrick Donne!"

VIII

Following Patrick Donne's introduction, our association president gestured hesitantly to his right before he turned, walked off the stage with a puzzled look on his face and stepped behind the curtain to his left.

Now the stage was empty. Where was Donne? Mary frowned and glanced in my direction, and I'm sure we both had the same concern as every other professional in the audience. Was there something wrong backstage, or was it just a little case of stage fright? Where was our fifth contestant?

And then, just as the murmurs in the audience began to swell in volume, a deep resonant voice echoed over the loudspeakers throughout the Regency Ballroom. . . .

"We are born for a higher destiny than that of earth. There is a realm where the rainbow never fades, where the stars will be spread out before us like islands that slumber on the ocean and where the beings that now pass before us like shadows will remain in our presence forever."

Patrick Donne was wearing a marvelously tailored glen plaid single-breasted suit, a white tab-collar dress shirt, an abstract jaquard print tie in several hues of blue, gray and tan and dark brown loafers. He was not smiling and he stroked his close-cut beard pensively for what seemed the longest time following his almost casual stroll to the lectern. Finally, in a very deep but hushed voice he said, "Those very special words you have just heard, written by an English novelist, Edward Bulwer-Lytton, before any of us were born, are perhaps as good a description as any ever provided mankind regarding what lies in store for us in that far-off place some call heaven."

I stole a quick glance at Mary. She was staring at Donne, and if she could feel my looking her way, she never acknowledged it. Now, for the first time in all the meetings I had attended at the convention, all I could hear was the audience breathing.

"Perhaps you are one of the many who have serious doubts that there is a higher destiny," Donne continued as he turned his head slowly to the right and then the left, "and that doubt is something only you can resolve with your God, if, indeed, you recognize a God. That, of course, is all up to you because faith is a lot like love—it can never be forced.

"Still, although only you can find your own way, after your life has ended, to that magic place where the rainbow never fades, I have an important message for you. One of the most difficult lessons we should learn in this life, and one that many of us never learn, is how to see and appreciate the beautiful, the divine, the heaven that lies about us right here on earth. Anyone . . . anyone . . . who has allowed himself or herself to be affected by events over which we often have no control, so that we despair of this precious life, is making a terrible mistake. Success, joy, wealth, love, fulfillment, are all available here . . . now! And yet many of us run for cover and hide, after fate has dealt us a bad hand, and from that moment on we live a life where tomorrow is as dark as tonight and instead of enjoying heaven on earth we wallow, unfulfilled, in our own private hell."

Donne stepped away from the lectern and raised both arms high above his head as that great basso-profundo voice reverberated throughout the room. "Those of you who have lost all faith in yourselves, in your potential, and in this tiny world which is the only one we have, please listen to me. I believe I have some suggestions that might help you change your life for the better. If you follow my suggestions and they don't work, you've really lost very little except some time and effort because you never believed your life could improve anyway, right? But . . . if I am correct, and from this day forward you could have followed just a few simple rules and altered the course of your life, taking you down a different path that might lead to gold and success, love and joy, peace of mind and contentment and perhaps, if you are truly fortunate, your own rainbow . . . if I am correct and you didn't bother to heed my words . . . my, my, won't you be sorry? So what have you got to lose? Are you with me?"

Amazingly, heads were nodding all around me. Professional speakers, all fully equipped with large egos of their own, rarely reacted to any speech in this way. Patrick Donne also nodded, turning his broad shoulders on us and walking very deliberately back to the lectern. Dead silence still prevailed. "Usually," he said, a slight frown appearing on his handsome face for the first time, "it takes me the better part of an hour to share some very simple suggested rules of living that, if followed, will change any life for the better. However, ladies and gentlemen," he continued, raising his right arm and glancing at his wristwatch, "even with the allowable extra two minutes I have only fourteen minutes remaining, but I'm still going to try to share with you, although in a somewhat condensed version, the actions you must take in order to enjoy a better life no matter how good you believe it is right now. Oh, and by the way," he said as he looked around, "I promise I won't get angry if you take some notes so that later you will be able to recall my—what shall we call them—suggestions for a more successful tomorrow."

Donne paused, clasped his hands together almost as if he were about to pray and said, "More than eighty years ago a great Canadian man of medicine, Sir William Osler, delivered a speech to the students of Yale University entitled 'A Way of Life.' Although Osler delivered scores of addresses and wrote many books in his lifetime, including a medical classic 'The Principles and Practices of Medicine,' Sir William may well be remembered for centuries to come because of his priceless advice to the youth of Yale. A copy of his original speech as well as his invaluable collection of books and manuscripts now have a home in Canada's great McGill University.

"Years prior to that Yale speech, Sir William was on an ocean liner. One day, while visiting with the ship's captain, a loud, piercing alarm sounded followed by strange grinding and crashing sounds below deck. 'Those are all our watertight compartments closing,' the captain explained. 'It's an important part of our safety drill. In case of real trouble, water leaking into any one compartment would not affect the rest of the ship. Even should we collide with an iceberg, as did the *Titanic*, water rushing in will fill only that particular ruptured compartment. The ship, however, will still remain afloat.'

"Osler, in his address at New Haven, remembered that unusual experience on the huge ship. He told the young people, 'Each one of you is certainly a much more marvelous organization than that great liner and bound on a far longer voyage. What I urge is that you learn to master your life by living each day in a day-tight compartment and this will certainly ensure your safety throughout your entire journey of life.'

"Osler continued, in words too powerful for me or anyone else to attempt to improve: 'Touch a button and hear, at every level of your life, the iron doors shutting out the Past—the dead yesterdays. Touch another and shut off, with a metal curtain, the Future—the unborn tomorrows. Then you are safe— safe for today!' "

Donne looked down as if he were grasping for the proper words. "Yesterday's failures and pains and heartbreaks are far too heavy a load for any of us to carry into the dawn of a new day. Leave them behind, all of them, and just walk away! And what of tomorrow? 'There is no tomorrow,' Sir William told his audience, 'the future is today!' Later he would write: 'Banish the future. Live only for the hour and its allotted work. Think not of the amount to be accomplished, the difficulties to be overcome, but set earnestly at the little task near your elbow, letting that be sufficient for the day; for surely our plain duty is not to see what lies dimly at a distance but to do what lies clearly at hand.'

"And so, my friends," Donne said, smiling for the first time, "my first suggestion you might wish to follow in order to achieve a higher destiny for yourself, right here on earth, is perhaps the toughest anyone ever made to you but, believe me, it truly works. Robert Louis Stevenson agreed with his contemporary, Dr. Osler, when the creator of his own *Treasure Island* wrote, 'Anyone can do his or her work, however tedious, for one day. Anyone can live sweetly, patiently, lovingly, purely, till the sun goes down. And that is all that life really means.'

"Let me repeat Osler's wise advice and my first suggestion to you. Live each day of your life in a day-tight compartment. This act alone will move you much closer to success and happiness.

"Another suggestion to assist you in achieving a better life here on earth is also from the past. It was without doubt the greatest secret of success ever willed to mankind, and it was delivered, almost two thousand years ago, by Jesus, in his Sermon on the Mount. In those powerful lectures to the huge crowd that had gathered, Jesus shared a great amount of wise advice with them. One of his rules of behavior, even after all these years, is probably not fully appreciated for the power contained in its words 'Whomsoever asks you to go with him one mile, go two!' Resolve right now, even as you are sitting here, that starting tomorrow morning you will devote more time and effort to please your clients . . . with no thought of extra remuneration or reward of any kind. Salespeople, you who normally end your day at five . . . continue until six so that you can devote more time to servicing your customers or perhaps even making a few more sales calls. Of course this type of activity, whether you are employed in an office or factory . . . no matter what your profession may be, actually . . . will not make you very popular with your peers because the name of the game, today, seems to be to do as little as possible for the check you receive. So be it. No one said you had to follow the herd. Just give a little more of yourself, in time and effort, in patience and caring, in helping and understanding. Do this tomorrow, and the next day, and the next, with no thought of any additional compensation. Try it for three months and then come to me, I dare you, and tell me your life has not changed for the better. Go the extra mile!

"Okay," said Donne, holding up two fingers. "I've now made two suggestions. Live each day of your life in a day-tight compartment and always go the extra mile, at home, at work, at play.

"Another suggestion. Never cut corners, never neglect the little things. Most of us break this simple rule many more times than we realize as we rush through each day, not realizing how much harm we are doing to our careers. Several years ago the great lyricist Oscar Hammerstein was being flown by a close friend on a sightseeing trip over New York Harbor in a tiny two-seater plane. When they eventually approached the Statue of Liberty, standing tall and proud more than three hundred feet above sea level, Oscar's friend banked the plane so that he could look directly down on Liberty's head, and what he saw amazed him. He remembered that this magnificent gift from the people of France had been erected in the harbor in 1886 and yet, as he looked down, he could see that every lock and braid of hair on the very top of the lady's head was as perfectly carved and polished as were all the fine details of her face and body and gown. But in 1886 there were no airplanes! Frédéric-Auguste Bartholdi, the statue's creator, could have saved months of tedious labor and costly expense by doing very little carving and polishing on the top of Liberty's head, reasoning that no one would ever see what had been omitted up there except possibly a few sea gulls and yet . . . and yet . . . every curl and braid is perfectly detailed and in place! There are no rough and unfinished areas! Never, never neglect the little things! Doing so can very often turn potential success into failure. Recently, an automaker, one of our big three, had to recall four thousand new and fairly expensive automobiles. Why? A tiny defective five-cent washer had been installed in the steering column!"

Patrick Donne paused, inhaled deeply, walked from behind the lectern toward the front of the stage, leaned forward and waved his right arm in a sweeping motion along the front row. "Well," he asked loudly, "are you all still with me?"

"Yes," they chorused, sounding like an exuberant first-grade class.

"Okay," he replied, now standing erect but remaining close to the stage front. "My next suggestion . . . never allow anyone to push your kill switch again. What's that . . . what's a 'kill switch,' you ask? Purchase an expensive automobile these days and you will probably also buy a burglar alarm . . . plus a little gadget called a kill switch. A few years ago those of us who had burglar alarms in our cars would merely step out of the car after we had parked it and turned off the ignition. Then, after double-checking to be sure the doors were all locked, we would insert a tiny key, probably in an opening in the fender, turn it and the alarm would then be set. If anyone tried to break into the auto, the air would be shattered with a loud, persistent scream, hopefully attracting enough attention to frighten the bad guy away. However, if the felon was bold enough not to be frightened off by the siren, after he was in the car he could still jump a couple of hot ignition wires in very little time, start the motor, and drive the car away, even as the alarm siren continued to wail. The kill switch changed all that for car thieves. Installed along with the burglar alarm, it is a simple-looking button wired to the ignition and hidden beneath the car's carpet in a place known only to the car's owner. Leaving the car, one would first push the kill switch button, make certain all doors were locked and finally turn on the burglar alarm. If a burglar broke into that automobile and the alarm was sounded, he could try till the cows come home and still never be able to jump any wires to start the car because the kill switch had completely cut off all power going to the starter. Oh, the lights would work, the windshield wipers would flap back and forth and the radio would even play, but the engine could not turn over and that car would not advance a single inch out of the parking lot!

"Now, I'm certain that only a very few of you here realize that all of us have a 'kill switch.' It gets pushed whenever someone puts us down or harshly criticizes our best efforts or makes fun of us . . . and, in one degree or another it's been happening to all of us since we were little kids. Ridicule, scorn, slights, insults—they all hurt and often their toll is so great that the little confidence we had managed to build up disappears until we finally stop trying to do better. How many parents, in moments of anger, pushed the kill switch of one of their kids by telling that little boy or girl that he or she will never amount to anything? How many kids then spend a lifetime working very hard to make their parent's prophecy come true?"

Donne paused again and tilted his head slightly. "Did I hit a nerve? Good! Just don't let it happen to you anymore. Don't push any more kill switches when you are with your kids and never, never let anyone push your kill switch either. Let me put it in perhaps a more familiar way to you. Never again give anyone permission to rain on your parade!

"Another suggestion. If you have been hiding behind 'busy work,' cut it out! It's something we all do now and then, but it can certainly put the brakes on a promising career and has, very often. You know the scenario very well. You are confronted with a real challenge, a project of some sort that is so large and important it might make a great change in your life if you handled it well. What do you say? 'Sorry, I'd really like to tackle that but right now I'm just too busy. Maybe later?' You're not too busy. You're just hiding . . . hiding behind piles of unimportant projects and papers and file folders that don't mean diddly in the larger scheme of things. Stop avoiding opportunity. Never hide behind 'busy work' again!

"Five suggestions. Note that I didn't say 'simple suggestions' because they certainly are not. There is enough power among them, when acted upon, to put a golden glow in your future. Live each day of your life in a day-tight compartment. Always go the extra mile, at home, at work, at play. Never neglect the little things. Never let anyone push your kill switch. Never hide behind busy work.

"If you follow those five, then the final rule of life I have for you will be easy. Never commit an act that you will have to look back on with tears and regret because you violated a law of God or man. Your most precious treasure is your self-respect. Guard it with all your strength. There is an anonymous poem which has been passed around for a few generations but it is still as wise and powerful as ever and I'd like it to be my gift to you as I take my leave. The poem is called 'The Face in the Glass.'

'When you get what you want in your struggle for self
'And the world makes you king for a day,
'Just go to a mirror and look at yourself
'And see what THAT face has to say.
'For it isn't your father or mother or spouse
'Whose judgment upon you must pass
'The person whose verdict counts most in your life
'Is the one staring back from the glass.
'Some people might think you're a straight-shooting chum
'And call you a great gal or guy
'But the face in the glass says you're only a bum
'If you can't look it straight in the eye.
'That's the one you must please, never mind all the rest
'That's the one with you clear to the end.
'And you know you have passed your most dangerous test
'If the face in the glass is your friend.
'You may fool the whole world down the pathway of years
'And get pats on your back as you pass,
'But your final reward will be heartache and tears
'If you've cheated the face in the glass.' "

Patrick Donne's voice had broken several times in the final few lines. He inhaled deeply and said, "I'm certain that all of you have probably gone on a long drive, sometime in your life, positive that you knew exactly the route to take to your destination. And then, after driving for a couple of hours or more, you suddenly realize that you are lost.

"You stop your car and open your glove compartment. But there's no road map there." Donne smiled. "The kids were playing with the maps, remember?

"Now you begin driving around, looking for a filling station, and you finally find one with a real friendly and helpful attendant. He opens his road map, shows you where you are . . . and then he shows you how simple it is for you to get back on course."

Donne turned his head slowly, sweeping the entire ballroom with his glance. "Well, for those of you who think you may have wandered off course a little bit in your journey through this tough life of ours, I hope that you will consider me just your friendly station attendant today . . . and when you get back on course, with your true destination ahead of you, if you happen to see a few broken branches along the way, please think of me. I left them there to mark your path to a higher destiny right here on earth. Have a good trip. I love you all!"

Everyone was on their feet, applauding, whistling and yelling. The ovation continued for more than five minutes, and somewhere during our constant clapping, Mary turned to me and held up both hands with all fingers and thumbs extended. Patrick Donne had scored a "10" with her and with me and with just about everyone else, it seemed.

I remember nothing about the final speaker, neither his name, his region nor the subject of his speech. I just sat politely in my chair, hearing nothing, trying to figure how best to approach the man from Blessings.

IX

When the telephone in our room rang, I picked up the receiver almost immediately since I had been sitting on one of the suite's three sofas with my hand on it. Jay sounded a little irritated.

"Bart, your damn line has been busy for over an hour. Is there trouble? Are you guys okay, or did the famous agent just take his phone off the hook so he wouldn't be disturbed by any nasty career climbers?"

"I'm sorry, old buddy. Been trying to locate Patrick Donne ever since Mary and I got back to this room. No one is answering his room phone and none of our people seem to know where he vanished to, not even our own president."

"Well, my friend," Jay chuckled, "I think I know where he'll be this evening, commencing around eight or so. You can bet all your treasury bonds that he's no early checkout. Mr. Donne will positively be attending our Night of Achievement dinner in order to pick up his check for a quarter of a million bucks as well as be crowned World Champion of the Lectern. A fine day's work, I'd say! Did you enjoy him? I mean, did he meet all your strict criteria, sir?"

"And then some . . . but where the hell can he be?"

"Beats me. Probably out celebrating somewhere. That's what I'd be doing. We'll catch up with him tonight, Bart, don't worry. I'll help. I want to be around when you reel this superstar in . . . if you do. Tell you what, I met a great member today, Sally Carver from Boston. Sally gives seminars on maintaining one's good health after fifty and she's got a figure that proves whatever she teaches must work. Anyway, I've invited Sally to go to the dinner with me and she accepted. How about the four of us getting together so we can dine at the same table, watch all the evening's festivities and then I'll help you corner Donne before the night fades away? What do you say?"

"I say it's an offer I can't refuse. Where shall we meet?"

"Well, you two are a few floors higher up than poor little me and, coincidentally, Sally is also on this floor. So why don't you two come by my room around eight and we'll all go down together?"

The staff of the Omni Shoreham had wrought still another miracle. As late as four o'clock in the afternoon, the Regency Ballroom had been filled with rows of folding chairs to accommodate every association member and spouse attending the contest to select the world champion. Now, only four hours after the contest had ended, the room held more than a hundred large round tables covered with red tablecloths, each table with fourteen place settings surrounding a giant vase of red roses. The ambiance of the huge room now seemed completely different from earlier in the day as the warm glow from glistening crystal chandeliers reflected off the golden-brown ceiling and shimmering stage curtain to form a perfect setting for the unique coronation that was about to take place.

The dinner was "black tie optional" and since Mary insisted that her attire for the evening was going to be a lovely evening gown she had purchased at Chermollie's in Manhattan nearly a year ago and never worn, I was duty bound to put on the white dinner jacket even though it felt a trifle tight.

Jay and his new friend were ready when we knocked on his door slightly after eight. Sally Carver was, indeed, a charming woman with not only a striking figure, as Jay had reported, but a lovely, almost wrinkle-free tan face forming a perfect setting for the largest blue eyes I believe I have ever seen. If the lady was only fifty, she was a miracle! Even as we were descending in the elevator, Mary and Sally had started chattering away. I glanced at Jay, nodded and winked. Like concerned parents, we both approved of his date.

Fortunately we found a table with four adjoining vacant seats not very far back from the stage. Neither Jay nor I knew any of the other speakers at the table, and so we went through the usual introduction routine all around. I missed several of the names because just as we started to introduce each other an orchestra of ten or so pieces, next to the stage, began playing an upbeat version of "We'll Meet Again." As soon as we had taken our seats, Mary tapped my arm and nodded toward the piano player, who was also directing the other musicians. "That's Peter Duchin," she shouted in my ear, "and he hasn't gotten a day older. Last time we saw him was at a wedding at the New York Hilton, five years or so ago, but I can't remember, for the life of me, who was getting married."

Jay was on his feet again. "Bart, if anyone comes by taking an order for drinks, Sally will have a Bloody Mary and I'll have my usual. I'm going to take a little scouting tour around the place to see if we can locate our man."

Unfortunately the Regency Ballroom was so congested with tables that there was no space available for dancing to Duchin's fine music, and so the would-be dancers began taking out their frustration by clapping loudly as well as pounding their feet. All that expended energy combined with laughter and loud conversations as well as the music to raise the sound decibels in the room almost to the point of torture.

Jay returned to our table just as the salad was being served. When I looked up he just shook his head, took his seat, saw that there were no drinks on the table except goblets of ice water, rose, dropped his napkin on his seat and headed toward the open bar. He returned in just a few minutes with a tray and drinks.

"Jay," Mary squealed, "you are absolutely amazing! How could you possibly remember that I drink Black Russians?"

"When it comes to women's drinks, I'm a master," he gloated. "When I need to find my garden tools, forget it."

Fortunately, everyone at our table seemed to know how to laugh, joke and relax, and so we all acted more like a bunch of kids at a school party than respected professionals from the world of public speaking and their spouses. The excellent roast beef dinner followed by huge servings of baked Alaska was as good as convention food ever gets.

Following a drumroll and fanfare from the two orchestra

trumpets, President Cobden finally stepped out onstage, smiling and waving again as he approached the lectern.

"Are we having fun yet?" he yelled into the microphone.

"Yesssss!" roared seventeen hundred adults.

"Are we all glad we came?"

"Yesssss!"

Cobden stood almost motionless at the lectern, obviously relishing the moment. "This is a historic evening in the history of our association," he said slowly, "an evening when one of our own is about to be recognized as World Champion of the Lectern! The Rostrum Professionals of America have played a huge part in promoting the growth of our profession throughout the world during the past several decades. However, as we continue to grow so that our membership now numbers in the thousands, we must never forget that small handful of visionaries who made all this possible, who had the courage and persistence and the burning desire to forge our organization out of little more than a dream. We are honored and so very proud to have had one of the six original founders with us throughout this convention. Ladies and gentlemen, will you all rise and join me in saluting the legendary Bart Manning!"

Reluctantly, very reluctantly, I finally rose to my feet as the applause and cheering grew in volume. Waving my arms and forcing a smile, I turned slowly in a full circle and then, feeling a little silly, sat back down as the chorus of sounds subsided.

Mary leaned toward me. "That was a first."

I nodded. "And, I hope, a last."

Next on the program was the presentation of the parchment scroll to those fortunate ten selected as new Masters of the Lectern. I had heard talk that there had been a special emergency meeting called with the board of directors earlier in the day to protest the masculinity of the award's title. This had become an annual and unscheduled element of each convention for the past ten years or so, but once again, I was told, "Mistress of the Lectern" had been rejected as the designation for those women fortunate enough to be honored with a scroll.

Of course, before the ten new "Masters" could be announced, all those who had been awarded the designation in past years had to stand as their names were called, bowing, smiling and enjoying another brief moment in the limelight. By the time Cobden had read his entire list, at least a hundred members were on their feet and looking down on the rest of us.

At long last, the ten new honorees, as their names were called, wended their way through the maze of tables up to the stage where the parchment scrolls were presented and each gave a brief acceptance speech. I knew none of them, but all ten seemed to be very popular choices with the entire crowd, and judging by their professionalism on the platform they probably all deserved the award.

When the final parchment recipient had returned to her seat, the ballroom lights began to dim gradually as the Duchin orchestra played "The Impossible Dream." Several spotlight beams drifted slowly across the curtain and stage until they all merged at the lectern as the ballroom continued to grow darker while two television cameras were moved closer to the stage on their tripods. The ballroom, after the music had ended, suddenly grew very still as Dick Cobden, holding hands with both, led an elderly couple up the steps to the right of the stage and then over to the lectern.

"Ladies and gentlemen," Cobden announced solemnly, "we

are now fast approaching that special moment that I'm sure you have all been waiting for. First, however, please say hello to Ted and Margaret Lee, who just happen to own the largest frozen dinner packaging empire in the entire world."

Both Ted and Margaret were obviously not accustomed to facing huge audiences despite their long status as respected leaders in the food industry. They both bowed very timidly to the applause as they nodded their heads and tried to smile.

"All of you, I'm certain," Cobden continued, "are familiar with Ted and Margaret's famous slogan, 'Our taste speaks for itself.' Well, very soon now, in a series of television commercials to be aired nationally, the World Champion of the Lectern, who is about to be selected from our own organization, will also be speaking for Ted and Margaret's fine foods.

"Through a series of regional contests," Cobden continued, "conducted during the past several months, the best speaker was selected from each area and these top professionals competed in a special program this afternoon which most of you attended. A special board of judges, all selected by Ted and Margaret's marketing people, then met in closed session and selected one speaker as the winner. That very talented individual, that spellbinder, is about to receive three very special prizes. First, he or she will be acclaimed as the World Champion of the Lectern, a title held by no other speaker in the world. Second," he said as he leaned down behind the lectern and raised a huge glass trophy, shaped as a lectern, high above his head, "he or she will receive this marvelous piece of Waterford crystal designed and created especially for this rare occasion. And finally, last but far from least, Ted and Margaret will present the winner with a check for a quarter of a million dollars!"

As if on cue, Ted Lee reached inside his white jacket, removed a yellow envelope and waved it high over his head as both television cameras edged ever closer to the stage.

"Ladies and gentlemen," Cobden shouted, "we have finally arrived at that magic moment!"

This time the two trumpeters in Duchin's band stood and the long fanfare from their horns echoed and re-echoed through the semidark ballroom. "I am most proud to announce that the World Champion of the Lectern ... from Blessings, Montana ... is Patrick Donne!"

Everyone in the ballroom was now standing and applauding. One of the spotlight beams moved slowly away from the lectern, across the stage to the right, past an area of gold curtain, until it came to rest on two wide brown doors with a red exit sign above. As if on cue, two waiters each pushed on one of the doors until they both opened wide, allowing Patrick Donne to enter the ballroom, waving and smiling. The audience remained standing and applauding long after Donne had joined the others at the lectern.

Finally, Cobden lifted the crystal trophy from the top of the lectern and placed it gently in Donne's arms, saying, "Pat, every member of the Rostrum Professionals of America salutes you. All of us envy you, also. What a great honor ... and you truly deserve it, sir. You were absolutely mesmerizing this afternoon!"

Applause broke out again throughout the room. Donne murmured a faint thank-you as he bowed his head.

"And now," Cobden continued, "we have two very famous

people here who would like to meet you. This is Ted and Margaret Lee and they have a special presentation to make."

Ted Lee moved closer to the microphone, glancing around nervously as he waited for the applause to end. "Mr. Donne," he said hoarsely, "my wife and I are both honored just to be on the same stage with you. You are truly a credit to your wonderful profession and we are certain that you will be a great messenger for us in spreading the news about our fine products. And so, with no further ado, Margaret and I would like to present you with your other prize as world champion . . . a certified check made out to you in the amount of a quarter of a million dollars!"

Patrick Donne shook his handsome head several times, as if in disbelief mixed with awe, after he was handed the envelope. Ted Lee grasped his hand and Margaret stepped forward to give him a warm embrace and a kiss on the cheek. Then Dick Cobden lifted the heavy crystal trophy from the top of the lectern, gestured toward the microphone, patted Donne on the shoulder and to our cheers, whistles and applause led Ted and Margaret off the stage and down to their nearby table with its small white pedestal sign marked #1.

Donne, still silent, stood very erect at the lectern, staring down at the envelope that Ted Lee had handed him. Finally, but very slowly and deliberately, he tore open the envelope and removed the check. He stared at it for several minutes, so long that some of us were becoming uncomfortable before he finally looked up and said, very softly, "Friends and fellow members, I am very touched by the great honor you have bestowed on me today. And Ted and Margaret, I thank you from the bottom of my heart for this lavish award. I daresay that most people labor their entire lifetime and yet never even come close to amassing a quarter of a million dollars . . . in one pile. And yet, Ted and Margaret, I cannot accept this check. . . ."

Reaction from the audience was instantaneous. There were gasps, shrieks, moans as well as several voices shouting "what?" "why?" "huh?"

I quickly turned and glanced toward the front row table where Ted and Margaret and our association officers were sitting. Margaret was holding both hands over her mouth, her eyes opened wide in disbelief, and Ted looked like everyone else in the ballroom, stunned, as if he couldn't believe what he had just heard.

Donne continued. "I cannot accept this check as it is made out, and so I beg the Lees to grant me a very special favor. A month or so ago it was my good fortune to visit the lovely city of Portland, Oregon, on a speaking engagement. Following my speech, an old and beloved friend of many years, knowing my compassion for all children, took me on a visit to the Dougy Center for Grieving Children. Here is a very special haven where children mourning the death of a loved one can share their fears and their experiences as they struggle through the agony of their terrible loss and begin the slow healing process. The Dougy Center is named after a brave little boy named Dougy Turno, who knew he was dying from an inoperable brain tumor, and yet his magnificent spirit and attitude about dealing with death influenced hundreds of lives before he passed on. All who met Dougy fell in love with him and were deeply touched by his message. As ill as he was, Dougy was always saying, 'I can go to hospitals and tell other kids not to be afraid to die!' Dougy died in early December 1981. He received his wish, 'a new life for Christmas.'

"The Dougy Center functions on the policy that all children from the age of three through the teen years can learn to cope with their loss if they are given the opportunity to express their feelings and feel supported by others. In only a few short years what began as one special lady's dream, Beverly Chappell, is now reaching out to grieving children in more than forty locations across our nation and Canada. All Dougy Centers, I learned during my visit to Portland, are nonsectarian and supported entirely through contributions. To continue and to multiply their priceless efforts of repairing the frightened minds and broken hearts of our little ones, they very much need our help.

"I came away from the Dougy Center, that day, touched as I had never been touched in my life, and so I made a resolution. I already knew, by then, that I was to be a finalist here, this week, and so that night when I prayed . . . yes, I pray every night . . . I promised God that if I were victorious in this competition I would donate my winnings, all of it, to the Dougy Center in Portland. However, if I take this check and cash it, as it is now made out in my name, I will probably have to pay at least a hundred thousand dollars of it in income taxes and that huge chunk would never get to the Dougy people. And so, Ted and Margaret, I do have a great favor to ask of you good people. I will perform the required number of television commercials for your company to the best of my ability, as the winner of the contest is contracted to do. However, I ask that you please destroy this check made out in my name and issue another, in the same amount, to the Dougy Center. That way the entire sum will be a charitable and nontaxable contribution and all of the quarter of a million dollars will go toward comforting and easing the pain of tomorrow's grieving children, and the next day's and the next. . . ."

Several people at the table with the Lees immediately began waving frantically at Donne while they pointed toward Ted and Margaret, who were both nodding their heads toward the lectern in the affirmative. A warm smile suddenly appeared on Patrick Donne's face as he said, very softly, "Thank you! Thank you both, for all the little ones whose lives will be changed for the better because of you. I have tried for many years to live the words of a very wise person that history is unable to positively identify. The words were first written or spoken by either Victor Hugo or George Eliot or possibly a Quaker missionary by the name of Grellet, but they have long been my life's premier rule. The words are: 'I shall pass through this world but once. Any good therefore that I can do, or any kindness that I can show to any human being, let me do it now. Let me not defer or neglect it, for I shall not pass this way again.' "

Donne looked around the room slowly before continuing. "Perhaps some of you might wish to join me in this mission. The Dougy Center, I know, would appreciate your contribution, both large and small. There are always so many tiny tears that need to be kissed away and so many tiny hearts that need to be mended every day. Sorrow never takes a holiday. These little people, unable to deal with their grief, must be taught that life is still precious and worthwhile and that they have our support, our love and especially our understanding as we

all pass, together, through this world. God bless you, everyone
. . . and that's from all the kids. . . ."

And with those words, the World Champion of the Lectern
walked swiftly off the stage . . . to the longest standing ovation
I have ever witnessed in my forty-year career.

X

A heavy rain had fallen all night on Manhattan, constantly punctuated by bright arrows of lightning flashes and deafening thunder. It was our second day home after the convention, and both Mary and I were still in our pajamas and slippers, lazily sharing the morning paper while we munched on our Thomas' English muffins on which Mary had applied, after toasting, generous spreadings of Smucker's sweet orange marmalade.

My mission at the Omni Shoreham had been a complete failure. After finding, in Patrick Donne, someone who possessed all the special qualities I was seeking in a speaker, I had lost him. When he had walked off the stage, following his dramatic acceptance speech, he passed through the same exit doors from which he had made his entrance and then, quite literally, had vanished. Even after Mary had grown weary and returned to our room, Jay and I continued our search for the man, not only throughout the hotel but in at least half a dozen hotel cocktail lounges within a mile or so of the Omni. No luck at all. In the morning, before we departed for home, I tried phoning his room once more but was informed by the operator that Mr. Donne had already checked out. Frustration. Anger. I wasn't accustomed to losing and I didn't even want to think about giving up my dream of getting back into the business I loved so much.

Just to rub a little salt in my wounds, the previous night the "CBS Evening News" had carried several minutes of Donne's convention speech and once again we heard that great voice saying "Sorrow never takes a holiday. These little people, unable to deal with their grief, must be taught that life is still precious and worthwhile and that they have our support, our love and especially our understanding as we all pass, together, through this world. . . ."

Dan Rather, to further emphasize Donne's touching words, remained silent and pensive for perhaps fifteen seconds before he looked directly at the camera and said, "With people like Patrick Donne around, I guess there is still hope for mankind!"

Jay had phoned later in the evening to tell me that Peter Jennings had also done a piece, praising the first World Champion of the Lectern for an amazing act of charity, on his "ABC World News Tonight." The final straw was to just read, on the bottom of the front page of that morning's *New York Times*, a three-column piece on the "angel of mercy" from Blessings, Montana, and the dramatic gift of his entire cash prize of a quarter million dollars to "a little-known but very worthwhile cause, the Dougy Center."

"More coffee, hon?"

I lowered my paper, nodded at Mary and forced a smile. She

had dealt with my moods for many years and since our return home had apparently decided that the best way to handle this one was to leave me alone, which she had done by losing herself in a pile of paperback romances.

"So what are your plans for the day?" she asked.

The phone rang before I could reply. Good thing. I had no plans for today . . . or any day. I walked over to the oak-paneled wall near the large window facing out on Park Avenue and lifted the receiver from its wall bracket. When I recognized the voice I almost dropped the damn thing.

"Mr. Manning?"

"Yes."

"Sir, this is Patrick Donne. Please forgive me for disturbing you. I'm in New York for a couple of days, meeting with Ted & Margaret's marketing people. Ever since I arrived I've been wondering how to get in touch with you since I was pretty certain your phone would be unlisted. Finally decided to wrestle with this ten-pound Manhattan white-page telephone directory anyway and, miracle of miracles, found your name! For at least twenty minutes now I've been trying to muster enough courage to call you. Sir, you have been almost constantly on my mind ever since the convention ended and I was wondering if the rumor that kept surfacing at the Omni had any merit. Are you really planning to come out of retirement and become an active agent once again?"

The look on my face must have alarmed Mary, because she jumped up from the table and was now standing by my side, her hand on my shoulder, looking both puzzled and worried. I tried to phrase my reply so that I not only responded to Patrick Donne but also relieved Mary's concern.

"The rumor is absolutely correct, Pat. After a year or so of sitting on my duff and being pampered by my lovely wife and cruise ship stewards, I decided that kind of life was not for me. I'm too damn young to just sit around and do so little that the highlight of my day is a jog in the park. I attended the convention hoping that I might discover a good motivational speaker or two to represent since my old stable of professionals are either dead of retired. I did find one. You! I even spent several hours after the contest trying to make contact with you . . . in vain!"

"You did? God, I'm sorry, sir, very sorry. I had no idea. Hope it's not too late. I would like very much to meet with you."

"Where are you staying?"

"I'm at the Plaza."

"Nice place. How about today? Any free time?"

"All of it is . . . until three."

Our kitchen clock read slightly after nine. "Okay, tell you what, meet me at my office at eleven, how's that?"

I gave him the West 44th Street address and he asked softly, "Sir, is that the same office you have occupied for more than forty years, the one *Time* magazine called 'Manning's sanctuary in the heart of Babylon'?"

"It's the only one I've ever had and compared to most of the offices on Park and Madison and Lexington it's not much more than a broom closet. However, it's mine and I love it. Wouldn't be happy anywhere else."

"Well, sir, you may not believe this, but there have been many times in the past few years, before you announced your retirement and as I got more and more involved with public speaking, that I imagined myself visiting you there, always wondering just what I would say to Bart Manning, and even more important, what advice Bart Manning would have for me."

"Well, let's find out. When you get there you'll find the old metal street-level door locked. Just ring the bell and I'll come on down and let you in."

"Mr. Manning?"

"Yes?"

"Thank you very, very much."

"You are more than welcome, champ! I'm certainly glad you called."

I had phoned Grace from the Omni on the morning that we were flying home, giving her the sorry news that I had failed in my talent hunt. I suggested that she just stay home for a few days until I decided what my next move was going to be, so I was alone when Patrick Donne rang our street-level bell. I dashed downstairs, unlocked the old door and let him in.

I'm not certain who was happier to see the other, but our handshake quickly turned into a warm hug before Patrick followed me up the narrow steps. He paused as I led him through Grace's small office, staring at our wall of pictures behind her desk.

Pointing, he said in a hushed voice, "That's Eric Champion, isn't it? I've got an old long-playing record of a speech he made to the National Safety Congress in Chicago back in the late sixties. He was so great!"

He pointed to another, smaller photograph. "General Goldfarb?"

"Yes, it is."

"I've read some of his speeches. Even on paper his words come alive. And I recognize that man, too," he exclaimed proudly. "Blandy. He played first base for the Boston Red Sox. Hall of Famer! You have certainly handled some great ones, Mr. Manning!"

"Yes, I did . . . and I miss them all. Come on into my office and please, no more 'Mr. Manning.' Call me Bart and I won't feel so ancient when I'm around you. How old are you, by the way?"

"I was thirty-two about a week ago."

"That's supposed to be a very fruitful and productive year in a man's life. Jesus did his most important works at age thirty-two."

Donne nodded and stared down at his hands. "But then they crucified him."

I didn't know what to say.

Donne leaned back in the old chair next to my desk and said, "How unusual, Bart. You're the second person in less than an hour to talk to me about Jesus."

"What do you mean?"

"Well, as you know, the Plaza is directly across from Central Park. After I had spoken to you I was just too wired to stay in that hotel room, so I took a long walk in the park. Shortly before ten-thirty I emerged from all that greenery, passed the statue of Bolívar, I think, and turned left toward Fifth Avenue, where I planned to catch a taxi to come down here. Suddenly this strange-looking street person began pointing directly at me, waving his old Bible and screaming hoarsely, 'You, you . . . this is your day! Life will change for you today! Remember the words of Jesus on the mountain, when he said, 'Ask and it shall be given; seek, and ye shall find; knock, and it shall be opened unto you.' He kept pointing at me and yelling, 'You, this is your day. Ask, seek, knock!' until I finally escaped into a cab on Fifth. Strange! Almost frightening to hear those particular words before coming to meet with you."

"Pat, are you a religious man?"

"Not really, I'm sorry to say. About once a month, on the average, I do attend Sunday services at a community church in Red Lodge, back home. I try to live by the Commandments but no . . . I'm not some kind of a religious nut, if that's what you're wondering."

"Tell me, was that street person screaming advice at you, on the corner of Central Park South and Fifth, in a wheelchair?"

Donne frowned and tilted his head sideways. "Yes, he was. You know this man?"

"No, but I had a similar encounter with him one morning while I was jogging home from the park a couple of months ago. Haven't seen him since, although I still take the same route home every day."

I didn't elaborate any further on my own curious confrontation. Instead, I said, "That was a great vanishing act you pulled after your powerful speech at the Omni. I had everyone but the FBI trying to find you."

He smiled. "I wish I had known. When I walked out those exit doors I went right down to the lobby and out the front door, where I jumped in a cab and asked to be driven to the Lincoln Memorial. Because of the time of night I'm sure the cabbie thought he had a real weirdo on board, and as I was paying him I told him to come back and pick me up at the very same spot in exactly two hours. Then I tipped him fifty. I managed to find a bench that was positioned so that I could sit and look directly at that marble masterpiece of Lincoln that was illuminated in such a manner that the stone seemed to glow. Before my long, solitary session on the bench, however, I walked up the long row of marble steps until the great man towered directly above me. On the inside left wall of the memorial, chiseled into the stone, is the Gettysburg Address, words that meant so much to me ever since I was in the first grade. Bart, way back then my beloved mother worked with me for days until I had memorized the words to that immortal speech. Then, on Lincoln's birthday that year, my mother encouraged me to tell my first-grade teacher that I could recite Lincoln's Gettysburg Address and so, naturally, I was asked to perform in front of my class. They applauded. They actually applauded! Before the day had ended, Miss Wray had taken me around to every classroom in our grammar school and in each class, to my great surprise, the kids cheered and applauded, even the sixth graders. I guess that lit the flame and the dream. Anyway, as I was standing in the memorial, so very close to that huge statue, I turned toward the interior left wall, bathed in warm light. I just stood there, alone, remembering how proud my mom had been and I read the words aloud with tears running down my cheeks. Then I retreated down the stairs to the bench I had found and just sat there with all my memories, trying very hard to put everything that had happened to me in perspective."

"And did you?"

"I think so. Bart, I need you. I'd like to be a great speaker, a real spellbinder, and I need your help to make my dream come true. Will you be my agent?"

"I'd be very honored to represent you, Pat. From what I've seen and heard, your potential is unlimited. I believe we might do very well together and what pleases me most is that I also like you as a person, not just as a commodity I'd be selling. However, some of my terms are rather stiff and perhaps after you hear them you might not be so eager to have Bart Manning handling you."

"For example . . . ?"

"My commission is twenty-five percent of the speaking fee we charge the clients for your performance. The client booking you assumes all charges involving your transportation to and from airports, hotel bill and meals. However, you arrange your own flights and report the charge to us. We will bill the client, collect and remit the total amount to you. All your flights are first-class. If they won't pay for a round-trip first-class ticket, you don't go, okay?"

He just smiled and nodded.

"And what are you charging, these days, for your typical one-hour motivational speech?"

"Well, Bart, the amount is always negotiable, depending on the organization. Usually runs between one and three thousand."

"Patrick Donne, you are the world champion now and the fee is ten thousand . . . not negotiable."

He briefly closed his eyes. "God!" He sighed. Then he looked directly at me and asked, "Would you mind if I continued to do a few fund-raising charity affairs at no charge as I've always done?"

"No problem. Now, you must understand that when we sign our contract I'll be handling you exclusively. Of course, by the terms of the agreement, as you will see, each of us is free to dissolve the contract with thirty days' written notice, no reason necessary, but while it is in force I will book all your speeches. Oh, I might split my commission with another agency if they contact me regarding booking you for one of their clients, but other than that every booking will involve just you and me and the client. Okay?"

"I have no problem with that. When do we start?"

"That depends a lot on you. How many future speeches do you have booked as of today?"

"Six, I believe. And the last one is sometime in October of this year."

"Then that won't be so difficult. Now, by any chance do you have any of your press kits with you? Do you use one to promote yourself?"

"I do use a press kit, Bart, but they're all in Montana. I'll be back home in a couple of days though. . . ."

"Send me a dozen or so. I've got a very talented advertising and promotion group here in the city who do a much better job than what I once put out for my people. How about glossy photographs?"

"There's a good eight-by-ten in the press kit and it's rather recent, but if you and your people don't like it, we'll get more."

"Great. That very first time we met, at the bar in the Garden Court, it seems you were telling my friend Jay Bridges and me about a cattle ranch that you had owned and sold."

"I sold it to my foreman when the speeches began to multiply. Never really had enjoyed all the thousand and one chores of a ranch, and when my dad died I probably would have sold it then, but it had been my mother's home since their marriage and I just didn't have the heart to ask her to move. So I kept at it until I lost her, four years ago, and when the speeches began to increase in number and I had a chance to sell the spread, I did. Kept five acres and a tiny three-room cottage, a messy combination home and office. Did all my own mailings and paperwork and bookkeeping and enjoyed it from the beginning. Still do. But I'm sure ready to graduate into the 'bigtime' with your help."

I grinned. "How about that plane of yours?"

"My Beechcraft? Flying was once my greatest passion, but I've grown rather weary of it. I'd probably sell the thing if I had the right offer. It's in a private hangar in a small airport just outside of Billings."

"Pat, there's something else I've got to ask as we get to know each other. You're a big, handsome guy, but I've heard no mention of any Mrs. Donne. What gives?"

"You really mean . . . am I gay?"

"No . . . no. I was just wondering . . ."

"Eleven years ago I was engaged to the most beautiful girl in Montana. I lost her."

"I'm so sorry. Forgive me."

"I lost her, but not the way you're thinking. She loved me but she also loved her church and I guess when decision time came, I didn't stand much of a chance competing against God. The girl I loved so much has been a nun, now, for a long time. We keep in touch. She's teaching third grade in a parochial school in San Francisco. We exchange Christmas and birthday gifts and lots of mail. I've just never found anyone I could love and cherish as much as I did Jean Foley, but I keep looking."

"Well, I'm sure a big, handsome guy like you doesn't have much of a problem getting dates."

He smiled shyly and shook his head. "Someday, I'll find that special lady."

I handed him a large file card. "Print your address and phone number on this and when the contract is drawn up, Grace will mail it off to you. In the meantime, as soon as we receive your press kit we'll go to work on a new one featuring the fact that you are now the official World Champion of the Lectern. We'll do live mailings to all my old friends, the meeting planners and should be rolling before you know it. Also, when you get home, send me the exact dates of your six scheduled speeches and their location. If we get lucky and have the opportunity, we'll book you around them. Oh, and one more thing . . . I'm pretty certain we could place you on a few national talk shows considering you've already been praised by Rather, Jennings and *The New York Times.* Any objection to flying back here once or twice if we're able to spot you on a few in the next month or two? Might generate some action and make my job easier."

"You book 'em . . . I'll do 'em. I don't know how long Blessings will continue to be my home base anyway. I've been in love with this city for a long time, despite all its problems and my being a country boy, so I might surprise you somewhere along the line and tell you I'm going to become a New Yorker."

"Great! It would make my job a lot easier, especially in promoting you as the best of the best to all the national media here. If I can help you in any way along that line, just give me a yell."

The young man rose, extended his hand and said, "Thank you for a great opportunity. I've dreamed of this for a long time. You won't be sorry, I promise you. I'll give you all I've got."

"Pat, I have no doubt of that. You were my only choice. I'm not sure you even realize what a powerful force for good you can be in this country and this very strange time in our history, when everyone seems frightened and worried as they struggle to keep from drowning in a sea of misery, fear, uncertainty and chaos. The world seems to be going to hell, Pat. They need to hear your voice, your words, your inspiration. I'll be in touch . . . soon."

Donne glanced at his wristwatch. "Let's see, I've got an hour before I'm due for a meeting with Ted & Margaret's people. I think I'll do what I've been promising Jean I would do every time I came to New York City. I'm going to pay a visit to St. Patrick's Cathedral. Never been there, but this is the perfect time. I just want to thank God for bringing us together and I can't think of a better place to do it."

XI

One of the wisest decisions I ever made in my professional career was on that morning, back in the mid-1970s, when I finally came to the conclusion, with assistance from Mary, that I needed professional help if I was ever going to get all the benefit possible out of the press kits, brochures and mailing pieces I had been assembling and sending out to potential corporate clients for years. Even though Grace had always handled loads of my paperwork such as contracts and mailing lists, not to mention at least half my phone calls, I was still spending long days at my desk in order to keep my full stable of twelve professionals fully booked and happy. Somewhere along the way I had started to bring work home and, of course, the easiest things to transport were the many legal pads, pages of rough draft copy and artwork necessary to put together promotional pieces. One evening, working late on our dining room table laying out a brochure for our newest speaker, Gilbert Cobb, Mary had brought me a cup of my favorite herbal tea. As she placed it gently on my desk, she said, "Hon, you look like hell. You must be exhausted. Tell me, please, why are you wasting our precious evenings sweating over promotional copy, when there are perhaps five hundred advertising agencies within a few blocks of here who would probably be delighted to do all that for you . . . and quite possibly . . . if you will forgive me . . . do it even better? What are you, anyway, one of our country's best agents, or a writer of ad copy?"

And so, on the following morning at my office desk, I had opened the NYNEX Business to Business Yellow Pages to Advertising Agencies. Mary had been wrong. There were closer to a thousand advertising agencies within just a few blocks. Now, completely confused, I slowly turned the fifteen or so pages of agency listings until a small one-column-by-two-inch display ad in italic print caught my eye. *Dandelion Productions. The seeds we release produce for years. Two decades of proven experience and results in everything from direct mail to celebrity promotion. Call us. Terri and Vic Darnley. 201 E. 50th St., 555-7849.*

Just one meeting with Terri and Vic was all I needed to convince me that I wanted those two bright people on my team. It is impossible to calculate how much they increased the number of bookings I was able to obtain for my people because of the creative and appealing promotional material they produced. Their wise advice regarding my mailings as well as the national exposure they arranged, commencing with Eric Champion, on talk shows and network morning programs such as "The Today Show" was priceless. The secret to their success, I am positive, is that the Darnleys really cared. They made it a point to personally get to know each of my speakers so that when we met to discuss future promotion possibilities, as we usually tried to do every Friday, they could offer, as Vic had once put it, "custom-made" suggestions because they truly were familiar with the person we were trying to sell to clients.

When Patrick Donne's press kits arrived by overnight mail, I immediately phoned the Darnleys. Terri answered the phone, and when I very briefly told her the purpose of my call, her voice broke several times when she said, "Bart, that is the best news I've heard in years. We sort of suspected something was up when we heard that you two were going to the speakers convention. Are you really getting back in the business?"

"With the help of you two, I hope. When can we get together and talk?"

"Well, tomorrow is Friday and Fridays have never been the same since you retired and our weekly meetings came to an end. How about ten tomorrow, here, like old times?"

"I'll be there!"

We spent the better part of Friday morning, after we had stopped reminiscing about our past triumphs and defeats, discussing the various avenues we might pursue to best promote Patrick Donne. I could sense that Terry and Vic had almost immediately picked up on my enthusiasm and eventually we came to several decisions on how best to proceed. We agreed that I was to contact no old friends or meeting planners or pitch Patrick Donne in any way until the new press kits had been prepared and mailed. Also, the Darnleys insisted that we needed much more dramatic photographs of Patrick than the one he had been using in his kit.

I pointed impatiently at the pieces from Donne's press kit which were now scattered across the top of Vic's desk. "I hope all this won't take too long. We should have his contract in the mail to him in the next couple of days."

Vic smiled. "Bart, you're just getting antsy because you've been on such an extended vacation. Okay if we phone him today and ask him to come back to the big city for a couple of days for pictures and a meeting with us? I'd like the Matteo Studios on Lexington to do the shoot for us. We've used nobody but Matt in the past ten years or so for all your people as well as most of our other clients. He's a true artist. We'll tell your man to bring a couple of his best tailored suits along, if he has any."

I smiled. "Don't let the fact that he's from Montana fool you. He's got them. In fact, I'll even bet his blue jeans are tailored."

Terry shook her head in wonder. "Bart, I don't think I can remember when I've heard you so gung-ho on a speaker. You're not building this guy up in your own mind just because you want to get back in the business so badly, are you?"

"Positively not! If you could have been with me at the convention, you would understand. Until I saw and heard this man, everyone else onstage there, including several so-called top professionals, had all struck out on my score sheet."

Vic scowled at some of the press kit copy lying on his desk. "And when he does come, Bart, and the sooner the better, we'd also like to have a long meeting with him so that we can really get to know the man. His clients all seem to be small companies in the Northwest. Not much here to impress a Fortune 500 meeting planner, so we'll need to find a handle or two we can use. Okay?"

"Of course. And you might ask him to bring that striking

Waterford crystal trophy he was presented as World Champion of the Lectern. Could make for some dramatic photos. Also, in case I've forgotten to say it up to now, you two have an unlimited budget on this one. Do whatever you feel you need to do."

Terri waved her index finger at me. "You'll be sorry."

I waved my finger right back at her. "Never have been yet. Just remember to remind Donne that time is of the essence. The sooner he comes east, turns on his charm for the camera and meets with the two of you, the sooner you'll be able to put together his new press kit. Once we have all that, we can begin our mailings and, hopefully, I'll be able to get on the phone on follow-ups soon afterward."

Terri phoned our apartment that evening as Mary and I were watching the eleven o'clock news. She had made contact with Pat on her first try. "What a magnificent voice that man has, Bart," she exclaimed, "and I didn't have to do a bit of selling to convince him of the urgency of our project. All he said was that if Mr. Manning wanted him, he'd be here. He said he'd come to New York next Monday afternoon and be at our office at nine on Tuesday. Isn't that great? That will give me all of Monday to get in touch with Matt and arrange for Donne's photo session sometime Wednesday. On Tuesday he and Vic and I will have our long getting-to-know-you chat. Oh, and I hope you won't mind, I asked him if it was okay for you to be present and he said he'd love it. Also sends you his very best and wants you to know he can't wait to get started. I told him we'd remit the cost of his airline ticket and cab fares and that he had a room booked at The Peninsula, charged to your account, okay? So how did I do?"

"Does Vic know what a lucky man he is?"

"I doubt it. Remind him, will you please, the next time you two are talking."

I phoned a surprised Grace on Saturday and asked her if she would please come in on Monday so that we could finish as-sembling the full mailing list of corporate prospects that she had been diligently working on when I had called from the Omni with the sorry news that my scouting mission had failed at the convention and we had no speakers to promote. Then Pat's phone call had changed everything. On Monday we worked together for perhaps two hours before Grace patiently turned to me and said, "Bart, I can handle this, as I've always done in the past. Why don't you go on home and rest up. You'll need all your energy and then some when we get the new press kit and you begin phoning and pitching all your meeting-planner friends."

I purposely delayed my arrival at the Darnleys' office by thirty minutes on Tuesday so that Terri and Vic and Pat could get to know one another a little and talk freely without my presence impeding things. Apparently the strategy worked just fine. When I was shown into Dandelion Productions' small and cozy oak-paneled meeting room where I had spent so many productive hours with Terri and Vic through the years, they all had smiles on their faces.

After shaking Vic's and Pat's hand and kissing Terri on the cheek, I lied and said, "So sorry I'm late. My broker phoned this morning and said he needed my autograph on a few papers and it took longer than we planned. Pat, how's your room at The Peninsula?"

"The room is superb and the entire hotel is magnificent!

Plus I've already discovered their three-level spa at the top of the hotel. A tough way to live," he grinned.

I turned to Terri and Vic. "Well, you two, what do you think of this guy? Are we going to be able to sell him to the world?"

Dressed in a loose-fitting light linen blazer over a black T-shirt, Patrick Donne smiled and raised his broad shoulders defensively, waiting for the reply that came from Terri. "Yeah, I believe you might be able to get this big cowboy a gig now and then if you're not too fussy."

Vic said, "Seriously, Bart, from what Pat has just told us, it appears that Ted & Margaret's national commercials are going to do a great deal of the groundwork for us. Pat, tell him what they're planning for the initial one which they're going to be running nationally for at least a month."

Pat smiled sheepishly and shook his head. "As I understand it, the first commercial will open with a loud trumpet fanfare as the camera zooms in on the Parthenon followed by the same treatment of the Colosseum in Rome, then Philadelphia's Independence Hall and finally, the Lincoln Memorial as a baritone voice-over is saying, 'The world has known many orators in the past such as Demosthenes, Cicero, Patrick Henry and Lincoln.' Then Bart—and you are not going to believe this since you know where I disappeared to after winning the speaking contest in Washington—as the camera slowly zooms in on the Lincoln Memorial the voice will say, 'Our century, as it draws to a close, has finally produced a spellbinder of its own who is the equal of any who have come before.' As those words are being spoken I will step out from behind Lincoln's statue and slowly walk down the memorial steps, smiling and waving, while the voice says, 'Ladies and gentlemen, meet Patrick Donne, World Champion of the Lectern!' As the camera zooms in for a head-and-shoulders close-up, I will do a fifteen-second spot telling the viewers how proud I am to be speaking for Ted & Margaret's great dishes and I will suggest a specific dinner, yet to be selected by their marketing people. End of commercial as camera fades back and up until we are looking at an aerial shot of Washington. They told me I'll be doing my part at the memorial next Wednesday and they plan to debut the finished commercial on '60 Minutes' and 'Good Morning America' in four weeks."

Vic turned toward me, grinning, as he raised both hands high above his head. "Who could possibly ask for anything more? Tell me, Bart, have you guys decided what kind of a speaker's fee you are planning to charge for Pat's presentations?"

"Ten thousand. Firm."

"Not enough! Not when you consider what some of the so-called 'celebrity' speakers are charging these days. Of course, we haven't heard Pat do his thing yet, but—"

Donne interrupted. "Would you like to hear me speak?"

"We'd love it!"

"Well, a week from this Saturday I'm delivering the keynote address to the Nevada Association of Realtors following their annual awards dinner at Caesars Palace in Las Vegas. If you two come, I'll arrange for tickets."

Terri sighed. "It's been much too long since I've tussled with those lovely, shiny slot machines."

"Ten years at least," said Vic, sounding just as wistful. "And I wouldn't mind a few hours at the roulette table again. Terri, let's go! The work can wait. We'll fly to Vegas on Friday and stay for three or four days or until we go broke, and we won't even charge Bart for any part of the trip. Aren't we nice? We'll call our Nancy at Welcome Aboard and set it up tomorrow."

Terri excitedly jumped up, pushed back her chair until it fell over with a crash, hurried to where Pat was sitting, embraced him and planted a noisy kiss on his cheek. "Thank you, my new and special friend," she shrieked. "You have just performed a miracle! My husband is actually going to get out of this office for a few days with his wife and just have fun! Fun! Thank you . . . thank you!"

"Great," Pat replied. "I'll be flying to Las Vegas on Friday, after I do my Lincoln Memorial bit on Wednesday, so there'll be plenty of time for me to arrange to get tickets to you for the Saturday evening dinner. And speaking of dinner," he continued as he looked around at each of us, "would you all please honor me as my guests for dinner this evening at The Peninsula? I realize it's very short notice, but we need to break a little bread to commemorate this new alliance. Bart, of course that includes your wife, too. I can't wait to meet her. The hotel, as you probably all know, has a lovely restaurant, The Adrienne, and great food. How about eight-thirty tonight?"

The Adrienne's soft shades of salmon pink, glowing in the warm light from elegant sconces carefully positioned around the restaurant, served as an ideal setting for our celebratory dinner, and Patrick Donne, as I had expected, was the perfect host. After toasting each one of us with a few kind words, Pat paused and turned to me, still holding his champagne goblet on high. "Bart, we've been tossing that word 'spellbinder' around for the last few days, but I think that Mr. Longfellow, in his *Tales of a Wayside Inn*, described that person best. Now, I haven't recited poetry in public since grade school, but here goes . . .

> 'He ended, and a kind of spell
> 'Upon the silent listeners fell.
> 'His solemn manner and his words
> 'Had touched the deep, mysterious chords,
> 'That vibrate in each human breast alike.' "

It was truly a relaxed and wonderful evening, and well past midnight when Mary and I finally arrived home. As we were both undressing, I asked, "Well, hon, what do you think of the man?"

"Bart, he is as impressive and charming up close as he was onstage. There is a special magnetism, an aura of some sort surrounding him that's hard to explain. He's appealing and attractive and yet I caught myself lowering my voice a couple of times when I was answering his questions . . . as a child might do when speaking to an adult who represented authority. And with that handsome face and beard he reminds me of some of the figures in religious paintings in our church when I was little. He almost looks as if he should be wearing a halo."

"Mary, what are you saying?"

"Bart, I'm sorry, I'm not really sure what I'm saying."

Vic phoned our apartment on Wednesday evening to report that the photo session had been a great success. "Bart, he actually brought four tailor-made suits, four different shirts, a dozen silk ties and three pairs of Ferragamos with him. Matt was really impressed and I'm pretty sure we'll have plenty of powerful shots to use. After Pat had said his farewells and returned to The Peninsula to check out, Matt told us that Patrick Donne could probably make a very comfortable living modeling clothes if he didn't make it as a speaker. Isn't that something? In any event, Terri and I will begin to play around with some promo ideas and we'll give you a call when we have the pictures in hand. And, of course, we'll be watching the man perform in person Saturday at Caesars. Then we'll really go to work."

Mary and I stayed up on Saturday night, watching *Barbarians at the Gate* on HBO until almost two on Sunday morning, hoping that Terri or Vic would phone us from Vegas with their review of Pat's performance. No such luck. We were both having a late breakfast of pancakes and sausage when the phone finally rang on Sunday. "Bart," said Vic, "Terri is on the other line in the bedroom so that we can both chat with you. Well, we saw our man . . ."

". . . and . . . and . . . tell me, for God's sake!" I exclaimed.

Then I heard Terri's soft voice. "Bart, he was absolutely fantastic! I've never heard a better speaker, and that includes your Eric Champion at his best! He had that crowd in the palm of his hand from start to finish, and that's tough to do with all the distractions in any of these Vegas hotels. That fee you were planning on charging, ten thousand . . . ?"

"Yes."

"We both believe you should double it!"

"Twenty thousand? Are you guys crazy?"

"No, we think you should double it and then offer a guarantee that no one who has had the responsibility of planning a

convention or even a single business meeting has ever heard
before."

"I'm listening . . ."

"Tell them all that if they hire Patrick Donne at twenty
thou and they are not completely satisfied, you will refund all
their money, including any expense charges you might have
collected, providing they notify you within thirty days of the
speech date. And we'll include a very special certificate of
guarantee attesting to all that in your promotion package."

Slowly, after I had managed to collect my thoughts, I said,
"There has never been anything like that before in the entire
history of public speaking!"

"Bart," Terri replied, "there has never been a . . . a . . . spellbinder like Patrick Donne before!"

XII

Ten agonizingly long days later I was finally back in Dandelion Productions' meeting room reviewing the Patrick Donne promotional material including a four-color brochure, cover letter and even a six- by nine-inch envelope with no return address, just my name in block letters in the upper left-hand corner.

Terri and Vic sat across the table from me in silence, watching intently as I studied the fruits of their labor. Their four-page brochure, probably the most important piece in any mailing no matter what one is selling or promoting, was as powerful a piece as any they had ever done for me. On its buff-colored cover page, framed in silver, was a picture of the Waterford crystal trophy that Donne had received for winning the championship contest at the convention. Above the photo, in simple black Times Roman lettering, was the question "Why Not Hire the Best in the World?" Inside were two striking photographs of Pat as well as simple copy, without a trace of hype, describing the man and his accomplishments from managing a huge Montana cattle ranch to being praised by Dan Rather, Peter Jennings and *The New York Times* all in the same week—an amazing trifecta!

I finally looked across the table at my old friends and smiled. "You have really outdone yourselves. It's all excellent—the photos, the copy, the layouts!"

I picked up the cover letter that would accompany the brochure, ostensibly written by me to each meeting planner, which opened with a brief announcement that I was now back in the world of public speaking and would appreciate their consideration for any future bookings they might have. The letter then went on to ask the recipient if he or she would kindly take a few moments to review the enclosed piece on the World Champion of the Lectern whom I now had the great honor to represent.

"This final paragraph," I said admiringly, "is a marvelous touch . . . casually mentioning the money-back guarantee without even making any sort of a big deal out of it. Can't you just see most of the meeting planners reading this letter to the bottom and then doing this great double take as they back up and read that last paragraph again to confirm what they had just read? Love it! And this Certificate of Guarantee promising all the money back if the meeting executives are not pleased with Donne's work looks more authentic than most of my stock certificates."

"Bart," Vic said, sounding very relieved, "we've got ten or twelve other great photos of the man that we didn't need in the material. Take them along, and if you decide you'd like to use any of them in your correspondence with meeting planners, just let us know and we'll have Matt run off as many as you want."

"Thanks. Okay, let's roll on everything. How long before we'll have printed stuff ready to drop in the mail?"

"Barring any foul-ups, we should have the finished kits in your office a week from today. How many do you want to start with?"

"Grace is going to mail to our whole list, so let's roll with three thousand."

On the day after Labor Day I phoned Patrick Donne with the news that early in the day we had made our mail drop to more than twenty-seven hundred prospects and that I was sending him several copies of all the material that had been mailed.

"What's next?" he asked anxiously.

"Well, I'll allow sufficient time for everyone to have received and looked over our package and then begin making follow-up phone calls, first to my old friends who have booked speakers with me through the years and then I'll just work our way down the rest of the list, slowly and securely."

I could hear Donne chuckling. "How many old friends, Bart?"

"Oh, a couple of hundred, I guess. So what have you been up to since you left Manhattan?"

"I gave three speeches . . . in Salt Lake City, Boise and Portland. Two more and I'll be out of work, Bart. Just kidding. I'm so darn proud to have you representing me. Can't wait to start my career in the majors. As they say, it's nail-biting time. To keep from going bonkers while I wait, I've been riding my Harley, just about every good day, up and down Beartooth

Highway. I guess I've probably made half a dozen round trips from Billings all the way down to Yellowstone National Park. Nothing better than stopping that bike near a few special spots and spending a little time sitting by a glacial lake or walking along the tundra that is so quiet I sometimes feel I can hear God speaking to me."

"Pat, you never mentioned that you drove a motorcycle as well as fly a Beechcraft."

"Not to worry, Bart. I've never done anything foolish in either machine and I'm so safety conscious, I'm boring. I'll be okay. Just trying to keep occupied until you turn me loose. Never enjoyed just sitting around waiting for something to happen."

"Please be patient for just a little while longer, huh?"

"I will. Everything is under control, trust me. By the way, would you like an audiotape of my speech . . . a real good one? The people heading that company in Boise where I spoke are old friends of mine and so, as a favor to me, they brought in a crew and recorded my talk and I took a few hundred bucks off their fee. You might want to make copies and send them to prospects who can't seem to make up their mind whether to book me or not. I guess I was in high gear that evening because even I think this tape is excellent. Shall I send it to you?"

"I'd love to have it!"

"What I also have is the master tape which is on a large reel with all kinds of information on the cover that I don't understand but I'm sure you will."

"Great! With that we'll be able to make copies with excellent fidelity. Call me when you receive the material I've just sent you and let me know what you think, okay? I probably should have cleared all of it with you before we went ahead and printed it, but I didn't want to lose another week and I was pretty sure you'd like everything anyway."

"I'm sure I will. Did you say the mailing went out this morning?"

"By first class. All of it!"

"The timing couldn't be better, Bart. Most likely I will receive it before this weekend and then, on Sunday, Ted & Margaret's first commercial will air on '60 Minutes' and be repeated Monday, Wednesday and Friday on 'Good Morning America.' When were you planning to commence with our phone calls?"

"Next Monday. Talk about luck!"

"Go get 'em, boss!"

I didn't have to wait until Monday. On Friday morning after I had returned from my daily jog, showered and dressed, I was sipping coffee in the kitchen, when Grace phoned from the office, her voice sounding a shade more high pitched than usual. "Bart, Harold Titus just called. He said his secretary had just brought his morning mail, including our promotion package which was an answer to all his prayers. He would like you to phone him as soon as you can. Can you believe it?"

Harold Titus had been chief meeting planner for Latimer Investments, a chain of large brokerage houses across the country, for at least ten years, and he had often booked my speakers for their annual national conventions which were always held in the finest hotels on apparently unlimited budgets. I can never remember Harold quibbling with me about a speaker's fee. Through the years we had become warm friends, and since their corporate headquarters was based in nearby Newark, Mary and I had enjoyed many dinners with Harold and his wife, Arlene, over the years. I immediately dialed the number Grace had given me and soon after I asked for Harold Titus, I heard a familiar voice say "Harold Titus's office."

"Peggy, how are you?"

She immediately recognized my voice. "Mr. Manning, I'm so glad you called. How are you?"

"Just great, and how nice to hear your voice again. How's that old grouch you work for?"

"Hold on, sir, and I'll let you find out for yourself."

"Bart? Bart, is it really you? Thanks for getting back to me so quickly."

"How are you Harold . . . and your pretty lady?"

"We're fine. Mary?"

"Tough as ever. Harold, it's been much too long."

"I know, and I've never been able to accept the fact that you were no longer in the business. Then I received your great brochure on this man Donne this morning, and I don't know whether I was more overjoyed to see you had come back to work or to think that you might be the answer to a terrible problem I have. Your mailing couldn't have arrived at a better time. It was truly an answer to my desperate prayers as I believe I told your assistant in the office—Grace, is it?"

"Yes, it's Grace. She just phoned me. I'm still at home. Tell me, how can I help you, old buddy?"

"Well, first of all, my vanity insists that I inform you that this old meeting planner now has a title after his name. For almost a year now I have been Harold Titus, Vice President, Meetings and Conventions."

"What great news! It was long overdue, my friend."

"Bart, I find myself in a very difficult predicament, one that I don't believe I've ever had to deal with before. A week from this Sunday, on the eighteenth of September, Latimer Investments is having its annual four-day national convention at Trump Plaza in Atlantic City. We expect a record attendance of around fourteen hundred of our top people and perhaps eight hundred spouses according to the latest reservation figures I've seen. On Wednesday, the final night, our featured speaker was to have been Alex Shelley, who, as I'm sure you know, has written four or five blockbuster books on sales and motivation. His latest has been on the *Times* best-seller list of nonfiction for over a year now. Well, yesterday afternoon Mr. Shelley's Ferrari blew a tire and rolled over several times on Route Ninety-five near Daytona Beach and our world-famous author is now in a hospital bed with both legs and one arm dangling loosely in midair. Tell me, is your world champion's schedule such that he can come be our keynote speaker next Wednesday evening?"

Despite all my years in the business, I could feel my heart beating. Wow! I tried to sound very businesslike. "Harold, Pat Donne still has two speeches to fulfill that he booked himself, before I took over, and I'm not sure what those dates are from memory, but Grace has them at the office. I'll check and get right back to you."

"Wonderful!"

"Wouldn't you like to know his fee? As I'm sure you noticed, we didn't mention that in the mailing."

"I know . . . but I did read your money-back guarantee. Very clever. Okay, what's his fee?"

"Twenty thousand plus the usual—first-class round-trip ticket from his home in Montana and room and meals, of course."

"Will do."

There was no conflict with Pat's schedule. He immediately phoned his travel agent and then reported back to me that if he departed Billings early on Wednesday morning, he would be at the Atlantic City airport, on United Flight 368, a little after four in the afternoon, plenty of time to prepare for the convention's grand finale.

I told him to go ahead and book it and someone from Latimer Investments would meet him at the airport and take him to Trump Plaza. Then he surprised me by asking, "Bart, are you still jogging in Central Park every morning?"

"I sure am."

"Well, if I come into New York City on the morning after the speech, Thursday, and take care of some business with Ted & Margaret's marketing people, who are getting ready for us to shoot the second commercial, how about if I joined you for your jog through the park on Friday?"

"I'd love it."

"What time do you roll out of your apartment to start your morning runs?"

"I'm usually out the front door at just about six-thirty."

"Okay, on Friday morning I'll be waiting for you in my jogging suit just outside your Park Avenue front door."

"You've got a date, and about the speech . . ."

"Yes?"

"Break a leg!"

I immediately phoned Harold with the news that Patrick

Donne would, indeed, be his closing speaker on Wednesday evening at Trump Plaza and that he was to send someone to the Atlantic City airport to meet Pat at a little after four.

"You've just saved my butt, Mr. Manning."

"And you've just made my day, Mr. Titus!"

XIII

Ted and Margaret's commercial on "60 Minutes," even though Pat had briefed me on its contents, was far more powerful than I had expected. Rare is the human being who would not appear small and insignificant standing next to the massive statue of Lincoln in the Lincoln Memorial, but when Patrick Donne stepped out from behind the white marble masterpiece by Daniel Chester French, nodding and waving, his powerful presence and warm smile, even on our television set, was compelling. When the commercial ended, Mary shook her head in wonder and sighed, "A star is born!"

On Monday morning I began phoning the names on my list of meeting planners with whom I had done business for so many years. Of course, each old friend had to be brought up-to-date on my activities, hear me explain why I had decided to jump back in the rat race and then we chatted about spouses and families and the condition of our health. Only after all those preliminaries were out of the way could I make my pitch for Pat, and throughout the day I heard repeated compliments on both our mailing brochure and Pat's dramatic appearance on that powerful commercial.

Corporate conventions are usually planned six to nine months ahead, so I was not in the least disappointed with the first day's results. My goal was merely to renew friendly contacts with those in a position to select big-name and celebrity speakers. The general reaction was that my old friends were happy that I was back and intrigued by Patrick Donne, most of them assuring me that they would certainly keep me in mind when planning commenced for their next convention, either regional or national. I followed the same routine on Tuesday, probably spending a total of six hours on the phone and renewing acquaintances with twenty-one meeting planners as well and learning that three of my old friends had passed on and two had retired.

At breakfast on Wednesday morning, Mary reached across the table and placed her hand on top of mine. "What's bothering you, hon? You seem to be a million miles away."

"I've been thinking that I should have gone down to Atlantic City to hear Pat do his thing tonight. After all, this is his first one for me and the very least I could have done is show up to give him a little moral support. It would have been nice. . . . "

"I don't think so, Bart. Patrick Donne doesn't need you hovering around and checking up on him. He's a big boy and your not showing up at Trump Plaza just confirms that you have complete faith in him. I really don't believe he'll be disappointed and I'm positive he won't let you down."

On Thursday morning I arrived at the office hoping that

Harold Titus would phone and report on Patrick Donne's performance as he had always done after booking one of my speakers in the past. Although I arrived earlier than usual, Grace was already at her desk and she greeted me with a smug smile. "Harold Titus hasn't changed a bit. He's already phoned. Shall I get him for you?"

I nodded and hurried into my office, picking up the phone on its first ring.

"Good morning, Bart."

"Harold, good morning. How did everything go?"

There was a long silence. After perhaps twenty seconds I asked, "Harold, are you still there?"

"I'm here, Bart."

"Something wrong? You sound strange."

"Well, my friend, I'm still trying to recover from last night. It was a closing session that no one who was there will ever forget, I guarantee it!"

By now all my inner alarm bells were ringing. Obviously something out of the ordinary had taken place at Trump Plaza last night, and Harold Titus apparently was still struggling to sort it out in his mind. I tried to sound casual but interested. "Tell me about it, Harold."

"Well, as you know, we were expecting a record crowd for this convention and we got it. The big ballroom had more than a hundred tables jammed into it for the awards dinner, which we always have on our closing night. The food was great and so was the music and entertainment, which we booked through the hotel people. They were a great help to us throughout the convention. After some dancing on a crowded floor, while the tables were being cleared, Robert Manson, our

vice president in charge of sales, went up onstage and announced the names of the leading producers for the first six
months of the year. Each was presented with a huge plaque,
and when they descended from the stage they walked over to
our table, where they received congratulatory handshakes and
hugs from our president, Horace Latimer."

"Sounds good," I said, still waiting for the ax to fall.

"Bart, table one, of course, is directly in front of center
stage. At that table sat Horace Latimer and his wife, Lucy, our
company treasurer and his wife, our vice president in charge of
sales and his wife, Sarah and me and . . . Patrick Donne.
When the ceremonies started, President Latimer and Lucy
turned their chairs around so that they were facing the stage.
After all the awards had finally been presented, one of my as-
sistants, Chuck Rosen, who had been a nightclub master of
ceremonies for years, approached the lectern and gave Mr.
Latimer a rousing introduction.

"As you know, Bart, Horace Latimer looks like a president
should look. He's tall, has great posture, chiseled features on a
tanned face and a full head of silver hair. When the entire
ballroom rose to honor our boss with a standing ovation, he
walked to the left side of the stage and up the steps slowly,
smiling and nodding at the crowd. At the lectern he patted
Chuck Rosen on the cheek, thanked him and proceeded to
speak to us for about fifteen minutes, telling us that he was
very proud of what we had accomplished during the first half
of the year despite a difficult economy and that he had complete confidence that we would do as well or better in the second half. Then he removed a folded sheet of paper from his
inside breast pocket and presented Patrick Donne, reading the

introduction perfectly, word for word, as you had requested. He waited for Donne to make the long trip to the lectern from table one, extended his hand and said, "Mr. Donne, I saw you in that commercial with your friend Mr. Lincoln. You both looked great!" And then, Bart, your man waited for the applause to end, still holding Latimer's hand, which he patted before he replied, "Thank you, sir. Knowing all that you have accomplished in your lifetime, I feel I am in the presence of greatness once again this evening!"

"That's my guy!"

"Of course, Bart, that produced another standing ovation and loud cheers. Donne waited calmly at the microphone until the audience had taken their seats again and Latimer had returned to his place at table one with his chair facing Donne and the stage."

I heard myself asking, "So how did the speech go, Harold?" Patience was never a virtue of mine.

"The speech was fabulous. Your man is as good as you said he was. The ballroom was soon very still, and that's always been my way of measuring whether a speaker is making it or not. Donne was powerful, dramatic, interesting, humorous and mesmerizing. Our people were truly spellbound. I remember that Latimer turned around in his seat, perhaps forty minutes into Donne's talk, nodded in my direction and raised his right thumb. Our president was obviously pleased and, of course, so was I. Then a terrible thing happened. . . . "

Now I held my breath.

"A frightening thing, Bart. Like everyone else in the ballroom, the people at our table were all concentrating on Donne and his message, and so the first inkling any of us had that something was wrong came from Donne himself. Like all good speakers, his head had been constantly turning from one side of the ballroom to the other, making eye contact with as many in our audience as he could, when he suddenly ceased talking in the middle of a sentence and leaned forward to stare down at Mr. Latimer, whose head had tilted backward as he clutched his chest with both hands. Before any of us could act, Donne leapt down from the front of the high stage, landing close to Mr. Latimer, whose eyes were now closed, his face covered with beads of perspiration as he moaned softly.

" 'My God,' I can remember his wife screaming, 'Horace is having a heart attack!'

" 'Someone call nine one one . . . get us an ambulance!' Donne roared as he knelt near Latimer, lifting him from his chair and laying him gently on the carpeted floor. Everyone was starting to crowd in, so the men at our table took it upon ourselves to keep them back. I watched Donne as he wiped off the old boy's face with a handkerchief and then began to stroke his forehead and cheeks as he said softly, and I believe I was the only one close enough to hear him, 'God, make him well, please. God, help him to breathe, please. God, help him to see, please. A sound heart is the life of the flesh.' He kept repeating the same words over and over as he placed the palms of both his hands on Latimer's cheeks and soon, so help me God, Bart, the boss's eyes slowly opened and his short, heavy breaths began to subside. It was an amazing thing to watch. Then Mr. Latimer tried to push himself up by his elbows, but Donne wouldn't allow it. The old boy just lay back on the carpet and I heard him say in a hoarse voice, 'I don't believe this was part of our scheduled program.'

"Well, Bart, the ambulance arrived rather swiftly and took Mr. Latimer away and everyone eventually filed out of the ballroom in a very shocked state. The few of us who had seen Patrick Donne in action, close up, didn't know what to say to the man except to extend our profound thanks. However, none of us quite understood what he did to bring our boss back from what appeared to be a one-way trip to the grave, although we all realized it was not the usual procedure for cardiopulmonary resuscitation. Those who had watched from nearby tables all went away telling each other they had witnessed a miracle and they were all asking, 'Who is this man?' "

"How is Mr. Latimer this morning? Have you heard, Harold?"

"I sure have, old buddy. He's out of intensive care and yelling like hell to be discharged. None of the hospital tests, including an EKG only an hour ago, give any indication that Horace Latimer had suffered any kind of seizure, heart attack or stroke last night. And yet, Bart, a few of us who were close by and have gone through the trauma of seeing someone struck down in the past will swear to you that the man had indeed suffered a heart attack. God knows he had most of the symptoms. He was clutching his chest. Pain! He had become very pale despite his tan, and there were beads of perspiration on his face. His breath was coming in short gasps and he had lapsed into unconsciousness before Donne laid him gently on the floor, wiped away his perspiration and began stroking his cheeks and forehead while he spoke to him. Bart, my mother dropped dead before my eyes when I was in my teens and she had all the same signs."

"Tell me again, what was Pat saying as he tended to Latimer?"

"As near as I can remember it was 'God, make him well,

please. God, help him to breathe, please. God, help him to see, please. A sound heart is the life of the flesh.' "

" 'A sound heart is the life of the flesh' sounds biblical, Harold."

"I'm afraid you can't prove it by me. All I know is that I thought we had lost our boss last night, but today he is still alive and well and I'm pretty certain that your man somehow saved his life. He's already checked out of the hotel, but when you see him please tell him that everyone who was in that ballroom last night will be forever grateful to him. And bless you, my friend. If you hadn't come out of retirement when you did, Horace Latimer would probably be dead this morning. God truly works in strange ways."

I continued to stare at the telephone after hanging up. There was a pain in the pit of my stomach.

XIV

Patrick Donne, looking very much like a Ralph Lauren ad in his black velour jogging suit and white Nikes, was leaning casually against the old red bricks of our apartment building on Friday morning, his arms loosely folded, when I stepped out onto the Park Avenue sidewalk for my morning jog at exactly 6:30 as promised.

"Good morning, boss," he called, flashing that handsome smile.

"Morning, Pat," I replied, extending a hand that he grasped firmly between his two huge palms. "Are you ready for a hasty round trip through the closest thing we New Yorkers have to heaven on earth?"

"Lead the way, sir," he replied, falling in beside me as I commenced a slow jog that I always maintained when coping with the usual wide variety of humanity found on Manhattan's sidewalks. Even at that early hour there were three occasions in the brief ten minutes it took to jog between my apartment building and Central Park when we were confronted by solitary old men in tattered clothes, crouching forlornly on the sidewalk and pleading loudly with passersby for money. Three times Patrick Donne stopped, removed cash from his wallet, placed it in the dirty hands of a grimy and disheveled panhandler who, in each instance, looked up gratefully at Pat and hoarsely said the same words—"Thank you, master."

As soon as we had crossed Fifth Avenue and entered the park with its lush greenery, our world immediately quieted down. Side by side we jogged along in silence, now at an accelerated pace, until we arrived at the Mall, that long, straight pathway lined with stately elm trees and busts of so many famous authors. Eventually we circled around the bandshell, went past the Bethesda Fountain and arrived at the Lake, a favorite spot for picnickers.

I could no longer control my curiosity. Slowing my gait, I pointed to a green wooden bench that faced the Lake and the park's only iron bridge, which had been made famous by decades of paintings, photographs and engravings.

"Let's sit for a few minutes. I've got to hear how the speech went."

Pat stopped jogging and smiled. "You mean your friend Titus hasn't reported to you on my performance yet?"

"Oh, he's reported all right. Gave you a rave review. Said you had that huge audience completely under your spell. I just wanted to hear all about it from the man himself."

Soon we were both seated with our legs extended to the stretch position on the newly mowed grass. "Well, Bart," Pat began, speaking slowly, as if he were considering each word, "I guess you would say that the speech was a success, but in that lovely hotel with its gorgeous ballroom one would really have to be a five-star dud not to be a winner on the platform. The room was perfect, the audience polite and receptive, and I gave them all I had. It being my first speech for you, I didn't dare let you down. On a scale of zero to ten, I guess I'd give myself a strong eight."

I nodded but remained silent, waiting for him to continue. Pat finally turned toward me and asked, "Did Mr. Titus tell you what happened toward the end of my talk?"

"He gave me some of the details. I figured I'd get the rest from you."

"Well," Pat sighed, "the speech had been going along pretty well and I was in the home stretch when I happened to look down at the head table, which was just in front of the lectern. Mr. Latimer had suddenly slumped backward in his chair as if he were having some sort of attack or stroke. I guess everyone was paying such close attention to me that I noticed he was having trouble before anyone else. I immediately stopped talking, ran around the lectern and jumped down off the stage to try to help the man if I could. I guess he was unconscious for a while, but he finally came to and was rushed off to the hospital. I phoned the hospital last night from my hotel here and they told me he was no longer in intensive care and was expected to be released sometime this weekend, so I guess it all turned out okay. However, I still like my ending to the speech better than his." He grinned sheepishly.

I leaned toward Pat and patted his shoulder. " 'A sound heart is the life of the flesh.' "

"What?"

" 'A sound heart is the life of the flesh.' Harold Titus, who was standing quite close to you when you were administering to Horace Latimer, said this was one of the phrases he believes he heard you repeating over the unconscious man. Some sort of prayer?"

Pat raised his head so that he was now staring over the water and trees toward the city's towering skyscrapers beyond. "Bart, those particular words are Solomon's from The Book of Proverbs. They are also part of a special prayer that I was taught when I was very young by an old Crow Indian who worked for years on our ranch. His name was Brightest Star and he was very kind to me when I was growing up. He taught me to appreciate the handiwork of God from the smallest worm or ant to the largest moose or pine tree. He taught me to have pity and patience and love for all living things, and that I should never allow a day to pass without doing good for someone, because I might never get the opportunity again. He also taught me how to say special words over anyone who was very sick and he assured me that God would positively hear me and consider my request."

"Have you used those special words before?"

He nodded. "They have never failed me."

"Are those the same words you repeated over Mr. Latimer?"

Patrick Donne nodded. Then he inhaled deeply, placed the palms of his hands gently against my cheeks and said, in that spine-tingling basso-profundo voice, "God, make him well, please. God, help him to breathe, please. God, help him to see, please, A sound heart is the life of the flesh."

He removed his hands and looked away. I started to say that it seemed to be a rather strange form of cardiopulmonary re-

suscitation, but I couldn't. Instead, I said, "An American Indian quoting Solomon. That's quite a twist."

"Why? We all share the same God. Someday the people on
this tiny ball of earth will stop cursing, hurting and killing one
another and realize that we're all from the same assembly line
no matter how different our fenders or wheels or paint jobs
are. We are truly all brothers and sisters. We all shed tears, we
all smile, we all feel pain, we all grow hungry. None of us
should lay our head on a pillow at night without planning to
reach out to another human being during the following day.
Even something as insignificant as a hug, if one has nothing
else to share, can be a precious gift."

A tiny sparrow suddenly swooped down from behind us,
landing only a few yards from our feet, pecking at what looked
like a discarded cookie.

"Bart, are you familiar with Oscar Wilde's great fable about
the happy prince?"

"No, I don't believe so."

"Seeing that little bird reminded me of it. It's one of my favorites on the subject of giving with no thought of any reward,
which I keep trying to sell the world. According to Wilde's
powerful classic, a very special and elegant statue of a happy
prince stood on a tall column high above a great city. The
prince's body was covered with thin leaves of fine gold, for
eyes he had huge sapphires and on his sword hilt there was a
large red ruby.

"One day, Bart, a little swallow who had delayed his winter
journey to Egypt much too long, paused on his hurried trip
south to put up for the night between the feet of the statue.
However, the swallow couldn't sleep because of the sound of

the prince weeping, so he flew up, landed on the prince's shoulder and asked him why he was crying.

"The prince replied that although everyone called him the happy prince, he was not happy at all. How could he possibly be happy, he asked the little bird, when from his station high above the city he could see so many people who needed help, food, care, love and tenderness. 'Will you please help me, little bird? Will you help me to give myself away?' The bird agreed.

"First, the swallow removed the ruby from the prince's sword and carried it down to a frightened young mother tending her sick child in a cold attic. Then the little bird flew all the way back to the prince, removed one sapphire eye and carried it down to an old man in a small shack who had not eaten for two days. Then he flew all the way back to the prince once more, removed the other sapphire eye and left it in the city at the feet of a little matchgirl. One by one, the swallow carefully removed all the leaves of gold from the prince's body and distributed them to the poor and helpless children of the city.

"And then the frigid blasts of winter struck, and since the prince's body was no longer protected, his leaden heart cracked. And, unable to protect himself from the cold, the tiny swallow also perished.

"One morning, God called his angels together and pointed down to the city, saying, 'Bring me the two most precious things from that place.' And when the angels returned they were carrying the cracked heart of the prince . . . and the body of a tiny dead bird. It's called 'love with no price tag,' my friend, and if we don't start learning how to live that way, our lives will all be worthless."

I nodded. "Thanks. That was very special. Those three panhandlers that we passed on the way here to the park . . . do you stop and give to all of them?"

He nodded, staring down at his hands. "Always. Every one of them is a work of God. There was a time in each of their lives when they had all the dreams and hopes and ambitions that you had, that I had. Teachers, parents and lovers cared for them, worked with them, planned with them. They had savings accounts, picked flowers, kept diaries, changed flat tires. They lived and laughed and could never have possibly imagined that one day they would be living in the gutter. They have hearts, Bart, and those hearts beat exactly like mine and yours."

"So you reach out to every one of them?"

"I do. I even bring that philosophy with me when I walk out onto the stage and face an audience. I'm really trying to do a sales job on each person in that crowd, trying to convince them to use the few simple but powerful principles that I share with them to build a better life so that they can fulfill their dreams without stumbling, again and again, until they also end up in a swamp of despair and fear. When I'm onstage, Bart, I give it my all, not for the fee I'm being paid . . . never . . . I'm working as hard as I do so that I can hopefully reach my audience and point out the way to a bright tomorrow for them. I don't know how many times I've looked out over the crowd, focused in on some well-dressed nice-looking guy or gal and pictured them standing on a corner somewhere, in dirty, tattered clothes, trying to sell pencils so that they could buy another bottle of cheap wine. Of course that's not what any of them, as they sit and listen to me, are planning for their future, but then, those panhandlers we saw this morning, when they were each ten years old, never expected to be standing, someday, on a busy Manhattan street corner, begging."

"You are truly an amazing man, Patrick Donne. I'm proud I'm your friend."

He shook his head violently. "I'm not amazing at all, Bart. There are a few simple lines from one of Emily Dickinson's poems that pretty much guide my life. . . .

> 'If I can stop one heart from breaking,
> 'I shall not live in vain;
> 'If I can ease one life the aching,
> 'Or cool one pain,
> 'Or help one fainting robin
> 'Unto his nest again,
> 'I shall not live in vain.' "

Patrick Donne rose, walked a few paces from the bench, extended both his arms in a sweeping motion and said, "Bart, look around this beautiful place you call heaven on earth. What do you know of its past?"

"Not as much as I should, I'm afraid."

"Well, you will admit that there is now an army of homeless people on the sidewalks of Manhattan, correct?"

"And I'm afraid the number is growing. . . . "

"Did you know that in the middle of the last century the so-called street people all gathered here? What is now Central Park was a dismal and smelly swamp, and all the homeless, along with their animals, camped here until Washington Irving, William Cullen Bryant and a small, powerful contingent of men who truly loved this city sold the public on establishing a huge park here. The winning design, after a hard-fought competition, earned a prize of two thousand dollars—imagine—and then the homeless fought, some to their death, to keep their only home when the city finally acquired this huge square of land and began clearing it. A tremendous army of tough, unemployed Irish immigrants, after years and years of digging and draining and landscaping, eventually produced this beautiful refuge for all to share."

"Pat, I'm ashamed to say I knew very little of that."

"This lovely place has been a haven to the homeless more than once, Bart. During Herbert Hoover's last two years of office, Central Park became the only address for thousands of unemployed and their long rows of flimsy shacks were known as 'Hooverville.' "

"Pat, how the hell do you know so much about this place? Research on Central Park . . . or the homeless?"

He grinned. "Guess."

Instead of walking all the way to the reservoir, on the park's eastern border, we turned before we got to the Pond and headed back south, past the children's playground, Conservatory Pond, Hans Christian Andersen's statue and the Children's Zoo before emerging through Grand Army Plaza and heading for the corner of Central Park South and Fifth Avenue.

I heard that unforgettable screeching voice before I saw him, leaning forward in his wheelchair, waving his Bible high above his head as he tormented and harangued each passerby.

"Beware of false prophets!"

"No man can serve two masters!"

"Refuse the evil, and choose the good!"

From his tattered red T-shirt to his dingy sneakers, he was dressed exactly as he was on that fateful day when I had suddenly turned south to avoid confrontation with him. As we approached, he saw me, pointed directly at me and screamed, "You! You! It is better to trust in the Lord than to put confidence in man! Hear me! You! You . . . !"

Suddenly the raving vagrant stopped screaming. Now, mouth open, he was staring at Pat. We drew closer and closer to the wheelchair. The old boy dropped his Bible in his lap, raised his hands clasped in prayer and, looking directly up at Patrick Donne, he said softly as we passed, "Hallowed be thy name. . . . "

XV

After showering, shaving and dressing I joined Mary in the kitchen for my usual second cup of coffee before heading to the office. She was frowning at me until I finally asked, "What's wrong?"

"So where is he?"

"Patrick?"

She shook her head and sighed impatiently. "Yes, my husband, Patrick, Patrick Donne. Wasn't he joining you this morning for your jaunt through Central Park?"

"He did. We parted just a few minutes ago. I tried to lure him up here with promises that you would make a batch of your special blueberry pancakes for him, but he has a plane to catch for Florida at ten. They're shooting Pat's second commercial for Ted & Margaret's Frozen Dinners at the base of a launching pad at Cape Canaveral, can you believe?"

"And it's okay with our government?"

"I guess. Most of the country is still talking about Patrick's first spot from the Lincoln Memorial. He said that the reception was so great that Ted & Margaret's have decided to run each of the final eight commercials for four consecutive weeks on '60 Minutes' as well as three times a week on 'Good Morning, America.' Talk about fabulous exposure. If the other commercials turn out to be as powerful as his first, I'll be getting more requests for speeches than he could ever possibly handle."

Mary laughed, kissed me on the cheek and said, "Poor baby. Oh, I almost forgot. Call Jay Bridges. He's at home. The number is on the pad hanging next to the kitchen phone."

"Something wrong?"

"I don't think so. The old boy sounded real upbeat. Asked me if I would please have my genius of a husband honor him with a call whenever it was convenient . . . if you can make any sense out of that."

I went to the phone and punched out the number Mary had scribbled on our message pad. Jay Bridges's familiar voice said, "Good morning. It's another lovely day here in Memphis."

"And it's not too shabby here in Manhattan either."

"Bart, you old fox, I've been tipping my hat to you for many years, but this latest stunt of yours calls for at least a touching of my knee to the floor in reverence. You certainly haven't lost your touch, that's for certain."

"Jay, what the hell are you talking about?"

"Oh, sure, this is all a surprise to you. I'm talking about that fascinating piece on your man, Patrick Donne, which happens to be on the first page of the Life section of today's USA Today."

"We don't take USA Today, so I have not seen whatever

you are talking about and I don't know anything about it. Do you have it handy?"

"I'm holding it, Bart. When the phone rang I figured it was you."

"Would you mind reading it to me . . . please?"

"It's a single-column piece, five paragraphs long, and considering that the subject of the piece is about the possible saving of a life, we have this amazing coincidence of it appearing right next to the Lifeline column . . . Lifeline, Bart, which always runs down the entire left-hand side of the first page of the Life section. The article has a bold heading which reads 'Does this spellbinder also perform miracles?' "

"Oh, God," I heard myself moaning.

Jay noisily cleared his throat twice and commenced reading. " 'Tall, handsome and with a commanding voice, Patrick Donne is one of that rare and rather exclusive group of professionals known as motivational and inspirational speakers. Is your company having its annual convention? If so, they could probably use a dynamic individual like Donne, after three days of dull business meetings, to send everyone back to their hometown on a high and positive note, prepared to set new sales records as they tackle the world again with renewed vigor.

" 'Few in the business of public speaking would question that Patrick Donne, ex-cowboy from Montana, is one of the best motivational speakers in the nation. Back in July, at the annual convention of Rostrum Professionals of America, an organization with thousands of members, Donne was victorious in a speakers contest against most of the top professionals in the business and was crowned World Champion of the Lectern.

" 'Donne's victory, however, was worth far more than a Waterford crystal trophy. The founders of Ted & Margaret's Frozen Dinners, sponsors of the oratorical "shoot-out," also presented the winner with a check for a quarter of a million dollars, an advance payment for his appearance in a series of nine television commercials "speaking" about their products. Donne shocked the huge crowd by returning the check as soon as it was presented to him, asking that another be issued, instead, in the full amount, to the Dougy Center, headquartered in Portland, Oregon, a nonprofit organization devoted to teaching youth how to better deal with the loss of a loved one. His touching and unselfish gesture attracted national attention at the time.

" 'Once again Patrick Donne is in the news. Last Wednesday evening he was delivering his powerful keynote address during the final evening of a convention of nationwide Latimer Investments representatives and their spouses at the Trump Plaza in Atlantic City. Toward the conclusion of his talk, according to some of those present, Donne suddenly ceased speaking, raced to the edge of the podium and leapt down into the audience, landing close to the table where company president, Horace Latimer, had suddenly slumped backward in his chair, clutching his chest and moaning. Latimer was obviously having an attack of some sort.

" 'In the confusion, no one is quite certain what followed except that Donne apparently lifted the stricken man from his chair and placed him gently on the carpeted floor. Then, according to one witness, he began to stroke Latimer's perspiring face as he spoke to the suffering man so softly that no one was able to hear his words. Soon Latimer had regained consciousness and was sitting up, even managing a faint smile at Donne before the ambulance arrived. Latimer spent the remainder of the night in intensive care but several physicians consulted all reported that there was no sign of any coronary damage and he has been released. Neither Patrick Donne nor his agent could be reached for comment, but there are many Latimer Investments employees who are quite certain that they were witnesses to a miracle, a true modern-day "laying on of hands." ' "

Fifteen minutes or more later, when Jay and I ended our telephone conversation, I still had not convinced him that I was not involved in any way with the *USA Today* piece. Most interesting, I thought, was that not once during our discussion did Jay ever ask me what Patrick had told me about the incident or whether I personally believed a miracle of any sort had taken place.

To help myself think clearly and rationally, I walked to my office, that morning, and by the time I arrived on West 44th Street I had decided to get some expert advice on how best to handle the situation before it got out of hand. I just didn't want the public at large, and especially prospective clients, to start thinking of Patrick Donne as anything but the magnificent speaker that he was. I phoned the Darnleys. Vic was out on business but Terri listened patiently until I had covered most of the details before she said, "Bart, Vic and I have seen the piece and already had a little chat about it. It upsets us too, primarily because it was projecting the wrong image of Pat, but we decided to say nothing unless you called and asked our opinion. Our opinion is that you should ignore the matter or, at the very least, treat it lightly. Vic and I were even making up questions that either of you might be asked about the affair by the media or potential clients and most of the answers we could come up with would only further confuse the matter. The most that should be done, if either you or Pat find your- self confronted with questions you cannot possibly avoid, is to just say that he only performed a little first aid just as any other human would have done under similar circumstances and let it go at that. However, our bottom-line advice for both you and Pat is to say as little as possible about the affair, vol- unteer no information and let time gradually erase the matter from everyone's memory. In a week or so it should have all faded away."

The Darnleys' advice, wise though it seemed, was not easy to follow. For several days after the article's appearance, al- most every phone call I made to meeting planners, as I contin- ued to follow up on my mailing, produced a question or two about Patrick's "miracle in Atlantic City" but gradually, as Terri had predicted, the entire matter seemed to have been forgotten.

Never before, not even at the height of Eric Champion's popularity, did I enjoy the success that followed in booking Patrick. Ted & Margaret's powerful and very memorable com- mercials, each presenting Patrick Donne as the World Cham- pion of the Lectern, shown to the nation week after week, soon made him almost as recognizable to the average Ameri- can as our president or Michael Jackson or Peanuts. Following his Cape Canaveral appearance, he delivered his Ted & Mar- garet's commercials while leaning against a goal post in the Rose Bowl, rounding a tight turn at the Indianapolis Motor Speedway in an Indy car, building a small campfire on a red ridge of rock over a breathtaking portion of the Grand

Canyon, strolling across the Golden Gate Bridge, softly strumming a guitar as he sat on the lush grass outside of Graceland, patting the Liberty Bell and rowing a small canoe on the still waters of Thoreau's Walden Pond.

The first four weeks of my contacting meeting planners had produced three future speaker engagement contracts, each at $20,000 plus expenses. In the following month Grace mailed out seven more contracts and then twelve during the third month. My problem then became one that all agents wish they had. Actually I had two problems. First, it became necessary for me to stay in constant contact with the promotion and publicity people at Ted & Margaret's so that I could coordinate Pat's scheduled speeches with the company's commercial shootings at the various locations. Secondly, as I continued to build on Pat's schedule, I had to find out from the man himself just how many bookings he felt he could handle each month without fatigue setting in and marring his performance. The speeches I had booked, so far, extended over a period of fourteen months and the most I had scheduled in any single month was five, which experience had taught me was just about anyone's effective limit considering that the engagements were scattered from Miami to San Diego. However, I wanted to discuss that with Pat, in person, and let him decide. Although I was now actually receiving several phone calls each week from meeting planners inquiring about Pat's availability and fee, I reluctantly decided to lay off making any further commitments beyond those speeches already booked until we talked face-to-face.

Pat had returned to his small spread in Blessings, Montana, but we usually spoke at least every other day on the telephone so that I could give him the latest tally of bookings made. Although his speaking schedule was not going to shift into gear for two more months, he wasn't at all concerned. He said that between the commercials that were being shot he was also working on a new and very important project that required peace, quiet and privacy. Even his planned move to New York was now on hold until the new undertaking was completed. He would be back in Manhattan in ten days, he said, to meet with Ted & Margaret's people again, and we could talk about his schedule. He also said if I were nice to him he'd even tell me about his special project.

And so, for the second time, Patrick Donne and I, at his request, jogged around Central Park soon after sunrise, only this time he came upstairs with me after we had completed our run and devoured at least a dozen of Mary's special blueberry pancakes to her great joy. After the kitchen table had been cleared, Mary poured a second cup of coffee for Patrick and me and then left us, saying, "Bart, I'll be upstairs for a while at the Wilsons. Joan has got to be at her bank this morning at ten and I promised I'd stay with Kathy. I shouldn't be more than an hour or so and Pat, in case you're gone when I get back down here, let me give you a hug now."

After Mary had left the room I said, "Kathy Wilson is a precious little nine-year-old who has spent the last three years or so in a wheelchair. She was hit by a cab right outside this building and her spinal cord was injured enough to paralyze the little sweetheart from the waist down. She loves Mary, and the two often go shopping together."

Patrick shook his head in admiration. "You are married to a very special woman, Bart."

"I know. And I also represent a very special speaker. Let's talk about him. I need to know how you feel about the number of speeches you can give each month. As you know, I've stopped booking until I know your feelings on the matter. If I keep making my phone calls and they keep calling me, who knows how many we can line up. What's your feeling?"

Pat sipped slowly on his coffee and exhaled deeply. "Let's set our limit at six a month."

"Six it is."

"Don't you want to know why I've decided on six?"

"Doesn't matter. If that's what you want, that's what you'll get."

"Bart, our fee is twenty thousand, right?"

I nodded.

"And your commission is twenty-five percent . . . five thou, right?"

Again I nodded.

"That leaves me with fifteen thousand dollars per speech. Six speeches per month is ninety thousand, and if we multiply that by twelve months, I will earn more than a million dollars per year. I cannot even imagine anyone making a million dollars in just twelve months, but that's now my goal."

"So you'll have more to give away?"

"I don't give it away. I just make a few investments in people. No big deal. There's an old saying that tells us we are rich only through what we give and poor only through what we keep. Any kind of charity is just a little love in action, that's all."

"Okay, we'll set the maximum number of speeches per month at six. Any exceptions?"

"I can be as flexible as necessary. If something special comes up, just call me and we'll deal with it. I'll also want to squeeze in some fund-raising appearances for charity whenever we can. No charge, of course."

"Done. Now . . . tell me about this new special project of yours."

Several minutes passed before he responded. "Well, as I've told you, Bart, I've been giving speeches now for about seven years . . . perhaps a couple of hundred in all. I love what I do and I truly believe I'm good at it, but I'm not convinced that we public speakers have as strong an effect on our audiences as many of us would like to believe. Several years ago I remember reading an article in *Disclosure* magazine that was very disturbing to me. A brilliant physician and educator with a long list of credentials, whose name I cannot recall, had written a provocative piece on learning in which he had stated that most of us are able to remember only ten percent of what we hear, ten minutes after we hear it. Well, I just didn't want to believe that most of the powerful points I thought I was making on the platform were going down the drain undigested, so I decided to quiz some of the members of several of my audiences almost immediately after my speech about the principles of success that I had covered. To my horror, the majority of those I asked actually couldn't recall much more than ten percent or so of all I had shared with them. Oh, they all said they had enjoyed the speech and I had fired them up to do better and they were certainly glad they had come, but when it came to specifics, they just mumbled things and tried not to look embarrassed."

Pat sipped his coffee, placed the half-empty cup in the

saucer and stared down at it. "I was pretty upset at what I had discovered and decided to kick it around with an old Montana friend, John Curtiss, who had been a high school principal in Billings before he retired to ski, read and play golf at the Red Elks Golf Club, where he and I played together quite often. We were sitting around, gabbing, one afternoon after he had whipped me pretty good on the course and I asked him, considering all his years of teaching, what he thought about that ten-percent theory that was really troubling me. He pondered for a while and then nodded his head, saying that it sounded about right. He was pretty certain, although he had never tried it, that if one read a chapter out of a history book to a ninth-grade class and then tested them on it, they would not score anywhere near as well as another ninth-grade class where you handed out books and asked them all to read that same chapter to themselves before testing them.

"Bart, I guess that what I remember most vividly is what John then taught me about Abraham Lincoln. He said that when Lincoln spoke at the dedication of the battlefield at Gettysburg, following famed orator Edward Everett's long speech, Abe's brief remarks attracted little if any attention. Lincoln, himself, was certain that his appearance and words had been a failure and a total waste of time. Later, however, when Lincoln's words were printed, they were acclaimed around the world . . . as they still are today, a hundred and thirty years later.

"Bart, after learning about my all-time hero, Lincoln, I did some research on my own—with all of it leading to the same conclusion—that the printed word somehow imbeds itself much more permanently on our brain than the spoken word.

Benjamin Franklin was an authentic genius and an excellent orator, but his wisdom and philosophy for a good life were taught to the world through his *Autobiography* and *Poor Richard's Almanac*. Napoleon Hill gave motivational speeches for years, but not until his 'steps to riches' appeared in print was he able to sell his ideas to millions. Norman Vincent Peale delivered his stirring sermons from the pulpit of his Marble Collegiate church, here in the city, for many years, but he reached national stature only after his thoughts on positive thinking appeared in print. Same with Dale Carnegie. The man was teaching night classes at the YMCA until *How to Win Friends and Influence People* was published. I am now absolutely convinced that messages delivered orally, no matter how powerful and dynamic, either in person or on tape, just do not compare in their power of retention with the printed word that one can read, reflect on, review . . . again and again."

"That special project. You're writing a book?"

Pat shook his head and smiled. "No, I'm trying to do something even more difficult."

"More difficult than writing a book . . . ?"

"I believe so. In a book you are free to use as many words as you believe you need to fully deal with your subject before moving on to the next chapter. What I'm trying to do is take those old and even ancient rules for a good life that I share with my audiences and convert them to a minimum of words and sentences that hopefully could be reproduced on a single piece of paper or cardboard. The fewer words the better, which is where the difficulty lies. This collection of wise advice, in whatever form I finally shape it, is going to be my special gift to everyone who hears me speak. Sometime toward the end of my speech I'll mention the small surprise they will all be receiving from me as they leave and then I'll ask them all to grant me one small favor. . . . "

I waited, saying nothing.

"Bart, I'm going to ask them all to read my little gift each morning before they start their day. I want them to get into the proper frame of mind to deal with the hours ahead, with all their challenges and pitfalls, temptations and dangers. I want them to follow my very simple road map along a path of life that will become much easier if they heed my advice, and if I can accomplish that goal, if I can affect more lives with assistance from the printed word, then so be it."

"And how is the project coming?"

He shook his head and sighed wistfully. "Very slowly. I don't even have a title for it yet, but I'm gaining. It's so easy to talk for twenty minutes about a secret of success, but it's very tough to write meaningfully about that same secret in just a twelve-word sentence. But . . . I'll make it. Should have it completed and printed before we really get rolling with our speeches."

Suddenly Pat reached into his side pants pocket, removed a key and placed it on the table in front of me. "Bart, what I'm working on is in a black looseleaf notebook in the top drawer of my old oak desk at my shack in Blessings. If anything should even happen to me before I get it finished and printed, I'd like you to have it to share with others, if you wish. Okay?"

Before I could respond, I heard Mary's voice in our hall followed by childish laughter and the now-familiar squeak of a wheelchair before Kathy Wilson appeared in our kitchen doorway, followed by Mary.

"Hi, Mr. Manning!"

"Hi, Kathy. How's my pretty girl?"

"Fine."

"Kathy, this is Mr. Donne. He's our new friend."

"I know. Mrs. Manning told me." Kathy turned toward Pat, who was now standing. Her left arm gently cradled a smiling teddy bear wearing a golden crown adorned with red jewels, gold lamé pants, a regal cape of soft purple velvet and matching velvet slippers. She placed the stuffed bear in her lap and rolled her wheelchair closer to Pat. Then she hastily ran her small hand over her long blond hair before extending it toward him and saying softly, "I'm very pleased to meet you."

"How do you do, Kathy," Pat replied as he leaned down to take her hand. "What's the name of your bear?"

"He's Prince Patrick, but I just call him Pat."

"Well, my name is Pat, too, and I'm really just a big bear myself. Is Pat here your best friend?"

Kathy nodded shyly. "Yes he is, after God and my mom and dad."

"What's that yellow tag hanging from his collar?"

"It says 'Pat, I love you.' I printed it myself and then signed my name, Kathy, underneath. See!"

"Well," Pat replied, "I want you to know that I think both you and your prince are very special."

The child suddenly extended both her tiny arms upward, and Pat leaned closer until the fingers of her hands were clasped tightly behind his neck. When the two finally separated, Pat kissed her softly on her forehead, lightly tapped both her knees with his fingers and said, "Be of good comfort, child."

There were tears in his eyes.

XVI

Mary reentered the kitchen wearing a light jacket and carrying her purse. "Bart, while I was upstairs Joan phoned and said that she was going to be tied up at the bank a lot longer than she expected, so Kathy and I are going out and doing some shopping. Should be back by noon."

"Okay. I'll be at the office all day. Now that Pat and I have worked out our numbers, I've got my work cut out for me. See you later, Kathy."

"So long, Mr. Manning. Bye, Mr. Donne." Kathy kissed the palm of her small right hand and waved it at both of us.

After they had gone, I turned to Pat, who was now sitting with his head lowered, both hands almost covering his coffee cup. "Are you okay?"

He glanced up, smiling wistfully. "I'm fine, just fine. Was just sitting here soaking in the atmosphere and special ambiance, if you will, of a real, honest-to-God kitchen that is lived in by people who love each other. Brought back memories of my mom and dad. I can still hear him cussing as he noisily loaded up our wood stove while Mother was trying to fry eggs and bacon in a giant black skillet. Memories, memories, memories . . ."

I patted Patrick Donne on the shoulder and said, "Don't you think it's about time you found someone to share a real nice kitchen with you along with that million-dollar income? Making any progress on that front?"

"Haven't had much time to look. It will all happen, not to worry. Are you going to the office today?"

"As soon as I shower, shave and get dressed."

"Walking?"

I nodded.

"Then I'll wait for you, if you don't mind. Keep you company. My morning is free."

"How long does Ted & Margaret's have you in the city this time?"

"All week. I'll be at the Plaza until next Monday, then back to Blessings for two uninterrupted weeks on my project."

When we finally arrived at my office, I invited Pat up but he said he had wasted enough of my time. That day, putting aside my mailing list and working on the names of meeting planners who had phoned me about hiring Pat that Grace had compiled, I made three firm bookings and two others said they would get back to me within the week.

On the following day I booked Pat two more times before noon, and after hanging up from making the second booking I strutted out into the outer office and saw Grace smirking at me.

"Did you say that you and Patrick had decided that his limit per month would be six speeches?" she asked.

"You've got it."

"God, Bart, at the rate you're knocking them off, he'll be booked solid for the next two years by the end of the month. I can't recall that we ever booked speakers two years ahead."

"I don't think I ever have. Remember how upset Eric used to get whenever I told him I had booked a speech for him even a year ahead?"

Grace grinned. "Yes, he would always ask us if we had some kind of a letter from God that assured us all that he would even be around in a year to give his talk."

"Well, two years is going to be our limit."

"What next . . . another speaker?"

"I don't think so. Not for a while, anyway. I'm enjoying this too much. No hassles. No struggles to make a sale. No fifteen phone calls back and forth to nudge someone to make up his or her mind. Hell, I don't even have to make a sales pitch to get this man a speaking date. Phenomenal!"

Grace nodded. "And those national commercials aren't hurting us any, that's for sure."

The phone rang. Grace lifted the receiver after the first ring and said sweetly, "Motivators Unlimited." She listened for a moment before saying, "He's right here." She waved the telephone receiver at me and said, "It's Mary."

I walked back into my office and picked up the phone. "Hi, hon."

"Bart, please come home right now!"

"What's wrong? You sound terrible. Talk to me. . . ."

"Everything is okay, but I still need you . . . now! And Patrick? Is he still in town? Try to get him, too. Please, darling.

Don't ask any questions. If you love me, just hurry home! And bring Patrick. Quickly. Please. . . ."

She hung up.

I phoned the Plaza and got lucky. As soon as Pat said hello I asked, "Do you have some free time right now?"

"Sure . . . what's wrong?"

"I don't know, Pat. Just received the strangest call I have ever had from Mary in all our years of marriage. She asked me to hurry home immediately and I was also to bring you, if possible. Will you come?"

"Of course."

"Okay, I'll grab a cab. You be out by the curb. Should swing by your hotel in less than ten minutes. Enough time?"

"I'm out of here," he said, and the phone went dead.

Our apartment door opened before I could insert my key in the lock. Mary's usually great complexion was ashen and her eyes looked as if she had been crying. When I took her in my arms she hugged me as if she were frightened and didn't want to let go. Her body was trembling.

"What's wrong, dear? For God's sake, tell me . . ."

"Nothing's wrong. You'll see. Patrick, thanks so much for being here. Now, come on into the living room, both of you."

Joan Wilson and her husband, Ted, were sitting quietly on our large sofa, holding hands and smiling. Next to the sofa sat Kathy in her wheelchair. When the child saw us, she dropped her teddy bear on her lap, waved both hands in our direction and said, "Hi, Mr. Manning. Hi, Mr. Donne."

In chorus we replied, "Hi, Kathy."

I turned to Mary. "Hon, what are you up to?"

She ignored my question. After introducing Pat to Ted and

Joan Wilson, she pointed to the two wing chairs directly across the room from where the Wilsons were sitting and said, "Bart, you and Pat sit there."

Pat looked at me and frowned. All I could do was shake my head and shrug my shoulders as we both took our seats obediently. Mary then walked to the center of our Persian carpet, directly under our chandelier, turned to Kathy and, sounding exactly like a bossy grammar-school teacher, asked, "Are you ready?"

Kathy smiled and nodded eagerly.

"Okay," Mary shouted, "do it!"

Kathy immediately placed the palms of both her hands on the wheelchair's two armrests. Then she inhaled deeply and pushed down with her arms. With the strain showing on her pretty face she gradually lifted her body from the chair and with the two foot supports turned upward, her feet slid downward until they were touching the floor. She continued pushing against the armrests until she was finally standing erect, her small and thin body swaying only slightly. Then she took a small step with her right foot, another with her left, then her right again, and she continued to step slowly and hesitatingly across the carpet, arms extended out from her sides as if she were trying to keep herself balanced on a tightrope. I'm sure we were all holding our breath. Finally, with a lunge she reached toward Pat and fell into his arms. She looked up at him and all of us heard her utter just two words—"Thank you!"

Late that night, long after Mary had turned off our bedroom lamp and cuddled up to my back, she asked, "Are you awake?"

"After this day, it's kind of hard to sleep," I replied slowly.

"I know. May I ask you one question . . . just one?"

"Shoot."

"Who is Patrick Donne?"

"Hon, I wish I knew."

In the months that followed, the speaking schedule I had been setting up for Pat gradually kicked into high gear and the man from Blessings soon found himself leading a far more hectic life than any he could have possibly imagined. Promoted, wherever he appeared, as the World Champion of the Lectern, Patrick Donne was one of the few speakers I ever knew who actually received standing ovations when he was introduced, and these same audiences, according to the reports received, always immediately settled down, becoming very quiet and attentive as soon as he commenced speaking. For sixty plus minutes Pat would share his dynamic and yet simple suggestions on how to live a happier and more productive life while he stood tall and compelling behind lecterns at the Anaheim Convention Center, the Boca Raton Resort and Club, Nashville's Opryland Hotel, the Arizona Biltmore in Phoenix, Boston's Hynes Convention Center, the Palmer Auditorium in Austin and the Wharton Center at Michigan State University to name only a few of the settings for his speeches.

The meeting planners who booked Pat, old friends and new contacts, represented corporations and organizations as varied as the auditoriums, ballrooms and hotels where he spoke. Some of his speeches, to audiences ranging in number from six hundred to more than eight thousand, were to United Consumer Club, the Association of Life Underwriters, Canada

Wide Magazine, Amway Corporation, Aim International, American Motivational Association, Alabama Association of Realtors, New Century Productions, Hill-Rom Corporation, Fruit of the Loom, Arbonne International, Re Max Real Estate, Ford Motor and yet he still managed to find time to do a fund-raiser for the Make-A-Wish Foundation in Phoenix.

Ten or fifteen years earlier, when Eric Champion and the rest of my speakers were at their peak, I had devised a system for meeting planners to rate the particular speaker they had employed. It was a very simple questionnaire with ten questions, each asking the meeting planner to rate the speech and the speaker on different qualities of the presentation from ten, "Absolutely magnificent," to zero, "Just plain lousy!"

Only once in all the years I represented Eric did he ever receive all tens. None of the others ever did. I had Grace resurrect the same rating system for Pat, and eight of his first twelve speeches from always tough-to-please judges gave Pat a perfect score! Five had even written on the comment lines beneath the questions that he had truly been the spellbinder I claimed he was!

In less than six months after his unforgettable evening at Trump Plaza for Latimer Investments, I had managed to book Pat solid, six speeches per month for the following two years except for both Decembers, when I could manage only one in each, which was no surprise or disappointment to either Pat or myself. Although the Ted & Margaret's commercials were coming to an end, Pat by now had become a familiar figure on national television, having appeared on all three morning network shows as well as "Donahue," "Regis & Kathie Lee," "Oprah Winfrey," "The Tonight Show" and a special with

David Frost, thanks to Terri and Vic's hard work. Whenever I called to compliment the two of them, Terri would always say that she wouldn't consider her work done until she had managed to get Pat on the cover of the *National Enquirer*. I was never sure whether she was kidding or not.

Pat was also honored by the Sales & Marketing Executives of Metropolitan St. Louis with the International Speaker's Hall of Fame Award, given to just one speaker each year, which was held by less than two dozen living Americans including such platform masters as Norman Vincent Peale, Bill Gove, Art Linkletter, Richard DeVos, Bob Richards and Cavett Robert, who had all been speaking to audiences for decades. Mary and I flew to St. Louis for that one, feeling very proud, and Pat's acceptance speech, when he paid homage to his late mother and father for instilling a dream of a better life in him, and me for helping him make it all come true, left very few dry eyes in the audience.

Pat and I continued to talk on the phone almost every day. He would phone from his hotel room if he had spoken on the previous evening, or from his home if he was between speeches. He would rate each of his speeches, using my system. He never gave himself a ten. Seven usually. Eight now and then. He always felt he could do better. Whenever he phoned from his home, I would also always ask him how his special project was progressing and he would tell me, as usual, that he was still struggling.

We didn't see much of each other for several months except for the few times when I had him booked in or close to Manhattan. I was constantly amazed, each time I heard him address a group, at how much he adjusted his speech for the specific audience. The man did his homework. He would casually drop the names of high-level company executives, mention some of their corporate goals and didn't even hesitate to name a product or plan that had bombed, although he did it in such a manner that no one took offence. I was also fascinated by the amount of practical wisdom that he shared, including so many success principles that he had omitted because of the time limitations at our speakers convention competition. Despite my love and respect for all my former speakers, I had to admit that he was without a doubt the finest orator I had ever heard, and yet there was not a single ounce of conceit in the man!

Grace Samuels, as she had always done so expertly for all my speakers of yesterday, made all the airline reservations for Pat's trips through our longtime friend, Nancy McLaren at Welcome Aboard, mailing first-class round-trip tickets to him at least three weeks prior to each scheduled speech. Pat had told her that he would prefer that she keep his commuter flights on small planes to a minimum because they made him uncomfortable, but every now and then it was unavoidable. Months earlier I had booked him to do his thing at a convention of Bonham Distributors' top salespeople which was being held at the lush Pilgrim Resort near Londonderry, Vermont. For that one, although Grace tried her very best, it was going to be necessary for Pat to fly into LaGuardia and then, five hours later, catch a commuter for the small airport at Keene, New Hampshire, where people from Bonham would meet him and drive him to the Vermont resort. That Pat was going to have five hours in Manhattan within a week was all Mary needed to hear.

At breakfast the next morning she said, "Bart, I checked with Grace yesterday afternoon and she said that Pat would be arriving at LaGuardia at exactly four in the afternoon, next Thursday, and was scheduled to depart at nine. Joan Wilson gave me the good news at lunch yesterday that little Kathy has been recovering so swiftly from all her problems that she will begin attending public school again when they open in two weeks. The doctors still can't explain her complete recovery anymore today than they could when we saw her first push herself out of her wheelchair that day, but after all the private tutors and nurses for three years, the kid is finally going to re-join her old gang at school!"

"What great news!"

"Bart, I'd like to throw a small party for Kathy on Thursday. No big deal. Just her mom and dad and you and me and . . . Pat. Kathy is always talking about him and Joan says she keeps playing over and over on her Sony Walkman that tape you gave her of Pat giving his speech. If I scheduled the party for late afternoon when he's here in the city next Thursday, do you think he'd mind coming? He could check his luggage at LaGuardia when he arrives, grab a cab, spend a couple of hours with us, make it back to the airport and still catch his plane for . . . where is it . . . Keene? I know it would make one little girl very happy."

I leaned across the table and kissed her nose. "Only a little girl, huh?"

Of course Pat said he would come to the party, and he did, ar-riving shortly after five on Thursday, smiling and radiant as he thanked us again and again for inviting him. "You both make me feel like family. Kinda nice," he said as he hugged Mary.

"Well," Mary said, "if you feel like family, then you won't mind my putting you to work. Come with me!"

Pat followed her into the dining room, where the two of them spent the next thirty minutes placing all sorts of school material throughout the room. They put lunch boxes in several colors, rulers, pads of blank paper, several small slate blackboards, boxes of crayons and wooden pencils beneath scores of thin streamers of red crepe paper that Pat, with the help of a small stepladder, draped in long strips from one end of the room to the other on which he hung several paper replicas of old-fashioned school bells. "Mary," I heard Pat exclaim, "you should have been an artist, or at least an interior decorator!"

After a great spaghetti and meatball dinner, Kathy's favorite dish, Mary and Joan cleared the table. Within minutes, Mary reentered the living room carrying, on a silver tray, a large chocolate sheet cake shaped like an open book and decorated with a light cream frosting. On one of the full pages, in frosting, was the word "Kathy" and on the other page was the numeral "4" surrounded by four lit candles signifying, as Mary quickly explained, that we were celebrating Kathy's entrance into the fourth grade at the local public school.

After the large cake had been placed directly in front of Kathy, she leaned over without being told and blew out all four candles accompanied by loud applause.

"Did you make a wish, Kathy?" Pat asked, cocking his head in her direction.

"I did but I'm not going to tell. When you blow out candles and make a wish and tell, it never comes true."

We sat at the table, talking, laughing, joking and even

singing two verses of "School Days" before Pat looked at his watch and said sadly, "I'm sorry, everyone, but I've got to leave this nice party. Duty calls. First, however, will all of you just stay put for a couple of minutes? I've got to get something out of the coat closet in the hall."

When Pat returned he was carrying a box wrapped in gold foil. He handed it to Kathy, saying, "Here's a friend who will always stand by and watch over you."

Kathy looked up at Pat and smiled, softly stroking the shiny paper.

"Look, Mom!" she exclaimed. "This little gold sticker on the wrapping says 'Neiman . . . er . . . Neiman-Marcus.' "

Pat smiled. "When I saw it in the store window in Dallas last week I knew it was for you, and that was even before I had been invited to your party."

Kathy ripped at the paper, opened the cardboard box, removed several sheets of white tissue paper and there was a lovely angel almost a foot in height. Her gown was a lustrous rosy pink and cranberry velvet trimmed with gold and satin rosebuds. Behind her tiny upraised hands were wings of gold, and a small halo surrounded her prim porcelain face.

"See," said Pat, pointing to a small card attached to her tiny bejeweled belt, "her name is Kathy . . . and underneath her name I printed 'I love you' and signed it, 'Pat.' "

Kathy held the small angel close to her face and squealed. "Thank you so much! I love her! I'll put her in my bedroom so she'll be close to me and I can always talk to her whenever I feel sad or lonely."

"Sounds good," Pat said, kissing Kathy on the forehead. "Now give me a hug, because I've got to go."

When Kathy released Pat there were tears running down her cheeks. She turned to her mother and said, "Mom, can I please talk to you in the other room before Pat goes away?"

"Sure," Joan replied, and she immediately went out into the hall with Kathy following. Soon Joan returned alone, saying, "Pat, I'm sorry, but can you please wait just two more minutes? Kathy has something upstairs in her room that she wants you to have."

"What's she up to?" her father asked, but Joan just raised both hands, frowned at Joe and shook her head. Soon Kathy was back, out of breath, carrying Prince Patrick. She walked straight to Pat and held the stuffed bear out to him.

"Here," she said. "You gave me a pretty angel to watch over me but you have no mother or father or wife or . . . or child to take care of you. Prince Patrick will. Just remember to call him Pat and he will be your friend forever. I showed you this before, the card hanging from his neck, remember? It says 'Pat, I love you.' And I signed it, see, 'Kathy'!"

Pat glanced indecisively at Joan, but she was nodding faintly. Only then did he reach out and take the regal teddy bear gently in his two hands, touching the bear's lustrous gold crown softly against his cheek. "What a very special gift. I will guard him well, Kathy, and give him love. Thank you so much. What a wonderful present. Are you sure . . . ?"

"It's not even enough. You made me walk again."

"Well, I'm very touched, Kathy. Prince Patrick, I mean Pat, will remain my close friend forever. God bless you."

"God bless you, too," she said, falling into his arms for a final hug.

When Pat finally released Kathy and straightened up, he

said quietly, "Mary, do you have a fairly rugged shopping bag? I know there isn't any spare room in my luggage, so I'm going to carry my new buddy, the prince, on the plane with me up to New Hampshire. And when I return home to Blessings, Kathy, I'm going to place him on a special shelf that is right above the headboard of my bed, where we can be close to each other, okay?"

Kathy's eyes opened wide. She nodded and smiled.

Then she reached up as Pat stooped over and held her angel close to Pat's cheek to give him a farewell kiss.

XVII

Our bedroom phone is on Mary's side of the bed. We were both awake by its third jangling ring. I lay in the darkness, heard Mary lift the phone from its cradle and mumble "Hello."

I could hear a man's deep voice talking. Mary turned on her bedside lamp and sat up in bed. Then she placed her hand on my shoulder and said, "Dear, someone in New Hampshire wants to talk with you . . . a Sam Harding."

Sam Harding? Sam Harding? Then I remembered. He was the meeting planner at Bonham Distributors who had booked Pat for his keynote speech in Vermont. Sam had confirmed with me only last week that he would personally meet Pat's plane when it arrived at the Keene, New Hampshire, airport.

I glanced at my alarm clock. It was slightly after two in the morning. Then I took the phone from Mary and said, "Hi, Sam, what's wrong?"

I heard no response.

"Sam . . . Sam . . . are you there? This is Bart."

"I'm here, Bart, but I don't know how to say this now that I've got you on the line." I heard a soft moan.

"What's wrong? For God's sake, tell me! What happened? Did Pat miss the damn plane?"

Sam's voice broke. "I wish he had, Bart. We've been here, at the airport, since ten, waiting for his arrival even though the area is covered by a very dense fog, because they had told us the plane was in the air. We have just learned . . ."

"What . . . what??"

"Pat Donne's commuter plane crashed into the side of Little Monadnock Mountain at just around eleven o'clock. When it hit the mountain it exploded in flames. By the time the police and fire department from nearby North Richmond could even get close to the impact site, there was nothing remaining of the plane but a small pile of smoldering ashes . . . nothing!"

XVIII

My United Airlines flight from Denver arrived at Logan Field in Billings exactly on time, and when I entered the airport terminal building I had no difficulty recognizing John Curtiss. During the last of our three telephone conversations that had been held over the months since Pat's death, I told him I thought I was finally ready to come to Montana. He said he'd be proud to come pick me up at the airport and drive me to Pat's little place in Blessings and that he would be the old boy waiting for me at the gate who looked like Santa Claus in civilian clothes.

John Curtiss was certainly at least my age, but he plucked my clumsy suitcase from the luggage carousel as if it were a small paper bag. I followed the big man obediently out to the parking lot. As we were driving away from the airfield, he said, "Mr. Manning, I sure hope you don't mind riding in my old Chevy pickup. I've lived with this tough old gal for a ton of years and I just can't bring myself to part with such a good faithful friend."

"Hey, I don't mind at all. She's a lot more comfortable than any Manhattan cab I've been in for the last five years. And please call me Bart."

He turned and glanced at me approvingly, nodding his head with its wide-brimmed old Stetson tilted slightly forward but still not hiding his white, bushy eyebrows. "Bart, I'm sure glad you finally decided to come. I realize how tough all this is because I do believe I know how much that young guy meant to you . . . and how much you meant to him. He talked about you all the time. Said you were a nice man as well as the greatest agent in the country. I do believe that if you told him to go give his speech on top of our Grasshopper Glacier out here, he'd probably do it. That's why I kept phoning you. I'm sorry I was such a damn pest."

I reached over and patted his broad shoulder. "No apology needed, John. I did promise Pat, more than once, that if anything happened to him I'd come out here and retrieve his project in person. Thanks to you, I'm keeping my promise."

"Soon after he signed on with you, Bart, he came to me looking and acting very intense and announced that he was going to start making a lot of money. Since he had no living relatives, he wanted me to be his estate's executor in a will he was about to have drawn up. I couldn't say no. Besides showing me where he kept his checkbook and bankbook and the folder with his mutual fund stuff, he reviewed with me, again and again, the need for my getting in touch with you if anything ever happened to him. I was to make every attempt to work out whatever arrangement would be necessary in order to get you out here so that you could take possession of something special he was writing that he kept in the top unlocked drawer of his old desk in a black notebook. Said you already knew all about it. When I asked him why he didn't keep it in a safety deposit box in one of the two banks in Red Lodge along with his will if he considered it that important, he said he couldn't because the project wasn't completed yet. I can remember asking him whether it wouldn't be a lot simpler if I just took whatever he had in that drawer and mailed it directly to you in case anything ever happened, but he wouldn't buy that. He didn't give any reason, just said you had to come get it. You know, Bart, I never could bring myself to ask what exactly was in the drawer, and he never told me. Then, of course, I spent a lot of time in his house at his desk after we received the terrible news, trying to clean up his few bills, deal with the many charities he contributed to regularly and wrap up his other financial dealings, which were few. Yet never once, as God is my witness, did I so much as take a peek into that damn top drawer of the desk to see what was so almighty important . . . although I sure was tempted."

"When we get there, I'll show you. Somehow I don't think Pat would mind."

"Well, as I was saying, I'm mighty glad you finally decided to come. You probably didn't know this, sir, but you had a deadline. Pat had instructed me that if anything ever happened to him and I contacted you about coming out here to pick up that mystery package and you still hadn't made the trip a hundred and fifty days after his death, then I was to figure that God did not think very much of his effort. After I had notified the electric company to come turn off the power, I was to torch the place and just walk away from it, although I could first remove whatever I wanted. He even gave me those instructions in writing so that I wouldn't get in trouble with the authorities. You were getting mighty close to that deadline, my friend. Nine days from now, as I reckon."

"Well, I thank God that I made it in time. I would have come sooner, but I went through my own little hell trying to deal with losing him. I've lost speakers and close friends many times through the years, but none hurt like this one. Patrick was the son I never had. He also had an incredible gift on the platform. They called him a spellbinder . . . and he was. Although the newspapers, radio and television were filled with the news of the tragedy for weeks, I still felt it my duty to call every meeting planner who had booked Pat for a future speech and every one of those conversations drove another spike into my heart. Then I got roped into a lot of interviews with reporters wanting to know what Patrick Donne was really like. John, I can remember Pat telling me that you were a teacher and high school principal. Did you ever have him in any of your classes?"

"Sure did . . . grades seven through nine."

"So what was he like as a kid?"

"Pat was a big boy for his age, but he never used his size or muscle to bully the other kids, only to break up their fights. He was also very quiet. A good student. No problems in or out of class. Loved animals and was always taking care of one or two stray dogs or cats that no one wanted. I remember he once tended a tiny bear cub for weeks after rescuing him from a deep crevasse in the mountains. One summer he also saved a little boy who was drowning in a pond near Red Lodge, and he was constantly running errands for old folks. A very special kid. My wife often said that he was practicing to grow up to be a saint, because he was always so filled with love for everyone . . . for all living things."

"He told me that you two played a lot of golf together."

"Well, we did until you started sending him all over the country. Yeah, we played a lot and I'm pretty certain that he usually let me beat him. That would be Patrick, never thinking of himself so long as he could make someone else feel a little better about life."

We rode along in silence for several minutes before John raised his arm and pointed at the panorama of craggy mountain beauty unfolding before us. "So what do you think of Big Sky country?"

"Awesome. Flying up from Denver, I thought that this must be what heaven looks like."

"We've been climbing a bit on this fine piece of federal highway since we left Billings, but we should be at the town of Red Lodge in about forty minutes. South of Red Lodge is what they call the Beartooth Range of the Rockies. In the summer months when it is open to traffic, the Beartooth highway will give you a mind-blowing entrance into Yellowstone National Park as you drive on roads engineered high into the mountains among glacial lakes and arctic tundra. Granite Peak is also in the Beartooths, and it's the highest mountain in our state at almost thirteen thousand feet. Red Lodge, my home for a lot of years, is a great place to live. No humidity, no mosquitoes. Never gets much above eighty in the summer and, at night, even in August, you usually still have to sleep under a blanket."

Soon after we had passed through Red Lodge, with its wide main street and countless stores displaying everything from cowboy boots and Levi's to bathing suits and television sets, we turned east at a small sign which read 308 and listed the names of four towns—WASHOE, BEARCREEK, BLESSINGS, BELFRY. John's old Chevy began to buck and sway as he struggled to keep it on course on the narrow, rutted dirt road. On both sides were green pastures as far as the eye could see. Cattle grazed everywhere, and on the horizon were more jagged mountain peaks, some still covered with snow.

John pointed ahead again, through his windshield. "Around ninety miles northeast of here George Custer ran into a lot more trouble than he was expecting back in 1876."

"Little Big Horn?"

"Yup. If you stand on that long sloping hill where Custer and his men made their last stand, I swear you can still hear yells and screams and shots being fired. There are a lot of gravestones there where some of the men were buried right where they had fallen. Now, New York man, I'm pretty sure you didn't even notice that we've already passed through the townships of Washoe and Bearcreek. Somewhere along here, on the right, is the big ranch that Pat's mother and father ran for so long. There, see that big clapboard house under all those red cedar trees? That's where our guy grew up. As you know, he sold all this land, except for a few acres, when his mother passed on and he decided he wanted to be a full-time public speaker instead of a rancher."

John leaned on his horn as we passed the driveway of what had been Pat's ranch, and several children as well as a couple of grown-ups turned and waved. Another young man in overalls who was driving a tractor in a huge yard on the side of the house looked up and tipped his baseball cap at John's obviously recognizable old red pickup.

In a few moments we turned left on an even narrower dirt road, this one flanked on both sides by pine trees so near that their lower branches rubbed against the side of John's truck as we went past. Suddenly we were in a small clearing on which sat a log cabin with a steeply sloped roof. At the rear of the cabin was some sort of storage shed over which hovered an ancient gnarled but still-leafy apple tree.

John parked and said nothing.

"Is this it?" I asked.

He nodded.

"Pat always referred to the place as a three-room cottage."

"Well, it does have three rooms—a small bedroom, a kitchen with an old wood stove and a living room with a fireplace that was also Pat's office—at least that's what he called it. That storage shed is where he kept his Harley before he sold it."

As I was opening the truck door John said, "You know, Bart, I plumb forgot to ask you what your plans were for tonight."

"Well, I just thought I'd spend the night in some hotel in Billings and then fly back to New York in the morning. My plane leaves for Denver at ten-fifteen."

"Sounds fine. You've got your key for this place, right? Pat said he gave you one."

I reached into my pocket and nodded.

"Good." He chuckled. "If it's okay with you, I'll just leave you to your business inside there, kind of let you mingle with Pat's presence, if you believe in that sort of thing. I've got a couple of errands to do in Red Lodge and then I'll come on back and pick you up and get you to a hotel in Billings. An hour okay?"

"Just so long as you come back, John. I don't know how well I'd survive out here."

He laughed. "Not to worry. Pat would never forgive me if I deserted you." He glanced at his wristwatch. "Four o'clock okay?"

"Perfect. John, I can't thank you enough for all this."

"Hey, you're a nice guy, Bart, but I'm not doing this for you. I'm just following Pat's orders. See you at four."

I watched as he backed the truck down the driveway. Then he rolled down the side window, stuck his head out and shouted, "Before I depart, let's be certain your key works, what do you say?"

I walked up to the faded blue wooden door and turned the key. I heard a soft click and then, with a little pressure, the door opened inward. I turned and waved at John as he gunned the truck's motor and roared down the dusty roadway.

The interior walls of the cabin were of rough, unfinished boards stained in a rust tone that gave the cluttered room an almost iridescent glow. I closed the door softly, feeling very strange and uncomfortable, as if I were in the presence of something I couldn't comprehend. Directly across from where I was standing was a large battered oak desk and an old swivel chair with a tattered pad on its seat. Stacked neatly on each side of the desk were several large plastic boxes in various colors, filled with file folders. To the right of the desk was a natural stone fireplace. I walked very tentatively toward it. The half-burned remains of a log were still in the grate, and above a thick wooden mantel hung a large, brass-framed reproduction of Dürer's "Praying Hands." On the mantel was an oval photo of a stern and unsmiling man and woman in sepia tone, probably Pat's mom and dad, and next to it was a photo of a young man in a football uniform posing awkwardly as he held his helmet against his thigh. There was no doubt it was Pat.

Every interior wall was alive with vivid colors from scores of hanging rugs, and stacked against each wall were piles of books. Next to a small twelve-pane window that looked out on the nearby woods hung several bridles, a small saddle and a piece of needlepoint depicting an Indian brave. On the other side of the desk was a cane sofa that looked completely out of place and an armless wooden rocker. A coffee table piled high with magazines was in the center of a large, oval braided rug that nearly covered the entire living room. The only sound I could hear was the wind blowing outside. Here was a magical place where anyone could have lived and shed all the tensions of life. A blessed retreat. An enchanted haven. I could almost feel Pat's presence. I think it was Pascal who once wrote that most of our misfortunes spring from not knowing how to live quietly at home, in our own rooms. The place fitted Patrick Donne perfectly. That a man who loved life as much as he did and knew how to live so well had to die so young was totally unfair. And far beyond me.

Adjoining the large room was a tiny open kitchen containing a cast-iron stove and a circular wooden table with several unmatching chairs. On a small end table next to the stove was an old-fashioned wooden radio and a glass jar filled with hard candy.

I moved slowly toward the closed door to my left and opened it just wide enough to see the bottom half of a bed covered by a rust and gold quilt. I couldn't bring myself to enter, so I quickly pulled the door shut, turned and walked back toward the desk. Even sitting in Pat's old swivel chair I felt un-comfortable. A black notepad and an old telephone were the only objects on the desk. I lifted the receiver to my ear and heard the familiar dial tone. How many times had Pat talked with me on this telephone? Was it during our final conversa-tion, before he came east for the last time, when he had proudly announced that he thought his special writing project was finally completed? "Bart," I can still hear that command-ing voice announcing, "I do believe I'm ready to take my little effort public. I'm going to have a printer friend in Red Lodge lay it out and then set the thing in two or three different styles and sizes of type and then I'll select one. Sure hope you like it. I don't know how many wastebaskets I have filled, over the months, trying to create a special but brief document that could change lives for the better. I truly believed my idea had merit, but it just wouldn't go down on paper in a way that sat-isfied me. I finally got so confused that I scuttled all my notes and went back to ground zero, setting just two criteria for my work. It had to be a code of life that could be read in no more than five minutes each morning, so that the principles of suc-cess would easily and quickly imbed themselves in one's con-scious and subconscious for the day. Also, it had to be the same advice I would give a son or daughter who came to me pleading for guidance on how to achieve a life of success, pride and peace of mind while avoiding all the sorry traps of failure. What I ended up with was pretty close to what I told you I had started with several months ago—the most powerful principles that I use in my own speeches, each condensed to as few words as possible."

I remember holding the phone and listening, saying not a

word as he continued. "Bart, as soon as I decided that the advice I wanted to give the world was exactly what I would share with those I love, everything seemed to fall into place. I just sat down the other night and started writing on a legal pad, and the next thing I knew it was dawn, and although there were a lot of crumpled balls of yellow paper on the floor, my project was done . . . and even I was satisfied. Amazing! I don't remember writing any of it. When I timed myself it took just a little under five minutes to read. Perfect! I'd like to distribute copies to everyone attending my future speeches so that it won't matter if they remember only ten percent of what I say so long as they have a daily reminder of some of the most important principles. At no charge, of course. Later I'm certain that between you and me we'll be able to figure how to get the message into the hands of many others who are hoping and praying, right now as we talk, for someone to throw them a lifeline."

There was a long pause. I remember waiting, again saying nothing. "Bart, we've got a world of hurting people who seem to have lost all faith in themselves and others. I believe that conditions are far worse now than they were fifty or a hundred years ago. So many just cannot cope and so they quit. They crawl into a hole and spend the rest of their days hiding in despair while others strike out in terror and panic and often end up bringing pain and even death to their fellow man. We cannot allow this world to continue on its present downward path. You and I may be only two wanderers on the beach of life, but we can make a difference to many. I truly believe that! Oh." He chuckled. "If you wonder where I got the title for my project, all I'll tell you for now is some of it came off the cover of an old model airplane kit box that I found in the shed the other day. Go figure . . ."

But now Patrick Donne was dead and it was all in my hands. I inhaled deeply and pulled open the long, narrow front drawer of his desk. The old black notebook was right where he had said it would be. I removed it gently from the drawer and placed it on the frayed crimson-colored desk pad. My hands were trembling. I looked up as I inhaled deeply and found myself staring at that memorable pair of praying hands above the fireplace. Then I shut my eyes, trying to get control of myself. The guttural hum of a commercial jet plane flying high overhead was the only sound I could hear except my own breathing. I took another deep breath, opened the notebook slowly and commenced reading. . . .

XIX

ASSEMBLY INSTRUCTIONS FOR YOUR NEW LIFE

You already possess all the tools and materials necessary in order to change your life for the better. In this world the greatest rewards of success, wealth and happiness are usually obtained not through the exercise of special powers such as genius or intellect but through one's energetic use of simple means and ordinary qualities.

Do not be deceived by the brevity of these instructions. Though they contain few words, they were all drawn from centuries of experience. Old seeds they may be, yet they are all filled with new life. Review them every morning before you begin your day. After they are planted in your heart they will grow into a wondrous garden of achievement and contentment that can be cultivated, admired and harvested as long as you live. . . .

Step One First, recognize that you are not a sheep who will be satisfied with only a few nibbles of dry grass or with following the herd as they wander aimlessly, bleating and whining, all of their days. Separate yourself now from the multitude of humanity so that you will be able to control your own destiny. Remember that what others think and say and do need never influence what you think and say and do. *Separate yourself from the crowd.*

Step Two As soon as you awake, seal yourself in a day-tight compartment so that you will live only for this day and its allotted work. Yesterday has vanished forever and tomorrow is only a dream. Refuse to allow painful memories of the past or hand-wringing concerns about tomorrow to befoul your thinking so that today's efforts are impaired. Get rid of both heavy loads, yesterday's and tomorrow's, so that you can advance swiftly today toward the good life you deserve. *Live each day in a day-tight compartment.*

Step Three Go the extra mile at every opportunity today and you will be following the greatest secret of success known to man. The one certain method of turning this day into a glorious success is to work harder, longer and more intensely than anyone expects you to do. Always render more and better service than that for which you are being paid and you will soon be paid for more than you do. *Go the extra mile!*

Step Four Realize that almost every adversity that may befall you today usually carries with it an equivalent or greater benefit that you will find if you have the courage to look. Collect your thoughts whenever you suffer a setback and ask yourself what possible good can be extracted from your misfortune. The scales of life always return to center, and if God closes one door to you, another will be opened. Never abandon hope. *Look for the seed of good in every adversity.*

Step Five Never neglect the little things. One of the greatest differences between a failure and a success is that the successful person will tackle chores that the failure avoids. Work done hastily, shortcuts taken, careless attention to details—these can all eventually wreak great havoc on your career. Constantly remind yourself that if it is part of your work, however small a task it may be, then it is important. History still reminds us of ancient battles that were lost because of a missing horseshoe nail. *Never neglect the little things.*

Step Six Never hide behind busy work. It takes just as much energy to fail as it does to succeed. You must constantly guard against the trap of falling into a routine of remaining busy with unimportant chores that will provide you with an excuse to avoid meaningful challenges or opportunities that could change your life for the better. Your hours are your most precious possession. This day is all you have. Waste not a minute. *Never hide behind busy work.*

Step Seven Live this entire day without allowing anyone to rain on your parade. The wounds to your inner self can be painful and long-lasting whenever anyone taunts or criticizes you. As you now begin to climb the golden ladder of success, you will constantly encounter those who will attempt to drag you down to their level. This has always been the way of the world, and if you permit it to happen to you, the pounding you receive will eventually cause you to cease your climb in order to avoid future pain. Just smile and walk away from it. Envy always implies the conscious inferiority of others. *Never allow anyone to rain on your parade.*

There are hundreds of other success laws and principles in the world, and most of them would probably help you advance toward the good life you seek. However, the seven you have just received, by themselves, have more than enough power, according to their past record, to make all your dreams come true if you will review them each morning and then apply them to the hours of your day.

As a wise man once wrote, realize that between your birth and your death the hours and the days and the years will probably be many. Yet there is no cure for birth, no cure for death, so you may as well be happy with your allotted interval and live it with pride, peace, honor, love and accomplishment. Follow just these few direct instructions every day and all that will definitely come to pass.

This very moment, through these pages, you have come to the crossroads of your life.

Your struggle has ended. God is nodding . . . and smiling.

XX

I closed the notebook slowly and stared at it for I don't know how long. Finally I pushed myself back from the desk, tucked the notebook under my arm and stood. I glanced at my wristwatch. If Curtiss was true to his word, he'd be returning for me in about fifteen minutes. I decided to spend those final minutes outside, breathing in some pure, sweet-smelling country air, but as I was heading toward the front door I paused and glanced toward the closed door to my right.

Without hesitation this time, almost as if I were being drawn by some force I could not ignore, I walked directly toward Pat's bedroom, pushed the door wide open and stepped inside. An old-fashioned canvas window shade had been pulled all the way down so that very little light entered from the outside. I hit the light switch next to the doorway, turning on a small wooden urn-shaped lamp that sat on an unfinished dresser. Above the switch, in a tarnished pewter frame, was an aged piece of parchment on which, in distinctive calligraphy were the words *Find something you love to do so much in your life that you would be willing to do it for free—Bill Gove.*

A reflected image in the large dresser mirror almost caused me to drop the notebook. Sitting on a shelf above the headboard of the single bed was a brown teddy bear, looking very much like the one Kathy Wilson had presented to Pat, with his golden crown, velvet cape, shining gold pants and purple slippers. Typical of Pat, of course, was that he hadn't divulged to little Kathy Wilson, on that ill-fated day when she had proudly presented him with her teddy bear called Pat, to watch over him, that he already owned one. I could still vividly remember her saying that since he had given her a pretty angel to watch over her and since he had no one to take care of him, Prince Patrick would watch over him from then on. I could even remember how Kathy had proudly shown Pat the yellow card hanging from her teddy bear's neck on which she had printed "Pat, I Love you" and then signed *Kathy* with her own hand underneath the words. Later that afternoon, before Pat had left our apartment, he had asked Mary for a rugged shopping bag of some sort so that he could carry his new friend with him on the small commuter plane to New Hampshire, since his luggage was all packed.

I moved closer to the head of the unmade bed, reached out and gently lifted the teddy bear from the shelf, cuddling him close to my face as if I were a child again, a lonely child. "Pat . . . Pat . . ." I heard myself sobbing. "I sure do miss you!"

A yellow card hanging from the teddy bear's collar cut sharply against my cheek. Remembering the card on Kathy's Prince Patrick, I held the bear at arm's length so that I could read the words on this one.

Dear God!

Dear God!

Printed in unevenly sized and spaced letters as a child would print were the words Pat, I Love you.

And beneath that precious declaration the card was signed . . .

. . . . *Kathy.*

· THE ·

Twelfth Angel

OG MANDINO

FAWCETT COLUMBINE
NEW YORK

A Fawcett Columbine Book
Published by The Ballantine Publishing Group

Copyright © 1993 by Og Mandino

http://www.randomhouse.com/BB/

Library of Congress Catalog Card Number: 98-96733

ISBN: 0-449-00577-1

Manufactured in the United States of America

Cover design by Michelle T. Gengaro
Cover painting by Michael Deas
Cover printed in USA

First Ballantine Books Hardcover Edition: May 1993
First Ballantine Books Mass Market Edition: May 1994
First Ballantine Books Trade Paperback Edition: August 1996

10 9 8 7 6 5 4 3 2 1

• THE •

Twelfth Angel

OG MANDINO

FAWCETT COLUMBINE
NEW YORK

A Fawcett Columbine Book
Published by The Ballantine Publishing Group

Copyright © 1993 by Og Mandino

http://www.randomhouse.com/BB/

Library of Congress Catalog Card Number: 98-96733

ISBN: 0-449-00577-1

Manufactured in the United States of America

Cover design by Michelle T. Gengaro
Cover painting by Michael Deas
Cover printed in USA

First Ballantine Books Hardcover Edition: May 1993
First Ballantine Books Mass Market Edition: May 1994
First Ballantine Books Trade Paperback Edition: August 1996

10 9 8 7 6 5 4 3 2 1

In loving memory . . .

Doug Turno

. . . the bravest little
guy I've ever known
&
Rev. Jack Boland

. . . the bravest big
guy I've ever known

A HUMBLE ACKNOWLEDGMENT

This book could have never been written without
the help and guidance of my son, Matthew. The
story line for *The Twelfth Angel* came from Matt as
well as the good counsel and advice that I needed
in order to do justice to this very special tale.

Og Mandino

Everyone's life is a fairy tale, written by God's fingers.

—Hans Christian Andersen

THE TWELFTH ANGEL

I

Solitary confinement.

Self-imposed.

For many days after the funeral I did little when I was out of bed except slump at my desk in the den for countless hours and think about ending my life. The phone was off the hook, fax machine disconnected, and all doors leading to the outside world were locked and bolted. Still, each day, what seemed like an endless stream of traffic had moved slowly up my long circular driveway, always followed by a mournful tolling of the door chimes until I finally ripped out some wires. Sympathy from my friends and neighbors was the last thing I wanted.

The past seventeen years. How special they had been. Filled with hard work, rewards, love, joy, success, achievement, laughter and even some tears. There had

been so many precious moments, such a long run of proud and unforgettable experiences, and now, even before my fortieth birthday, life was suddenly no longer worth living.

Occasionally I would push myself away from the desk, rise, and move slowly around the room, pausing to stare at each of the framed family photographs on my walls. Memories. The good times and special occasions depicted in each picture were still so vivid to me that I could almost hear voices and laughter. Was it Lord Byron who wrote that we can see farther through tears than with a telescope?

I turned my high-back wooden swivel chair slightly to my right, reached down to the bottom drawer of my large oak desk, tugged at the handle and it slid open silently. Inside, resting atop a telephone directory and several seed catalogs, where I had placed it yesterday after a long search through still unopened packing cartons in the garage, was the dull-finished .45-caliber Colt automatic pistol that I had bought, secondhand, during a rash of house burglaries back in Santa Clara, ten or so years ago. Next to the old weapon was a box of cartridges, a full box. I hated guns, always have, and after three test shots in the basement of a San Jose gunshop, I had never fired the damn thing again. Now I placed the lethal instrument on my desk blotter and stared at it, running my fingers slowly along its scratchy surface. On the flat side of the barrel, just above the trigger, was the small outline of a rearing horse and the words *Government Model, COLT, Automatic Caliber .45.*

I raised the muzzle end of the gun with thumb and forefinger, stared down the barrel and despite my shattered state of mind a name suddenly flashed through my self-pity to add to my confusion—Ernest Hemingway. *Dear God! A ghost from my childhood!* I had discovered Hemingway's books in the local library when I was ten, and that summer I devoured everything of his I could find. It was after reading *For Whom the Bell Tolls* for the second time that I made my decision. When I grew up, I would be a writer, a famous writer, and I would find adventure in all parts of the world like Hemingway. What a wonderful life that would be! And then . . . and then my hero let me down. One day in 1961 he placed the business end of a loaded shotgun to his head and pulled the trigger. I had a terrible time dealing with that. Why would anyone be foolish enough to do such a thing? Why? No rational answer came from the grown-ups I queried. Why? Why? What could possibly cause a man to take his own life, especially a big, tough, smart guy like him—a man who had so much to live for? I leaned forward and peered down the gun's barrel again, shaking my head as my eyes filled with tears. *Mr. Hemingway, please forgive me for judging you and thinking you were dumb to do what you did. Please.*

I turned my back on the gun and gazed out the picture window directly behind my desk. Just below was a wide deck that extended across the entire rear of the new Cape Cod–style house. Rolling slightly uphill, away from the deck, were several acres of dark green lawn, studded with white Adirondack chairs, a horse-

shoe court, cedar picnic table and benches, and two six-foot-tall golf pins with red practice flags, set approximately a hundred and thirty yards apart so that I could practice with my short irons. At the far side of the lawn was a long single row of newly planted privet hedge, and beyond them was a meadow with several huge granite boulders, tall blueberry bushes and a small pond filled with noisy green frogs. Behind the meadow was a stone wall and a thinned-out woodland of pine, birch, maple, and a few ash, extending to both my left and my right as far as I could see. Raindrops suddenly began to fall, splashing against the window and diffusing my view until the outside world through the glass looked more like a painting by Monet. Forty-four acres of heaven on earth. Sally and I had fallen in love with the house and grounds at first sight. Bought it the very same day the realtor showed it to us.

Sally . . .

I was now sitting in almost exactly the same position as on that Saturday, just a month ago, when she had walked into the den, stepped around my desk and hugged me. "Well, hometown hero," she asked proudly, "are you ready to greet your public?"

"I'm not ready but I am nervous. Hon, I haven't seen most of these people for a lot of years. I can't believe this old town is doing this."

"Why shouldn't they? The people of Boland are very proud of you, John Harding. Your mom and dad spent their entire lives in this community. You were born here, went to school here, were a three-letter man in high

school as well as president of your senior class, went on to college and became a baseball All-American. Now, here you are, just twenty years later, moving back to your hometown while you are being acclaimed by the entire business world as the newly elected president of Millennium Unlimited, one of the largest and most powerful computer companies in the computer industry. And . . . and . . . you're still so young! Why shouldn't these people honor you? Real heros are getting tougher and tougher to find in this crazy world of ours, and this town of Boland, as well as the rest of New Hampshire, has every right to pay tribute to you and all that you have done with your life. In the past few weeks most of them have seen you on *Good Morning America* or the *Today* show and read about you in *Time* and now they can't wait to see you in person, especially the old-timers who knew your folks and remember you as a little boy. I was chatting with a Mrs. Delaney down at the post office this morning and she told me that the town hasn't been in such a frenzy since Commander Alan Shepard, from Derry, dropped by for a clambake supper after he had become the first American in outer space—and that was almost thirty years ago!"

New Hampshire was a completely new experience for Sally, whose roots were all in Texas. We were both recruited out of college by a Los Altos firm that manufactured portable adding machines. Three months after we met, we married. Smartest thing I ever did in my life. In the years that followed, we probably moved our skimpy collection of furniture and clothing six or seven times up

and down what would later become known as Silicon Valley as I kept changing companies in my persistent climb up corporate ladders. Sally was a rarity of the age. She insisted that all she wanted to do was stay home, be a housewife and mother—and my cheerleader. She was all of those and more to me, and seven years ago we were blessed with a healthy son, Rick.

Just two years ago I had assumed the vice-presidency of sales for Vista Computer in Denver and after I was fortunate enough to double the company's dollar volume, both years, I was approached by an executive headhunter for the position of president of Millennium, third largest manufacturer of computer software in the world. The board of directors, it seemed, had voted unanimously, after two years of decreasing sales volume, to go outside the company for leadership. It was a dream come true for me, both the opportunity to head my own company and also to return to my New Hampshire roots.

Since the company's headquarters and main plant were in Concord and my old hometown of Boland was only about a thirty-minute drive away, on good roads, Sally and I decided to look for a home in Boland, and we got lucky. Of course our West Coast furniture was completely out of place within the traditional architectural styling of the new rooms, but that didn't faze Sally a bit. Almost overnight she was deep into books and catalogs on early-American and colonial interiors and she solemnly assured me that before we had our first house party for Millennium's executives, our new home

would be furnished in a manner that would make even Paul Revere proud, providing we didn't run out of money first.

"Well," I sighed, after Sally had finished singing my praise, "they said they wanted us down on the town common at two, so I think we had better get going. Where's our son?"

"Rick is in the living room, sulking. He's not very thrilled about his usual Saturday afternoon baseball game with his friends being fouled up by adult doings, but since it's his birthday next Wednesday, he's struggling hard not to lose any points."

I grinned. "Well, let's go take our bows and get on with our lives."

11

I remember so vividly the rare sight of heavy traffic on Main Street as our Town Car inched past automobiles parked on both sides of the recently tarred pavement on that Saturday morning. Drawing closer to the common, we began to hear the brass and drums of a marching band.

The township of Boland, population five thousand plus, founded in 1781, was such a typical small New England community that it almost looked like a Hollywood set. Along its two-lane, maple tree–lined main thoroughfare were three old spired white churches, one small restaurant, a grocery and hardware store, police station and town offices sharing the same aging red-brick building, a Grange hall, two filling stations and a branch bank. Not a single new building had been erected along the town's downtown "business" district

since I had gone off to college in '67, and only a huge stone foundation remained, now nearly covered by weeds and brush, from a fire four years ago, that had totally leveled the Page Public Library, my favorite hangout as a youth. That spacious Georgian-style building had been erected through a generous bequest from one of Boland's most successful citizens, industrialist Colonel James Page, and his gift to the town had also included sufficient funds to fill all the library's shelves with books. Unfortunately neither while the edifice was being erected nor in all the years it had served the people of Boland had any of the town's officers ever thought about making arrangements to insure their most beautiful municipal building, and the small town, despite several attempts, had never been able to raise the necessary funds to rebuild after the fire. Across from the library ruins was the bench-lined common, and at its northern site stood the bandstand with a new coat of light-blue paint.

"Wow," exclaimed Rick as he leaned closer to the front windshield, "look at the crowd of people, Dad! Are they all here for us? If they are, can I please just stay here in the car and wait for you two?"

I pointed ahead at the banner that hung tautly across Main Street, WELCOME HOME, HARDINGS . . . BOLAND IS PROUD OF YOU! "See that, Rick? That greeting includes you, fella!"

My son tugged at his baseball cap and puckered his lower lip. "Why me? I didn't do nothing."

"Well . . . you are a Harding, right?"

"Yes."

"Then you are an accomplice. You're in this with us."

A uniformed police officer standing close to the sidewalk near the commons began waving his arms frantically as soon as he spotted my car. He gestured toward an empty parking space that he must have been saving for us. As we stepped from the car, to loud applause and cheers, the officer raised both his arms protectively. "Welcome, folks. Will you three kindly take each other's hand and follow me closely to the bandstand? Please don't stop to greet old friends during this trip, because if you do, we'll never get to that platform before sunset. There will be plenty of time for all that later, but right now they need you up there," he said loudly as he nodded toward the bandstand. The townfolk were sitting so close to each other on the common's newly mowed grass that many had to stand in order to make room for us, but with the officer's help we finally did reach the bandstand's steps, where we were greeted by a smiling man with a huge crop of white hair.

"Welcome, John," he shouted above the band's rendition of "Hail, Hail, the Gang's All Here!" "I'm Steve Marcus. Don't know if you remember me but—"

"Steve, of course I remember you. Our class treasurer, played left field your junior and senior year . . . and I heard you now have your own law practice in Concord. You look great and haven't changed at all—except for the color of this . . ." I said as I ruffled his hair.

On the bandstand, seated in a half circle of wooden folding chairs, were the other guests. Steve walked us

down the row, introducing Sally, Rick and myself to the three town selectmen, the fire chief, police chief, high school principal and the pastors of the town's three churches. I knew none of them from my early days except one of the selectmen, Thomas Duffy, a retired judge who had been a good friend of my dad's.

"John," he said in his fondly remembered basso-profundo voice, "my only regret is that your mother and father are not here today to take part in this very special occasion."

"Mine, too, sir. Judge, you are looking just great!"

"And so are you, son, so are you."

Steve paused before the next chair but made no introduction. Instead, smiling slightly, he asked, "Do you remember this lady, John?"

I leaned closer. She was a tiny woman, wearing a delicate summer floral-print dress, her silver hair pulled back tightly in a bun, a small white-cloth handbag resting on her lap. She looked up at me almost timidly, through rimless glasses, and there was a slight quiver in her lower lip as she moaned and reached up with both hands toward me.

"Miss Wray," I gasped, "is it you?"

She closed her eyes and nodded. I knelt down to embrace my first-grade teacher, that special person to whom I owed so much because she had instilled in me a passion for books that had contributed toward every step I had been able to take up the ladder of success. I kissed her cheek gently and said, "Now this truly is a special day!"

Miss Wray nodded while tears ran down her wrinkled cheeks. After I had introduced her to Sally, she motioned toward Rick and asked, "Is this your son, John?"

"Yes. This is Rick, Miss Wray. He'll be in the third grade this fall."

"Rick," she said in a firm voice, placing her small hands over my son's, "I hope that you are as proud of your father as we all are. We knew, even when he was very young, that he would be an important person someday."

Rick finally found his tongue and asked, "Did you really and truly teach my dad when he was only in the first grade?"

"I certainly did. Almost thirty-five years ago."

"Was he very smart when he was little?"

Miss Wray nodded vigorously. "If I could have promoted him directly into the third grade, I would have done it. That's how smart he was!"

I felt a hand on my shoulder. "Sorry to break this up for now," Steve said apologetically, "but everyone is ready to start the program. John, you and Sally and Rick take those three empty seats in the center and we'll get started."

First we all stood and sang "The Star Spangled Banner" accompanied by the Boland High School Band in its familiar uniform colors of maroon and white. Then one of the clergy gave a brief invocation followed by a buxom woman with a lovely voice singing the Streisand classic "Memories" while I held my wife and my son's

hands very tightly, thanking God again and again for all my good fortune.

Judge Duffy then rose slowly, walked to the micro-phone with no introduction, tilted the instrument slightly upward, cleared his throat and said, "Ladies and gentlemen of Boland, this is indeed a special chapter in the history of our old town as we gather here to honor one of our own for all that he has made of his life in such a few short years. I am most proud to say that I was a friend of Priscilla and Leland Harding. I can re-member when John was born and how proud his dad was when we met outside the bank and he shoved a ci-gar into my shirt pocket. Leland's pride in his son would have multiplied through his later years had he lived. John was an all-star shortstop in the Boland Little League, he was a member of the National Honor Soci-ety and he graduated from Boland High with straight A's. During his senior year he captained both the foot-ball and the baseball teams and was an all-state forward in basketball. Also, during his senior year on the base-ball team, his batting and fielding were so sensational that he won a scholarship to the college with perhaps the finest baseball program in the nation, Arizona State University. During his senior year at Arizona State, John was batting more than four hundred and had major-league scouts drooling before torn knee cartilages sadly ended his dreams of a big-league career. . . ."

Main Street had obviously been closed to traffic as soon as the program had commenced, but what amazed

me, as I sat and listened to Judge Duffy, was the behavior of the huge crowd. Except for an occasional cry from a baby, everyone was, or seemed to be, hanging on the judge's every word. I wasn't sure whether they were captivated by his marvelous oratory or my record.

The judge continued, still without referring to any written notes. "As broken-hearted as John Harding was when his baseball-playing dreams came crashing down, he still graduated near the top of his class in 1971, was recruited by a California high-tech firm and now, in less than twenty years, he has certainly made it to the major leagues in the business world! As most of you know, our beloved young friend was recently selected to become president and chief executive officer of a computer company, perhaps the largest in New England, with annual sales of more than a billion dollars—that's a thousand million, in case you've forgotten your high school arithmetic, folks! The media, from our own *Concord Monitor* and *Manchester Union Leader* to the *Wall Street Journal, USA Today* and *Forbes,* have all joined the loud chorus singing the praises of John's managerial style as well as his character. If you have had the pleasure of seeing him on national television recently, you cannot help but like as well as respect this bright young man. However, what makes me most proud is that when John came east to assume leadership of his company, he chose this town as the place where he wanted to settle with his family. Oh, he could have selected many high-fallutin' communities around Concord, but he picked Boland. He's home

again, right back on the land where he spent so many happy years growing up, back with the people who remember him and still love him!"

While the applause grew louder and louder, Judge Duffy turned toward me, smiling as he reached into his jacket pocket and withdrew what seemed to be a large bronze medal dangling from a wide red ribbon. "John Harding," he said in his best courtroom voice, "would you kindly come forward to receive a small token of how these good people feel about you?"

The medal was at least three inches in diameter. The judge held it close to his face and said, "On this medal are the words, 'To a favorite son, John Harding. Boland is truly proud of you.' Our town seal is on the other side along with the state's motto, 'Live free or die!' " He held the medal high above his head as the crowd roared, turned and draped the red ribbon around my neck before embracing me. Then he limped slowly back to his seat.

The people had risen to their feet, applauding and cheering, and the band suddenly began playing "The Impossible Dream." I turned toward Sally. She was crying, but Rick was standing and applauding. I just stood at the microphone until the music ceased and the crowd quieted down.

"Friends and neighbors," I began as I tucked the heavy medal inside my sweater to prevent it from banging against the microphone. "I thank you from the bottom of my heart for this warm and very special gesture of

love toward myself and my family. Also, I deeply regret that even though we have lived among you now for almost two months, I have been so busy in Concord, taking over the reins of Millennium, that I still haven't had time to visit with many old friends from the past, and I beg your forgiveness. I shall correct that omission as soon as possible. Before too long, I promise you, the Hardings will throw the barbecue to end all barbecues at our home, and when we do, all of you are invited!"

I waited until the cheering subsided. "One of the things that has amazed me since my return is how many of you have never left Boland. You were born here, grew up here, went to school here, got married—and now you're raising your kids here. How wise! You all know a good thing when you see it. I cannot think of a better environment in which to live a happy and peaceful life than right here, in the heart of New Hampshire.

"Like Judge Duffy, I, too, wish my mom and dad could have been here to share this special moment with us but . . . but . . . I'm sure they are watching, just as I am certain that I could have accomplished very little without their love and guidance. I thank you all for coming. This day is without doubt the highest point of my life."

And then, only two weeks after the celebration, my life plummeted from its peak to the utmost depths of anguish and despair. Sally and Rick were on the Everett Turnpike, going south to Manchester to do some shopping, when an old Ford pickup truck, heading north, suffered a blowout of its left front tire, careened across

the center strip of grass and struck Sally's station wagon head-on. Both Sally and Rick were killed on impact. . . .

. . . I don't remember how long I had been staring out the rain-streaked window in my den before I turned back to the desk and the Colt .45. I opened the lower-right desk drawer again, removed the box of cartridges and placed it next to the weapon. Then I tipped the container until several ugly-looking brass cartridges rolled toward me. This was it. I wanted to die. Very much. I wanted the pain in my heart to stop, and there was no medicine available anywhere that could relieve my agony. Living without Sally and Rick was a punishment I did not have to endure a moment longer. I removed the empty cartridge magazine from the pistol and began stuffing bullets into it. Easy. Finally I was ready. I shoved the magazine back into the gun. *Hurry! Don't think about it! Just do it!* I raised the gun to my forehead.

"Dear God," I sobbed, "please forgive me!"

And then an angel—yes, an angel—saved my life!

III

*A*t first it sounded like distant thunder. When it persisted, in an almost rhythmic beat, I realized that the thumping sounds were being made by someone pounding on the rear of the house clapboards. Then I heard footsteps on the deck and a voice shouting, "John . . . John . . . are you in there? Answer me, please. Open the door, any door . . . even a window! John, it's Bill West. Can you hear me, old buddy?"

Bill West? Could it be? He had been my closest friend during all the growing-up years in Boland, as close as any blood brother could have been—from that first day of kindergarten when two frightened little boys shared the same seat in an old yellow school bus to our double-dating in his dad's green Buick for our high school senior prom. Bill West? Bill West? My comrade, teammate, fellow Boy Scout, confidant and alter ego. Was that re-

ally Billy's voice calling me from my deck? Even before Sally and I began our house hunting around Boland, I had tried in vain to make contact with him. Eventually I had learned that although he still lived in town with his wife and two sons, he was in Santa Fe, on a three-month sick leave from his company, recuperating from a triple-bypass operation that had almost killed him.

The sound of pounding grew nearer and louder. Quickly I jerked open the desk's right-bottom drawer, dropped the pistol and cartridge box on top of the phone book and seed catalogs and slammed the drawer shut. I certainly didn't need any witnesses to my suicide, especially my oldest and dearest friend.

Suddenly there he was, peering in my picture window, his hands shielding his eyes, yelling, "John . . . it's Billy West . . . answer me, please. John!"

I stood and moved close to the window. Bill staggered back several paces before he recovered his composure, grinned and pointed at me. "Hey, old buddy. Finally found you! It's me, John. . . . Bill . . . Bill West!"

I forced a smile and then motioned for him to come closer to the window so that he could hear me. "There's a door down at the end of the deck," I yelled, pointing to my right. "Go on down there and I'll unlock it for you!"

We embraced for several minutes and then stepped back but not so far that we released our hold on each other. The palms of Bill's two hands were patting my cheeks while my fingers were locked tightly behind his neck. We were both crying.

Bill spoke first after removing a handkerchief and blowing his nose. "Hell of a reunion, isn't it? I'm so sorry, John."

I tried to answer but couldn't. Bill placed his hands on my shoulders and said hoarsely, "I had read all about your big move up to Millennium. Aunt Jessie phoned us in New Mexico to give us the news about Boland's planned welcome-home celebration, but my doctor insisted that if I truly loved my family, I should just lie around in a hammock in Santa Fe for another couple of months before coming back. He said I could celebrate with my old friend later. But when Jessie called again with the terrible news about Sally and Rick, I couldn't stay out there."

"Bill," I said softly, "you should have listened to your doctor. Thanks for caring, but there's really nothing that anyone can do for me, I'm afraid. Hey, let's not stand out here. It's a lot more comfortable in the living room."

We sat in silence until Bill finally said haltingly, "It's a . . . a . . . lovely room, John."

I stared down at the antique Heriz carpet and shook my head. "Sally kept promising me that by Christmas she'd have it looking just the way we wanted. I think I've only come in here once since the accident, and even then I could only stay a couple of minutes. My pretty lady is everywhere I look. I can remember the afternoon we bought that Queen Anne armchair and walnut slant-front desk in Conway and the rainy Saturday morning when we were shopping for vacation clothes and came home with this Chippendale sofa instead."

Bill looked around the room slowly, pausing to study the oil painting of clipper ships sailing in Portsmouth harbor, the Shaker rocking chair with woven-tape seat, the oversize fireplace with its carved walnut mantelpiece and flintlock rifle hanging above its shelf and the eight-foot-tall grandfather clock in the corner nearest to us.

"Magnificent," he sighed just as the clock chimed the quarter hour.

I nodded. "Sally's favorite . . . of all the furniture."

Bill forced a smile. "How long has it been since we've seen each other?"

"High school reunion. Our tenth, wasn't it? I only came for that one. Then I got too busy."

Bill shook his head. "That's a dozen years ago! Where the hell is the time going?"

"Old buddy, I don't know . . . and I really don't care."

"They tell me that no one has seen you around town since the funeral. Have you been locked up in this house all that time?"

"No. Every night after dark I walk down the driveway and clean out my mailbox. I don't have any other reason for going outside. The freezer is pretty full, and there's still some wine in the cellar."

"What about your company? I know they've had plenty of problems during the past few years and I would think that they probably need their new leader at the tiller almost every moment to guide them out of their troubled waters."

I hesitated. The words were tough to say. "Bill, two days after the funeral I wrote to my best friend on Mil-

lennium's board and tendered my resignation, stating that the company certainly deserved more, far more, than I felt I was able to offer them, since it had become a terrible struggle for me just to get out of bed in the morning. It didn't even hurt to write that letter, which gave me a good idea of my state of mind. I had truly buried all my hopes and dreams with Rick and Sally. A couple of weeks have now passed, and I still feel the same way."

"That's a rough, tough board of directors who sit around Millennium's oval table. Six years ago, John, I used up a lot of sweat and tears putting together their pension plan. I've got thirty years of experience in insurance and pension plans, but they made me earn every cent of my commission, and then some. So what kind of response did you get to your letter?"

"One I never expected. They would not accept my resignation. Gave me a four-month leave of absence, with pay, and suggested that I meet with them sometime soon after Labor Day. In my letter I had suggested the names of two vice presidents, both recruited by me, either of which I believed would do well as my successor. The board did name one of them acting president and chief executive officer for four months."

"So . . . you'll be back on the job in September?"

I said nothing.

"John?"

What could I tell him? That I never expected to serve another day as Millennium's president? That I didn't even want to *live* another day . . . and as soon as he de-

parted, I was going to finish what he had interrupted and kill myself?

"John? John, I'm so sorry. It's much too early for you to begin thinking about going back to work. How inconsiderate of me even to ask. I just came by to offer you my love and my sympathy and to find out if there was anything I could do to make your load a little lighter. Like the old days, remember?"

I patted his knee and mumbled, "Thanks."

Bill rose to his feet, frowning and looking down at me. "I also came for another reason. I need a favor, a favor that no one I know can handle better than you."

"Just ask."

"My station wagon is parked in your driveway. Will you please come for a ride with me?"

"What?"

"A ride. I'd like to take you for a short ride. Won't even leave town, and I promise to have you back here in thirty minutes. I swear!"

Thirty minutes. Such a tiny morsel of time. Time. The world's most precious commodity and increasing in value every day. Franklin had called it the stuff from which life is made, and here was my oldest friend asking me now for *just* thirty minutes, with no idea that if he had come pounding on my window thirty minutes later, he would have found my dead body.

I shook my head. "Sorry, old friend, but I don't think I'd make much of a riding companion, even for that short a time. The last automobile I rode in was a long black Cadillac behind a hearse."

"Humor me, John. You don't have to be a good riding companion. Don't say a damn word if you like. Just come with me, please. Please."

I went.

Neither of us spoke until we had reached Main Street, but when we passed the common and bandstand, Bill said, "They tell me this old town gave you quite a coming-home celebration." Immediately he made a wry face, pounded on his steering wheel and said angrily, "I'm sorry, John!"

I didn't reply. Bill turned right after passing the Baptist church, drove over a small covered bridge and by the time we had passed the old town cemetery, with its leaning thin headstones of slate, I knew where he was taking me. Within minutes we had pulled into a paved parking lot whose far side was guarded by a chain-link fence at least twelve feet tall, on which hung a long blue-and-gold wooden sign proclaiming, in Old English lettering, that we were at BOLAND LITTLE LEAGUE PARK . . . as if I needed a sign to tell me.

I could feel my heart pounding as I followed Bill through the opening on the right-field side of the park between the end of the wire fencing and wooden outfield wall, which curved in a gentle arc from the foul line in right to a deeper point in center to the foul line in left. The number 202, in vivid yellow, was freshly painted at the very edge of the fence in both right and left field, indicating the footage down the foul lines. I remembered hitting a home run over the fence in dead center field, during my last year of Little League, and on

the following day my uncle had measured where the drive had cleared the fence—247 feet!

When Bill and I arrived in center field, he stopped, extended his hand to me and said warmly, "John, now you are really home."

I inhaled deeply and turned slowly to my right until I had completed a full 360-degree circle. Then I turned and did the same thing in the opposite direction before I said, almost in a whisper, "Amazing, truly amazing. The park looks exactly as it did thirty years ago! Lots of fresh paint, new wood, neat fencing and a much better parking lot, but it's still our old field! Look, Billy, they still have those small billboard-type ads plastered along the outfield fence in right and center . . . and some of those companies were advertising back when we were playing. And then in left field the wall is just painted green—no ads—exactly like the left-field wall in Boston's Fenway Park that we've always called the 'Green Monster.' "

I pointed up at the scoreboard high above our heads in center field and actually smiled. "Remember how our dads had to climb that ladder alongside the scoreboard platform and post the score, inning by inning? The parents would draw for that duty before the game, and the person whose name was drawn, the 'loser' he was called, was given the numbers on wooden squares, and he would climb that ladder after each inning and hang the proper number of runs scored."

"They're still doing it, John."

I walked slowly toward the infield until I was standing

at my old position, shortstop. Bill stepped back on the grass to the left of where second base would be and we stared at each other. Suddenly and impulsively I slapped my hands together, crouched as if to field a hard-hit ground ball, swept it up in my hands and tossed the invisible ball to Bill, who had moved over and was standing on "second base." He reached up as if to take my throw, turned and threw toward where first base would be. Double play! I applauded.

Arm in arm we walked slowly toward the pitcher's mound. "Look at the grandstands," I said with a sigh. "They haven't changed them a bit! Twenty or so rows high, from behind third base all around the wire backstop behind home plate to just behind first base. Wow!"

Bill nodded. "Seating capacity hasn't changed. Those grandstands hold slightly under a thousand fans. Not bad for a town of only five thousand. Let's go have a seat," he said, pointing to the dugout behind third base.

"Now those are different," I said. "We just had benches, but these are real concrete dugouts, sunk into the ground with steps up to the playing field and a roof overhead. Big-league stuff!"

We stepped down into the dugout and sat on the wide green bench. "The field is in great shape," I said. "This place must get a lot of tender loving care."

"Yes, they're just about ready for the season's start in three weeks. Tryouts are this Saturday morning. The field is ready—but I'm afraid the league isn't."

"What's that mean?"

"Well, with the exception of one year in the past

twenty, we've always been able to come up with enough kids to fill our four-team league with at least twelve players on each squad, and it looks like we'll have enough personnel again this year, just barely."

"So what's the problem?"

"John, my two boys are now in college, so it has been many years since they were involved in Little League. I can't say the same for their father. As you remember, it is tough for many of the players' dads to offer their services as coach or manager because they have jobs that would make it difficult for them to be at most practice sessions, whereas I pretty much make my own hours. So each year I continue to offer my services as coach, and if any of the four team managers can use me, well, I'm his for the season."

"Bill, I think that's great. With your knowledge of the program and experience dealing with these kids I'm certain you're a great asset to any team."

"I hope so," he said. "Anyway several months ago Tom Langley, whose boy was the league's all-star catcher last year, had been selected by the league president and board members to be one of the four managers this year, and he asked me to assist as coach. I agreed of course. Then my angina acted up, and I was pretty sure I'd be out of it this year, if not forever. But when I heard about your . . . your trouble, I had to come home in case I could help in any way, and now there's another reason for staying. The league needs me. It seems that Langley was promoted by his company, a month ago, and has already put his house up for sale and moved to Atlanta.

So, one of our teams needs a manager, and there's not much time."

We had been friends for many years. I was almost positive I could sense what was coming. Bill leaned close to me and said, "John, remember I told you that I needed a favor?"

I couldn't look at him. "I thought you just wanted to take me for a ride."

Bill chuckled. "Well, I do in a way. A twelve-game ride. The league officers were a little bit intimidated by your position and success and were hesitant to contact you, especially in light of your great loss, so I offered to explore with you the possibility of your managing a Little League team this year."

"Old friend," I said sadly, "I can't even manage my own breakfast, much less deal with a dozen hyperactive kids straining to break loose from parental authority. I could never do it."

"John, we're all convinced you would make a fine Little League manager. With your background you are familiar with the program and its goals, would be a wonderful teacher and role model and your players would certainly learn plenty from your baseball savvy as well as how to handle victory, defeat, and how to treat your teammates and your opponents. I remember a lot about you, my friend. I know the kids would love you."

"But that love has to flow both ways, Bill, and I'm afraid all of mine is now buried in Maplewood Cemetery."

"I'll help you, John. I'm a damn good coach. And now

that Millennium has given you the summer off, this would be a great way to fill your time for the next couple of months. Might be the best kind of therapy for you, old friend."

I shook my head. "Sorry," I muttered, "I just can't do it."

Bill stood, walked slowly up the dugout steps and headed toward home plate. Suddenly he paused, turned toward me and said, "John . . . our last year of Little League together. Remember it? We went undefeated. League champions. Do you happen to recall our team's name?"

"Of course I do. We were the Angels."

Bill nodded. "Well, that happens to be the team that doesn't have a manager this year!"

I closed my eyes for I don't know how long. Then I heard myself asking, "Did you say tryouts were on Saturday morning?"

Bill leaned toward me and said softly, "Saturday at nine. Please consider it, John. I'll drop by around eight-thirty in case you've changed your mind, okay?"

"What day is today?"

"Thursday."

I was several steps behind Bill as we walked slowly on the thick green grass toward the right-field opening and parking lot. Suddenly I saw Bill stumble, quickly regain his balance and reach down. When he turned, he was holding the most bruised, battered and weathered baseball I had ever seen. He placed the ball in my hand and turned away without saying a word.

IV

I couldn't bring myself to go inside, after Bill dropped me off at my front door, so I circled around to the rear of the house and walked across the lawn toward the meadow. Dense clusters of tiger lilies in full bloom formed their own aimless and natural maze all the way back to the tree line, and already a dozen or so tall wild blueberry bushes were covered with white blossoms. I stepped closer to one of the bushes and rubbed the palm of my hand gently against the frail flowers. Sally and Rick and I had walked this same path before we had even moved in, and I still remember how excited Sally had become when I showed her the blueberry plants. She had waved both arms high in the air, extended outward to include every nearby bush, and shouted, "You two guys pick them when they're ripe and I promise to bake all the pies and muffins you can eat!"

After gently snapping off a tiny branch of buds and placing it in my shirt pocket, I walked hesitantly down a small slope to the oval pond and sat on the same flat granite boulder, at water's edge, that the three of us had shared that day. We had been told by the realtor that there were both perch and bass in the water, and I had promised Rick that soon after we moved in, he would have his own fishing rod and I would teach him how to use it. I never got the chance.

When I finally returned to the house, I entered through a side door of the attached two-car garage and tapped the overhead light switch. Since I hadn't driven my Lincoln in more than three weeks, I walked around it slowly, checking to be certain that none of the tires had gone soft. The other parking stall, of course, was now empty. Except for two tiny brown oil spots on the cement floor, there was no sign that a car had ever parked there. Along the left wall, nearest the hallway entry to the kitchen, was Rick's red twenty-inch still-scratch-free Huffy "Street Rocker" bicycle, his seventh-birthday present.

In the kitchen I made myself a cup of instant coffee to wash down what had become almost a daily diet: saltine crackers and peanut butter. As I sat at the antique pine harvest table that Sally had insisted on buying, with its matching six chairs, after she had learned that it had been made before George Washington took his first oath of office, I found myself staring at that unique and decorative piece of needlework called a sampler that was facing me on the kitchen wall. More memories.

Some were of my beloved mother, sitting in her wicker rocker after the day's work was done, humming softly as she cross-stitched rows of alphabets, flowers, country landscapes, fruit, and even entire poems on face-towel-size squares of tea-dyed linen, using threads of every color imaginable. Her patience, when handling the tiniest of details, as well as her talent, had won scores of ribbons at county fairs throughout New Hampshire despite some very tough competition.

The sampler in our kitchen, consisting of twelve rows of different-style letters of the alphabet, both upper and lower case, had been my mother's wedding gift to Sally and me and it had hung in every kitchen we had ever occupied throughout our married life. "Some people hang old horseshoes in their home for good luck," Sally had once told my mother, "but in our house it's the precious sampler you gave us." In none of our many kitchens, through the years, had it looked as much at home as it did in this country setting. At the bottom of the framed piece, framed but with no glass—"like they did it in the old days," I remember my mother saying—was her name and date when the work had been completed, *Elizabeth Margaret Harding, August 1954.* I had been all of four years old.

Sitting in that very still kitchen, sipping coffee and making cracker crumbs, I was staring almost hypnotically at the busy sampler I had lived with for so many years of my life when I suddenly remembered how my mother had always dealt with death, even the loss of my

father. Mom was very religious, and whenever there was a death in Boland, of either a stranger or a friend, she would make it a point to attend the wake, whether it was at a funeral home or at the person's house. When I was very young, she would often take me along rather than leave me in our neighbor's care. Now, sitting in my kitchen with her sampler before me, it was easy to remember how she went about comforting those in mourning. I'm pretty certain that her powerful words of consolation never changed throughout the years, and recently I caught myself using them to accompany my sympathy at a friend's loss.

My mother, after embracing the grieving spouse or child or parent, would say, very gently, "You must cry no more. Wipe away your tears. Just remember that where your Robert is now, he wouldn't change places with any of us!"

I leaned forward and buried my head in my arms. *John, I could almost hear my mother's soft voice again, you must cry no more. Wipe away your tears. Just remember, please, that where your Sally and Rick are now, they wouldn't change places with any of us!*

On Friday morning I was awakened by the guttural roar of power mowers. Bobby Compton and his Homestead Landscaping crew were doing their weekly thing. Instead of pulling the pillow over my head, as I had done in the past few weeks, I rolled out of bed, showered, shaved, put on fresh blue jeans and a clean sport shirt and went outside to greet Bobby. When he saw

me, he put down his weed trimmer and hurried toward me, extending his hand and saying, "I'm so sorry, Mr. Harding."

I nodded. "Thanks, Bob."

"We've been mowing here each Friday, even though I didn't have any luck trying to contact you. Was that okay?"

"Of course. I'm glad I've got you. The place looks great!"

"Is there anything special you'd like done?"

"No, just keep doing what you're doing."

"Mr. Harding, I ran into Mrs. Kelley at the village store yesterday. She's awful worried about you. Said she's come by here several times and also tried to phone you often but had no luck."

Rose Kelley had been hired by Sally to be our one-day-a-week cleaning lady. Within only a few weeks we had grown to love her, had virtually adopted her into our family. Rick had even begun calling her Nana.

"Thanks, Bob. I'll get in touch with her. You guys have a good day."

"You, too, sir."

I had orange juice, coffee, and two dry bagels before calling Rose.

"Mr. Harding, oh, dear God, it's so good to hear your voice again!"

"It's good to hear yours, too. I miss you and I know I need you. Please forgive me for not calling you before this. . . ."

"Oh, I understand, sir."

"Anyway, the place is getting messy and dusty. I haven't done much around here since ... since ..."

"I know, and I'm so sorry. How about today? Can I come now, or would it inconvenience you?"

"Now is fine ... or come whenever you like. Just knock hard on the front door, Rose. There's something wrong with the doorbell."

She was at the front door in less than twenty minutes. After a long hug and a few tears, she straightened her green bandanna and headed for the downstairs broom closet. Although Rose was over sixty and couldn't have weighed much more than a hundred pounds, she was incredibly strong and she proved it again by the way she muscled our powerful vacuum cleaner through every room in the house. Before dark, with only a short pause to eat a small lunch she had brought, as always, in a paper bag, the place was looking immaculate. When the old girl came into my studio, to say good night, I jumped up, went over to her and kissed her cheek.

"Next week?" she asked. "Thursday as usual?"

I held out my hand. In it was a duplicate house key that Sally and I, only days before the accident, had discussed giving her. "Thursday is fine. And now you've got your own key so that whenever I'm not here you can still come in and take care of business, okay?"

She nodded and her eyes grew moist. Then she bit her lower lip several times, inhaled deeply and said, "Mr. Harding, as I was going around cleaning, there were ... ah ... there were lots of Sally's things, here and there, you know. I didn't know how to ask you what

you wanted done with them, so I just kind of left everything where it was."

"That's okay. I'll do some picking up, although I'm
afraid that even after everything of hers is put away, she
will still be in every room."

Now there were tears running down Rose's cheeks.
"And I didn't know what to do in the child's room either,
so I just made the bed, put some toys in the toy box and
dusted."

"Thanks, Rose. See you next week."

I returned to my desk and sat, chin in the palms of
both hands. What was I doing? Maintaining the
grounds? For what? Dusting and vacuuming the house?
Rick's toys being picked up? Why? What difference did
it make? Damn! Damn! I jerked open the lower-right-
hand desk drawer and stared at the ugly loaded gun.
Same old questions exploding in my head. What was
there to live for? Who was there to live for? Who? On
my desk was the aged brown baseball, its cover cut and
scuffed, that Bill had stumbled over and handed me as
we were leaving the baseball park. I picked it up and
held it against my cheek. *Oh, God, please help me!*

V

❧

*O*n Saturday morning I had already walked down the driveway and was leaning on my mailbox, waiting, when Bill pulled up in his old Buick. He looked both surprised and pleased at seeing me but said nothing as we rode along, for at least five minutes. Then, still staring straight ahead, he shook his head several times and said, "I'm very proud of you, old buddy."

"Well, I think it would be wise if you withhold judgment for now. I'm not sure I know what I'm doing or whether I'll be able to see this thing through. The odds are great, Bill, that I'm probably going to let you down and run away from this commitment, and sooner rather than later. You've got to understand and be ready if I can't hack it."

Bill reached down and handed me a Masonite clipboard that had been next to him on the car seat. "I

typed up a list of all the player applicants last night so that you can make notes while you're evaluating the various kids in the tryout. That red number before each name will be on a piece of heavy paper pinned to the back of each boy's shirt, which should make it easier for the coaches and managers who are judging talent to identify the kids and jot down their opinions and ratings for each of them. We're trying it this year for the first time. Should make the Monday-night player draft a lot easier and certainly speed it up."

"And what's this other number, the one after each name?" I asked.

"That's the boy's age. Just to refresh your memory, the magic date is August first. Kids must be nine before that date and not thirteen until after that date in order to play—ages nine to twelve, as it has always been. By sheer chance we happen to have no nine-year-old applicants this year, but there's a good mix of tens, elevens, and twelves."

"Some of these names are underlined. What's that all about?"

Bill grinned. "Well, I figure the other three managers have a little jump on you since they've lived here for years and know most of the kids. Also, they all managed last year, so they've got a pretty good reading on the available talent. The names I underlined are the twelve kids I think are the most outstanding athletes. The three names with double underlines are the best three pitchers, at least as I remember their performances from last year. But this is your team," he said, patting my knee,

"and your flock of Angels will all have been selected by you."

"However, you will share your expert opinion with me, correct?"

"If you ask for it," he said, smiling.

As soon as we stepped out of the car, in the Little League parking lot, I could hear them—the children—shouting, laughing, calling out to their fellow players, accompanied by an almost rhythmic thump of baseballs being caught in leather gloves. It was still early, but obviously most of the playing candidates were already on the field doing whatever they believed was necessary to attract some manager or coach's attention.

It had been one thing for me to walk out on a quiet and empty field the other afternoon with Bill, but this was much tougher. I don't know what I expected, but the kids didn't look much different or sound much different or even act much different from the way my young buddies had, almost thirty years ago, when this field had been the most hallowed ground in the entire world to me. I closed my eyes, listening to the sounds, and tried to remember my very first Little League try-out. I was just a few days past my ninth birthday, nervous and frightened, and my dad had driven me here, to this same field, in his pickup. Just before I turned away from him, in the parking lot, and ran out on the diamond for the first time, he extended his hand, smiled and said, "Break a leg, son!" I knew what he meant because that strange phrase had come up at dinner one night, and mother had patiently explained to both of us

that those words were how show people always wish each other good luck before a performance. Break a leg!

"John?"

I opened my eyes. Bill was several yards away and frowning. "Are you okay?"

I shrugged my shoulders and nodded. He pointed toward the first-base dugout. "Let's go meet the league officials while we've got time."

Boland Little League's president, Stewart Rand, was already an acquaintance, since he was an officer in the local savings bank and we had met on that morning when Sally and I had opened our checking and savings accounts. He rose from the dugout bench when he saw us approaching and extended his hand toward me before Bill could say anything. "Mr. Harding, I can't tell you how pleased we are to have you with us. We all welcome you, with open arms, as well as extend to you our deepest sympathy. Thank you for your willingness to share your time, your effort and your considerable baseball knowledge with our youngsters. I'm certain they will be better players and citizens because of your counsel, leadership and example. Forgive the speech"—he grinned—"but I truly mean every word of it. You are a very special man, and I'm glad we've got you."

I mumbled my thanks. Then Bill introduced me to Nancy McLaren, the league's secretary-treasurer, followed by three members of the board, the other three managers and their coaches as well as several parents, all of whose names I forgot soon after the introductions.

At last, in response to a single shriek from a whistle that had been hanging around President Rand's neck, the players ceased their throwing and running and noisily took seats in the lower rows of stands behind the dugout. Parents, who had been scattered throughout the grandstand, now began moving to positions in upper rows, behind the boys, in order to hear, while the league president waited patiently for everyone to get settled, waving and nodding constantly to people calling out his name. When the chattering in the stands finally subsided, he raised his right hand and said loudly, "Good morning, parents and players and friends of Boland Little League. My name is Stewart Rand. As this year's league president, I welcome you to the opening session of what will be our forty-fourth year as a chartered Little League. That means that, through the years, we have proudly sent several thousand of Boland's youth out into the world, imbued, we hope, with qualities of teamwork, fair play, courage, persistence and discipline that have made them better adults and better citizens."

Stewart Rand paused, smiled and then said, "We have a good deal to accomplish in the next couple of hours or so and we shall try, with the generous assistance of our managers and coaches and several parents, to give every player an opportunity to show what he can do at bat, on the bases and in the field. And, while all that energy is being expended on our historic field, our four team managers, upon which so much responsibility rests for the next two months, will also be moving around the field from group to group, observing and judging and

making notes so that on Monday night, at the draft, they will be able to assemble four good competitive teams for our exciting twelve-game pennant race."

Bill and I had been standing, with the other managers and coaches, behind Rand. Bill turned and said softly, "I'll get together with you later." Then he moved slowly toward the league president just as Rand was saying, "And now I'm going to turn this morning over to an old friend of mine and many of you, Bill West, who will co-ordinate the various activities."

The tryouts lasted until well past noon. Each player was allowed half a dozen swings at the plate, hitting pitches tossed by one of the coaches who had the unique ability to throw ball after ball in the strike zone. During the long hitting session at least six boys took their turns behind the plate, catching. Four were allowed on the infield at one time, while the batting was taking place, and they were told to go to their position of choice and to field anything that was hit toward them. While all this was happening, another coach and parent were stationed in deep right field, behind the foul line, hitting towering fly balls to a second group of youngsters. After perhaps forty-five minutes the outfield group came in to the dugout, batted, and then assumed positions in the infield, while those who had been batting and playing the infield moved to the outfield. As all that organized chaos was transpiring on the field, another, smaller group had gathered behind the first-base dugout, where there was a pitching rubber and plate. They threw to catcher candidates for more than half an

hour while all four managers watched intently. Often, at the request of a manager or coach, another young athlete would be called in from the field and asked to pitch for several minutes with the emphasis on control—how many pitches were near or over the plate.

Not until just before noon did I get a chance to confer with Bill. Swinging a bat as he would a golf club, he came over to me and said, "Well, skipper, what do you think?"

I handed him my clipboard, saying, "Pretty tough to really evaluate all these kids in just a couple of hours, but I did take a crack at grading them numerically, ten down to one, plus jotting down a few comments to help me remember some of them on Monday night at the draft."

He studied my board for several minutes, nodded and handed it back. "John, you don't need any advice from me. What did you do about pitchers?"

I handed him the clipboard again and said, "I marked the best pitching prospect P-one, the next P-two and so on, but of course everything will depend on when we get to draft. Whoever drafts first will no doubt go for my P-one, he's that much of a standout."

Bill nodded. "You're absolutely right. Todd Stevenson was not only the best darn pitcher in the league, last year at age eleven, he also batted over four hundred, hit five or six home runs and played first base when he wasn't pitching. He was very special. Didn't you say you were rating the kids from ten down to one?"

"Yes."

"But there's nothing next to this kid's name," he said, handing the clipboard back to me.

"I know. Number thirty-six. God love him, he's so tiny and slow and uncoordinated that . . . I just didn't know what to put down. But he never quit, never stopped running and never seemed to get down on himself after missing pitch after pitch at the plate. Do you know him?"

Bill leaned closer to the clipboard and squinted. " 'Timothy Noble.' No. Must be a new family in town."

I pointed toward the group in center field still taking turns catching fly balls from a coach's bat. "Third from the left, Bill. In those baggy pants. See him? Your list shows he's an eleven-year-old, but he's got to be the smallest player on the field."

As we were talking, the little guy moved away from the other players, who turned and watched, nudging each other and snickering. Obviously the next fly ball to be hit was his to catch. Leaning forward, he flexed his knees and pounded his right fist into his glove again and again.

"My God!" I said half aloud.

"What's the matter . . . what am I missing?" asked Bill as he glanced around the outfield.

"Nothing . . . nothing."

How could I tell him that Timothy Noble, not much bigger than my beloved seven-year-old, looked just like Rick from a distance as he crouched and leaned forward on his toes, waiting. The coach swung his bat and arched a long fly ball toward Timothy, who circled

helplessly beneath the ball, waving both his arms toward the sky. As the ball descended, he first turned to his left, then to his right and began to run, but somehow his feet got tangled and he fell headfirst onto the grass while the nearby group of players moved close to each other, almost in a huddle, with several holding their hands over their mouths as they fought back giggles.

A few minutes later the youngster failed, once again, to get under a fly ball hit to him, and it landed several feet away. He raced toward it, picked it up and threw it back toward the batter. The ball landed no more than forty feet from where Timothy had been standing and the other players turned away, smiling. Timothy momentarily brushed the back of his right hand against both eyes.

"He sure is tiny," said Bill. "How old did you say he was, according to our list?"

"Eleven."

"Well," sighed Bill, "he's certainly going to be a challenge for the manager and team who end up with him. Probably will be one of the last kids drafted. Still, according to the rules, he's going to have to be played in each game, for a minimum of six defensive outs, and he'll have to go to bat at least once per game. I'm afraid that any balls hit in his direction, wherever he'll be playing, even for two innings, could prove very costly."

We looked up to see Timothy Noble on the move again. This time he overran a tall, lazy fly ball that dropped behind him. As he tried to stop suddenly, his

tattered sneakers slipped on the grass and he fell, tumbling over onto his side. Still, he jumped up quickly, wiped the grass clippings from his T-shirt, yanked down firmly on the bill of his old baseball cap, retrieved the baseball, ran in several steps toward the coach who had hit it and threw the ball with so much effort that he fell over backward. The ball, after completing a small airborne arc, rolled along the grass until it finally came to rest at the batter's feet. Those who were watching cheered loudly while they mockingly applauded. Timothy Noble turned, faced his hecklers and tipped his cap.

"Look at him, Bill," I said softly. "The kid is smiling."

V I

$\mathcal{S}$aturday afternoon, or what remained of it after tryouts had ended, was spent behind my house, on the deck, reading, rereading and highlighting in glowing yellow many paragraphs in the *Little League Baseball Official Regulations and Playing Rules*.

Soon after I had started my second pass through the sixty-four pages of rules, I found myself reading a small piece, written by the Chairman of Little League Baseball, in which he briefly presented leadership qualities by which any local manager could be evaluated. Many of them sounded familiar to me until I realized that the traits necessary for good leadership, including many I had worked hard to acquire and live by in my own business career, were universal and as old as time and that they would certainly work in successfully guiding a Little League team as well as they worked in any board

room: compassion, understanding, setting a good example, cooperation, teamwork, reaching toward mutual goals, encouragement, praise, and always striving to improve. Each of the activities listed were indeed vital to a good leader, in any enterprise, but somehow I had never expected to find such wise and valuable advice in a baseball book of rules.

Reviewing the hundreds of "shalls" and "shall nots" among the pages of playing rules brought back memories of my own Little League experiences, but they faded quickly from my mind. The Chairman's brief but powerful message was forcing me to take a long look at myself, and what a sorry image it was. John Harding, widower, no immediate family, currently on "employment leave," despondent, aimless, potential suicide. Should that John Harding be leading a Little League team? Never! What I was about to become involved in was foolish and irresponsible, and those great kids I saw trying so hard this morning certainly deserved far better than me. How could I encourage them? How much sympathy and compassion did I have to dispense? How could I make any attempt to understand their home life while I was struggling to deal with the grim fact that I no longer had one of my own? And how could I possibly set a good example for them, fill them with enthusiasm and desire, teach them how to think positively—and never quit, never quit(!)—when I, their manager, their leader, was ready to quit the greatest game of all—life—and really didn't care if I even lived to see another sunrise? This situation was truly my fault.

In my depressed condition I had bought Bill West's great sales pitch because he had always been such a special friend, but it just wasn't fair to those young and impressionable boys at an age when they already had enough problems. Not fair! However, I still had time to bail out. Then I remembered how Sally had always acted as my manager whenever I had been confronted with situations in the corporate world that I didn't think I could handle and didn't want to deal with. She would cup my face in the palms of her hands, look straight into my eyes and say, "Hon, I've never, ever seen anything or anyone beat you and I positively have never seen you give up. You can handle this problem just like you've handled every other. Just be yourself and you'll come out fine."

I shoved the rule book into my back pocket and slid open the glass door leading to the living room. After walking slowly across the room, I paused a yard or so away from the fireplace, leaned forward and stretched out my arms until both hands were tightly gripping the wooden mantel. I stared down at the hearth. To my right was a small copper pail filled with kindling wood and an old folded newspaper, and next to it was a brass log holder piled high with split maple logs. Sally had insisted that we really couldn't claim to be official residents of our new home until we christened it with our first fire in the fireplace, so she had quickly located a local source for wood and had it delivered and stacked along one wall of the garage. I recall, so vividly, that chilly evening back in March when I had come home

late after a very rough day at Millennium, found a roaring fire in the fireplace and a proud wife anxiously waiting for my reaction. With her tiny hands clasped tightly together, as if she were pleading for mercy, and blue eyes opened wide, she had asked anxiously, "Well, how did I do?"

I remember saying, "You've just bought yourself another chore, lady, especially on Christmas morning."

Rick was already in bed, so the two of us had sat on the sofa, very close to each other, holding hands and touching heads, staring contentedly into the gold-and-crimson flames. . . .

I pushed myself back from the mantel, turned and stared at the empty sofa, feeling so lost and alone. Then I pulled back the black-mesh screens covering the fireplace opening, reached inside and opened the chimney damper and within ten minutes I had a fire blazing. After stacking logs on the fire, as high as the top of the andirons, I slid the mesh screens closed and slumped down on the sofa—only now it was early June and I had no Sally to hug. . . .

For municipal budgetary reasons it had almost become general practice throughout New Hampshire in the past twenty years or so to have consolidated school districts, each composed of students from clusters of small adjoining towns. But the very independent town of Boland had remained autonomous, with its own school system. And so, when Bill West drove into the parking lot at Boland High School on Monday evening, it was another

trip backward in time. Twilight was falling, but I could see that the red-bricked, single-story exterior looked almost exactly as it did when I had graduated in 1967. Inside we walked down a polished-tile corridor. The walls, which held several cork bulletin boards filled with notices and student artwork, were painted in familiar beige. I paused outside one of the doors, on which the gold numeral four was printed high on the frosted glass. Bill turned, staring at me until I pointed toward the door and explained, "My homeroom. Senior year. Suppose it's okay to peek inside?"

"Don't see why not."

The door was locked.

We continued down the hall and entered Room 8, where the draft was scheduled to be held. Stewart Rand and Nancy McLaren were both standing near the teacher's desk. Behind them, on the large blackboard, were printed the names of every player who had participated in the Saturday-morning tryouts.

"Good evening, gentlemen," Stewart called out. "Please take seats anywhere, and we'll be ready to commence in just a few minutes. Thank you."

First I followed Bill as he went up aisles, shaking hands with his old friends. Although I had met them all at the tryouts, I was introduced to the other team managers and coaches once again. We found two empty seats near the front and tried to force ourselves behind two small desks.

"I guess we've both grown a little since the late sixties," Bill said, chuckling as he tapped his stomach.

Stewart Rand began striking the side of a drinking glass with a ruler, and all conversation and laughter gradually subsided.

"Okay, everyone, before we begin this year's draft, let me quickly review a few points. The fact that a player was on one particular team last year does not automatically place him on that same team this year. There is no team-player carryover. All players will be drafted by you to the team on which they will compete this season. Is that understood?"

Rand glanced around the room until several heads nodded.

"I've been asked why there are no girls involved in our league. They are, of course, entitled to participate as well as the boys, and of course they have in many past years. However, the girls' softball program in this town, for all age groups, has become so popular that apparently the young women seem to have elected to compete in their own league, so this year, for the first in several, our teams will be composed totally of males.

"Now . . . before we begin our drafting process, I ask a small favor. Would each of the managers kindly stand, introduce himself, name his team and tell us in a few short sentences what he hopes to accomplish this year."

Rand waited patiently until a well-muscled man wearing a New York Yankee T-shirt rose and said, "My name is Sid Marx, and I understand I shall be managing the Yankees with the help of this fine gentleman, sitting to my right, Don Pope. This will be my third year as manager, and I'm honored to have these kids under my care.

My fervent hope and prayer is that Don and I can teach them some of the many values they will need to live a life filled with success—and more important, peace and contentment."

A tall, gray-haired man in a well-tailored business suit stood and said, "My name is Walter Hutchinson, and I'll be handling the Cubs along with Coach Alan LaMare, who could not attend this evening because of business. This is my second year in the league, and although I look forward to improving my last-place finish of last year, I realize that there are other goals in our program than just winning baseball games. I know only too well, from my own life's experiences, that participating in Little League can be a wonderful training ground in helping to shape the character of our young men."

"My name is Anthony Piso," said a short, stocky man who had been sitting in front of me. "I'm probably the only grandfather managing a Little League club in all of New Hampshire, but this year the Pirates will be handled by me and this man here, Jerry White. I've been managing for six years, and for the first three of those years my grandson, who now lives in Arizona, was on the team. He's the one who got me into this. During my years as manager I've won two championships and look forward to building another good team, which will probably be my last, since my doctor doesn't think that getting excited as I do, during the games, is doing very much for my cardiac condition. I hope to walk out, at the end of this season, with my head held high, but even more important, I want to make some contribu-

tion, once more, toward helping a dozen kids take another step in the right direction on this tough road called life."

There was a slight rippling of applause as Piso took his seat, grinning. "Just like a politician," someone behind me said loudly, and everyone turned toward the old boy smiling. Puzzled, I glanced at Bill.

"Tony is Boland's town treasurer, John. Has been for more than twenty years, I guess. Now it's your turn, buddy."

I rose, inhaled deeply and said, "My name is John Harding, and I'll be managing the Angels, with a lot of help from my friend, Bill West. I'm extremely honored to be a part of Boland Little League again, after so many years, and I truly appreciate the opportunity you have all given me to teach and work with these fine boys. I fully realize that I have much to learn about this important position and I hope that I can count on all of you for advice when I seek it. The precious lives that have been entrusted to us deserve every opportunity to develop to their fullest potential. I'm honored to be part of this program."

Stewart Rand, smiling slightly, nodded in my direction and said, "Gentlemen, thank you. And now . . . the big moment! The rules governing our player-selection process are quite simple. You four managers will each draw a number from this old baseball cap of mine. The manager drawing number one will select first, number two, second, and on through each of the four managers. Then, in order to keep things fair and to equalize the

talent among the four teams, we will select in reverse order in the second round. The manager who drafted
fourth in the first round will draft first, the manager
who drafted third will select second and so on. Since
there are forty-eight eligible players, there will be a total of twelve rounds. As soon as you have drafted a
player, Nancy will bring you an information card with
his address, parents' names and phone number. You will
want to phone the young man to inform him as to
which club he'll be playing for and also give him the
time and place of your first practice.

"One final point of order. Sid and Walter have sons
who will be playing in our league this year. They are
both excellent players, and so, in keeping with our local
rules and custom, they will be considered as having
been drafted by their father's team as part of the second
round of the draft. I believe this is fair to all four teams.
However, if anyone objects, let's hear from him now."

There were no objections.

"Okay, gentlemen. There are four folded slips in this
cap. Will each of you kindly come up here, remove a
slip from the cap and hand it to Nancy."

I was last in line, so Stewart reached in for me,
handed my slip to Nancy and I returned to my seat. She
opened all four slips, made notations on her legal pad
and handed the pad to Stewart.

"Gentlemen, here is the order in which you will draft
to commence things. Beginner's luck! John Harding of
the Angels will draft first; Sid Marx of the Yankees, second; Walter Hutchinson of the Cubs, third; and . . .

sorry, Tony, Anthony Piso, Pirates, will select fourth. Are you prepared to draft your first Angel, John?"

"I am. The Angels take Todd Stevenson."

Sounds of moaning and groaning filled the classroom. Sid Marx turned and grinned in my direction, saying, "Todd will pitch his game a week and win them all, so you've already got six victories in the sack. Win just three out of the other six and you've got yourself a championship."

"Sid ... Sid ... if only it were that easy," Bill said with a sigh.

"I know. Only kidding, John."

The entire draft took almost two hours. Very often coaches and managers checked and rechecked their notes, and on several occasions they went out into the hallway to confer in private. It was obvious, from the beginning, that these men were really familiar with the available talent. Fortunately I had Bill West and I leaned on his judgment heavily as we went through round after round of selections.

Finally we were in the last round of the draft and there were only four candidates who had not been chosen. Heavy lines had been drawn through all other names on the blackboard as well as on every manager's and coach's list of players. Bill leaned toward me, reached out toward my list and pointed to one of the names through which there was still no line drawn, Timothy Noble. I glanced over at him. He was shaking his head from side to side. The eleven players we had selected so far seemed like a well-balanced group. I was

pleased with our team, at least on paper. Now, just one more selection.

It didn't take long. Piso, Hutchinson and Marx all had their pick ahead of us, and after they had made their choices, there was only one name remaining on the blackboard without a white chalk line running through it.

Timothy Noble became my last . . . my twelfth Angel.

VII

❧✳❧

$\mathcal{F}$or the next three weeks each of the four teams in our league practiced two afternoons a week, usually from four P.M. to six P.M. One weekly practice session for each team, according to the schedule Nancy had distributed after the Monday-night draft, was at Boland Little League Park, and the other was on a smaller baseball diamond behind the park, owned and maintained by the town, adjacent to the playground, which boasted swings, sandboxes, seesaws and even several horseshoe courts for the older folks.

Following our weeks of practice, the official season would commence. Each team was scheduled to play twelve games, two games a week for six weeks, with four games played against each of the other three teams. All games would be played at Little League Park on Monday, Tuesday, Wednesday and Thursday evenings,

commencing at five P.M. Should a game be rained out, it would be rescheduled for Friday evening or Saturday morning. Actually two postponed games could be played on Saturday if necessary. After each team had completed its twelve-game schedule, the two with the best won-lost record would play one game for the league championship.

On our way home, after the draft, Bill West offered to phone the players we had selected to inform them that our first practice would be at Little League Park on the following Tuesday afternoon at four, but I told him that if I was going to manage the team, then I believed it was my duty to get on the phone. He looked surprised, then pleased, then grinned and nodded his head approvingly.

Shortly after seven on Tuesday evening I settled down at my desk in the den to notify twelve young men that they were now Angels. Shuffling the individual player cards that Nancy had handed us following each of our selections, and reading the names on our roster, one after another, made me think that we had not only drafted for Little League but also for a little League of Nations: Todd Stevenson, John Kimball, Anthony Zullo, Paul Taylor, Charles Barrio, Justin Nurnberg, Robert Murphy, Ben Rogers, Chris Lang, Jeff Gaston, Dick Andros and Timothy Noble.

Bill West had left me with a gentle warning when he dropped me off after the Monday draft. Most of the kids were familiar with him, the other three managers and every coach, but I was a stranger in town, an unknown factor that might cause our players some unease

and uncertainty, at least at first. It was a wise observation, and I thanked him. Before making any phone calls I scribbled some notes on a legal pad, outlining a simple procedure for me to follow once I was on the phone as well as some key words to use. Dialing each player's phone number, I would ask for him first after identifying myself, no matter who answered the phone. I would then welcome the boy to the Angels, tell him he had been selected because he was a fine ball player and that our first practice was scheduled for next Tuesday at four. I would then ask if the boy had a ride to the park and someone to pick him up at six after each practice. Many, I discovered, got around Boland quite well on their bicycles. I had forgotten how independent country kids always are. After chatting with the player I would ask to speak with his father, introduce myself to the gentleman, tell him that I was proud to have his son on my team and ask him to call me, at home, anytime, if there was anything he wished to discuss concerning his son during the season. I would close by mentioning that I was looking forward to meeting every parent at one of our practices or games soon and that I would certainly be grateful for their support. If the father was not at home when I phoned, I would have a similar conversation with the boy's mother. My final phone call was to little Timothy Noble.

"Timothy Noble?"

"Yes."

"Timothy, this is John Harding, Little League man-

ager of the Angels. I'm calling to tell you that you will be playing for the Angels this year."

"All right!!!"

"First practice is next Tuesday at four o'clock at Little League Park. Can you make it okay?"

"Yes, sir! I'll be there!"

"Will you be able to get a ride to the field and then home? Practice will end at six o'clock—always."

"I have a bike, sir. I'll be there. Mr. Harding, could you please tell me some of the other guys on the team?"

"Sure. Todd Stevenson, Paul Taylor, John Kimball, Anthony Zullo—do you know any of those fellows?"

"I'll be playing with them? Wow! They're all great. We'll have a good team, a super team!"

"And I'm counting on you to do your part, Timothy. Now, is your dad around? I'd like to talk with him if I may."

The little guy's lilting voice immediately fell several octaves, and he replied swiftly, in a flat, husky monotone with no hint of emotion, "My dad lives in California."

Caught off guard, I hesitated. How to reply? Finally I said lamely, "Oh . . . well, could I speak with your mother?"

"She's not home from work yet."

I glanced at my watch. Exactly seven-forty.

"Oh. Ah . . . okay, Timothy, we'll see you on Tuesday afternoon."

"Yes, sir. And . . . Mr. Harding, sir?"

"Yes?"

"Thank you very much for picking me. I'll try hard to do good for you."

I hung up slowly. My heart was suddenly pounding. While talking to Timothy I had turned my head to the left. Among a cluster of framed family photographs, hanging on the wall nearest me, was a color enlargement of my Rick wearing a slightly oversize baseball cap, staring intently at the camera while he crouched menacingly with his aluminum baseball bat cocked behind his right shoulder. I rose, walked slowly from the room out onto the deck, sank limply into the chaise rocker and remained there, staring off into the distant woods until long after darkness fell.

It was a tortuously long seven days, waiting for the team's first scheduled practice session. I worked very hard at trying to fill every waking moment with some sort of activity, either of body or mind or both, so that I didn't stumble and fall into that always nearby pool of despair. I would force myself out of bed at seven each morning and after breakfast went off for a long hike through the woods behind the house. Then I would take my red practice shag bag of golf balls and my short irons and stroke shot after shot from one golf pin to the other in our backyard. After darkness I would jog for perhaps an hour, return, shower, and put on my pajamas and robe. Then I would sit at the kitchen table, despite the far more comfortable chairs in other rooms, and try to read. During the years of struggling up corporate ladders, I had acquired a large collection of some of the

world's best self-help and inspirational books to assist in my climb, classics such as Allen's *As a Man Thinketh*, Hill's *Think and Grow Rich*, Peale's *The Power of Positive Thinking*, Stone's *Success Through a Positive Mental Attitude*, and Danforth's *I Dare You*. Now I spent countless hours each evening, searching through these and scores of other books, hoping to find special words of wisdom or consolation that might help me to deal with the pain of my loss. In an old leather-bound nineteenth-century anthology of wise sayings I finally discovered some precious words of solace from Benjamin Franklin and Antiphanes, a Greek dramatist from the fourth century before Christ.

At the funeral of a close associate Franklin had told mourners, "We are spirits. Our friend, as well as all of us, were invited abroad on a party of pleasure which is to last forever. His chair was ready first and so he has gone before us. We could not all conveniently start together and why should you and I be grieved at this, since we are soon to follow and know where to find him."

Amazingly, more than two thousand years earlier, Anthiphanes had written, "Be not grieved above the measure for thy deceased loved ones. They are not dead, but have only finished the journey which it is necessary for every one of us to take. We ourselves must go to that great place of reception in which they are all of them assembled and, in this general rendezvous of mankind, live together in another state of being."

Once again I remembered my mother's similar advice to those mourning the loss of a loved one. Accepting

that advice, whoever was giving it, required a giant leap of faith. God, how I wanted to believe their words!

During that long week of waiting I renewed two other common activities of life, answering a telephone and driving an automobile. Don't know what made me pick up the phone on Wednesday morning to hear Bill's surprised voice on the other end. After that he called every morning just to check on me. As to the driving, I went nowhere in particular, just backed my car out of the garage one afternoon and drove around the back roads of New Hampshire for a couple of hours. In spite of all my efforts, however, I still went into my den at least once each day, pulled open the bottom drawer of my desk and stared down at the gun. Once I picked it up and held it cupped in my hands for several minutes. The deadly thing felt very cold, almost as if it had been packed in ice.

Even though I pulled into Boland Little League's parking lot early, for our first practice session, Bill West was already there ahead of me, removing two large canvas bags from his car's trunk, one containing catchers' equipment and boxes of baseballs and the other filled with batting helmets and bats.

"Let me give you a hand," I yelled, coming up behind Bill and lifting one of the bags. Together we walked through the fence opening and turned toward the nearest dugout, behind first base, as the players who had arrived early came running toward us while, in the parking lot, several car doors slammed as mothers dropped off their hopeful athletes.

Bill passed out some baseballs, suggesting that the boys pair off and begin warming up. Some were dressed in blue jeans and T-shirts, others wore last year's now-tight baseball pants. Some had baseball shoes, others wore sneakers, high and low. Soon we had two rows of six players, tossing balls back and forth, a few very serious and obviously nervous, while others were laughing and loose. Bill and I casually walked behind first one row of six players and then the other, introducing ourselves to every boy. Each was told, as we shook hands, that I was John Harding and he was Bill West. The word *coach* would be fine for both of us if they didn't want to call us by name, and we said that there was no need for 'sir' or 'Mister.' Also, as we chatted with each new Angel, we asked him what position he liked to play and if he had participated in Little League last year. Gradually we could sense that all players were beginning to relax. The smiles multiplied.

It was amazing to me how much we managed to accomplish during that first practice. Bill West sent groups out to the shortstop and second-base positions and hit several balls to each player, who had to field the ball and then throw it to first, where there were two candidates for that position. I stood in short right field and observed how players moved and reacted to Bill's hits. Two of them, Anthony Zullo and Paul Taylor, fielded flawlessly and threw to first with good accuracy. The Taylor kid, in a tight T-shirt, had a great upper body, which I was sure had taken a good deal of time and effort to develop.

We repeated the same procedure with our outfield candidates, hitting several ground balls and fly balls to each of them. We also had them throwing the balls they fielded back to our only catcher candidate, John Kimball, looking for strong arms that might be converted into another pitcher or two. Two players, Charles Barrio and Justin Nurnberg, looked very fast and competent and could throw.

Eventually Bill hit three fly balls to little Timothy Noble. Two he failed to get under and the third caromed off his glove and rolled far behind him. The ground ball hit to him went right through his open legs.

At our second practice session, on Thursday, we commenced by putting a tentative team on the field based on our observations from the first practice, with Bill hitting both ground and fly balls to each position while I walked around and offered suggestions on the best way to catch a fly ball, how to position oneself to best handle a ground ball and, most important, how to throw a baseball properly. I was very impressed by our catcher, short, muscular John Kimball, who had two years of Little League under his belt and a cannon for an arm. Any baseball team, amateur or professional, without a good catcher plays under a terrible handicap. We were very fortunate to have Kimball.

During our third practice, at the other ball field behind Little League Park, we concentrated on hitting. I threw batting practice so long that my arm began to tremble as Bill made notes on his clipboard pad. Both of us stopped play often to correct batting stances, strides

and swings. There was no doubt that Todd Stevenson, our star pitcher, was also our best batter. He hit several of my pitches out of the park, and his smooth left-handed swing was a joy to watch. Our catcher, Kimball, whom the players had already nicknamed Tank, also hit well, as did Paul Taylor and a tall boy, Justin Nurnberg, who looked like he might be our first-baseman during the games that Todd pitched. Then, when someone else pitched, we would put Todd at first base so that we'd still have his potent bat in the lineup, and we'd probably move Justin to the outfield, although he was a much better fielder at first.

Eight players looked like certain starters, even after only the third practice session—Stevenson, Kimball, Zullo, Taylor, Nurnberg, Barrio, Murphy and a great fielder but weak hitter, Ben Rogers, who was a natural at shortstop. Three other players, Chris Lang, Jeff Gaston and Dick Andros, showed potential and were certain to get better with practice and experience. And then there was Timothy Noble, who had been the last to bat. I had tried to pitch the slowest possible balls to the little guy, but his stance was so awkward and his swing so choppy that I felt embarrassed for him as his new teammates giggled each time he swung at the ball and missed, until I turned and stared at them and it became very quiet.

I glanced at my wristwatch. We had sent word home to all parents, via their sons, that we would not run any practice beyond six P.M. so that dinners could be planned accordingly. It was now five minutes to the hour. I clapped my hands together several times and

yelled, "Okay, guys, that's it for today. See you all Thursday, at four, on Little League Field!"

Most of the boys immediately raced to the parking lot and their bikes or their waiting car ride home. Timothy, however, was still standing at the plate, looking very concerned, swinging the bat he was holding back and forth. I glanced toward the dugout where Bill was loading bats and helmets into one of the canvas bags. There was no one else on the diamond when I walked slowly toward the plate and said, "Timothy, can we talk for a minute?"

"Sure," he replied, his voice quivering slightly.

"Timothy," I said, "I believe that if you work very hard and put in some extra time and practice, you could become a good ballplayer. The more we practice something, the better we get at it. It's kind of hard to work very long with one player when all the guys are here, but I think I can help you with your hitting and fielding if you let me. Tell me, would you be willing to spend an extra half hour after practice, just with me, concentrating on a few basics? I know that with a little work we can really improve that swing of yours, and maybe I can give you a few tips that will help you handle fly balls and grounders a lot easier. We have three more practices before the games begin. What do you say?"

Knees bent, I had been crouched down so that I was talking to him at eye level, and for a brief moment as he took a half step forward I thought the little guy was going to leap into my arms.

"I'd like that very much," he said, biting on his lower lip.

"Would your mother mind? Might mess up a couple of her evenings. Late dinners. What do you think?"

"That would be okay. She works at Edd's Supermarket in Concord and doesn't get home until around eight o'clock. She works from eleven to seven, Monday through Saturday."

I didn't understand why, but I found myself fighting to hold back tears.

"Okay, Timothy, we'll do it. How about tonight? Want to start right now?"

His brown eyes opened wide, and for the first time I noticed the faint band of freckles that ran from one cheek to the other, across the bridge of his nose. He nodded vigorously.

"And Timothy, we don't have to say anything to the other kids. We wouldn't want them to think I'm playing any favorites here, okay?"

He nodded again.

I turned toward the dugout. Bill West, although he was too far away to hear us, was watching and smiling. Finally, and before I could say anything, he said, "John, I'll leave the bag with the baseballs and bats right here. You two have fun. I don't think you'll need me. I will see you both on Thursday."

"Good night, Bill."

VIII

༄ ✿ ༄

$\mathcal{T}$he Angels, as a team, made far more progress than either Bill or I had dared expect of them during our final three practice sessions in the ten days leading up to our first game. In all sports, I'm certain, the majority of coaches spend most of their time concentrating on the mechanics of playing well. Our challenge was to teach the fundamentals of fielding, hitting and running, as well as the rules of the game, to active, energetic youngsters who are at an age when concentration on any one subject for more than five minutes is usually a major achievement.

During each of the practices we devoted the first hour to hitting and running the bases and the second hour to fielding and reviewing the playing rules. Beginning with the fourth practice, I asked Todd Stevenson, Paul Taylor, Charles Barrio, and Justin Nurnberg to

come to the park thirty minutes before the others and to commence strengthening their pitching arms by throwing to either Bill or myself so that we could further evaluate their potential. Todd, of course, was without question our ace pitcher, while the other three would compete for spots in our pitching rotation. According to Bill West, both Taylor and Barrio had pitched at least one winning game during their previous season of play, and Nurnberg threw so hard that we couldn't ignore him.

For the batting sessions Bill and I split the pitching time, tossing soft throws across the plate while the other, standing off to the right of the batter, would make countless suggestions and corrections, ranging from having the youth try another and usually lighter bat to positioning him nearer or farther from the plate or showing him how to stride smoothly through the swing instead of lunging at the ball. Bill asked Paul Taylor, our muscular third-baseman and now pitching prospect, to try spreading his feet until they were as far apart as his shoulders were wide. With this more comfortable and solid batting stance, an enthusiastic and now-excited Paul began hitting long fly balls over the fence in center and left field. Ben Rogers, our shortstop and smooth fielder, seemed to chop down on every pitch, either missing the ball completely or driving it into the dirt. It amazed us that someone who fielded with such grace looked so awkward at the plate. We worked on leveling this quiet and unsmiling young man's shoulders and hips just before he swung. Soon his

bat was making much better contact. After hitting three consecutive long fly balls to center and left he caught one of my pitches flush, and I watched the ball sail down the left field line until it cleared the fence by at least ten feet. Dour Ben was actually smiling when he jogged past me to the outfield.

To accomplish as much as possible in the limited time available, we also tried to combine base running with our fielding drills, stressing again and again how important it was for our base runners to know exactly where that baseball was at all times, since they should run the bases with as much aggressiveness as they could. We also worked on the fundamentals of bunting, and timed all our players with a stopwatch, again and again, not only from home plate to first base but also from first to second. Little Tony Zullo and Todd Stevenson were easily the fastest, while Tank Kimball, our catcher, took so long to get from first to second that Bob Murphy, our team comedian, said he was much too slow to be called Tank.

The final thirty minutes of practice were devoted to reviewing the playing rules. We realized that there was no possible way we could cover every rule and subclause in the entire sixty-four pages of *Little League Baseball Official Regulations and Playing Rules*, but we concentrated on as many as possible, covering situations that we believed might arise again and again, such as why one should guard against getting hit by a ground ball as he is running the bases, when he can and cannot leave a base once he has reached it safely, and especially what his

demeanor should be toward spectators, opposing players and umpires, and the penalty for acting otherwise.

Of course I now had an additional activity to help occupy my mind and a little more of my time: the practice sessions, one on one, with Timothy Noble after our regular team practice. On the afternoon following our third practice session, when he had both surprised and touched me by quickly accepting my offer of some additional coaching, the two of us first sat alone in the quiet dugout and had a long chat.

"So tell me, Timothy, have you been playing baseball most of your life?"

Sitting on the bench, quite close to me, his short legs didn't reach the ground. He stared down at his dangling feet for several minutes before shaking his head slowly and replying, "No. My dad was in the army and we lived near Berlin in Germany for a long time, and the kids there all played soccer. I liked soccer, but I wasn't very good. Couldn't run fast enough. Then we came back to the United States last year, to live here in Boland, but pretty soon Dad went away from us and he never came back and my mother was sad. Then she got a divorce."

Again, as on the telephone, Timothy was speaking in a flat, emotionless monotone, sounding almost like a toy robot. *My father is gone. There, I've told you. Now let's not talk about that anymore.*

"So you've only been playing baseball for a year or so?"

He nodded vigorously, brushed back loose strands of

blond hair that had escaped his old baseball cap and smiled. Then he threw out his tiny chest, kicked forward with his two legs, clenched both fists, raised them above his head and shouted loudly, "But day by day, in every way, I'm getting better and better!"

"What did you say?" I gasped.

"Day by day in every way I'm getting better and better!"

I couldn't believe my ears. Impossible! I inhaled several times, trying to calm myself, unable to grasp how the little guy had just managed to repeat the very same powerful words that had once played such a vital role in *my* life. One of the greatest and most positive influences during my early years of corporate-ladder climbing had been a tiny book written by a turn-of-the-century French healer, Emil Coué, titled *Self-Mastery Through Conscious Autosuggestion.* Coué believed that he could help others rid themselves of nearly every affliction, from serious physical problems to negative mental attitudes, if they learned to make positive and healthy suggestions to themselves again and again. Coué eventually became a great cult figure, and his lectures attracted thousands, both in England and in the United States back in the early days of this century. Vast audiences listened and believed that it was possible to rid themselves of scores of life's illnesses and wounds by merely repeating their positive goals and desires again and again. The Frenchman's work was best exemplified by his most famous self-affirmation, "Day by day in every way I am getting

better and better!" Millions repeated those words, aloud and to themselves, time after time, day after day, and so did I after I discovered them in a thin black-leather volume in a secondhand bookstore. That powerful self-affirmation worked for me. Primarily because I *believed* the words. They kept me optimistic and hopeful. My mental attitude, despite any temporary setbacks, always remained positive. I *knew* things would be better tomorrow. I *was* somebody! I *would* succeed! It was almost impossible to think negative thoughts while announcing to the world and to myself that "day by day in every way I am getting better and better!"

Coué and his process of conscious autosuggestion faded from popularity long before the great depression, and he had his share of critics, as do all pioneers in the fields of medicine and psychology. But from my own experiences I knew that positive thoughts programmed into my subconscious mind through self-affirmations, either repeated aloud or to myself, produced positive results, and my favorite was "Day by day in every way I am getting better and better!"

"Timothy," I asked after I finally closed my mouth and took another deep breath, "where did you learn that saying?"

He frowned and glanced at me suspiciously. Finally he said, "From Doc Messenger. He's nice. He's very old, but he always takes care of me and my mother when we get sick. When I saw him the last time, he played catch with me and told me if I kept saying those words, lots

of times each day, I would get better at whatever I was doing, even playing baseball. Doc Messenger is nice. He comes to see me practice, sometimes."

"Oh, was he here today?"

"Uh-huh. He was sitting behind first base all by himself. Today he was wearing a cowboy hat. He waved at me. He has a white beard."

"Has he taught you any other sayings?"

Timothy nodded, threw out his small chest and said, "Never . . . never . . . never . . . never . . . never . . . never give up!"

I knew that one too. Winston Churchill's commencement address to a graduating class at Oxford. Eight words . . . eight very powerful words. Then the great man turned away from his audience and walked slowly back to his seat.

"Do you believe those words, Timothy, that one should never give up?"

He nodded. "I never give up."

We spent our first practice working on Timothy's hitting. I would stand next to him, also holding a bat, and ask him to imitate my stance and swing. Worked better than I had hoped. After ten minutes or so I began pitching to him while correcting any variances in either his stance or his cut at the ball. Before long Timothy was taking short strides into my pitches with a level swing and even following through while maintaining his balance. He only made contact a few times, but I could see that his confidence was gradually building, and he seemed to be enjoying our routine. We even spent time

practicing bunting, and although he had difficulty pivoting and keeping his arms relaxed, I finally had him crouching and bending his knees until he dropped several fine bunts down the third-base line.

That evening, at home, I phoned Bill.

"You okay?" he asked quickly, unable to hide his concern.

"For the moment."

"How did it go with your little Angel?"

"Fine. Fine. He's getting better and better. . . ."

"What?"

"Nothing. Bill, I was wondering, are you familiar with a Doc Messenger in this town?"

"Everybody is, John. Old Doc Messenger has practiced here for a long time. He was a big man on the staff at Johns Hopkins and came here to Boland after he retired—to grow a few tomatoes and hit some golf balls, he told everyone. Then Boland's only doctor suddenly moved to Seattle, and this township had no one to take care of them, so the old man decided to come out of retirement and he's been Boland's savior ever since. Even makes house calls for sick kids and old folks. Why are you asking about him? Something wrong, John? Need a doctor?"

"No, no. Timothy was telling me about the good doctor. Seems like he's quite a special man. According to Timothy I guess he's even come to a couple of our practices."

"I thought that was him sitting high up, back of first base, wearing that old hat of his. Never gave it another

thought when we got busy. Didn't figure him to be spending time at a Little League practice."

"Timothy said he came to see him."

"Well, since he probably helped deliver most of our team into this world, as well as the rest of the league, I imagine he's keeping his eye on all of them. Quite a guy! Must be almost ninety, but he can still hit a golf ball a long way, believe me."

During our final two practice sessions Timothy and I worked on his fielding and base running. On fly balls I began by merely tossing them up into the air, coaching him to hold his hands over his head and catch the ball with both. After he had caught perhaps ten tossed balls in a row, I grabbed a bat, sent him out to shallow center field and began hitting gentle pop-ups. It seemed to take him far too much time to see the ball in flight before he moved toward it. I wondered if his eyesight was at fault, but he said he had been checked at school in May and they had told him that his vision was normal. Could it be his reflexes, perhaps? I didn't know. Also, his running was terribly slow, whether he was chasing after a fly ball or going from base to base, and the expression on his tiny face, when he ran, was always one of great effort. I finally asked him, "Timothy, does it hurt you to run?"

"No," he gasped. "I just keep trying to make my legs go faster, but they don't. They will, though, you wait. They will. I'll never give up . . . never! I'll be faster!"

Following our final preseason practice each player received his official Angel uniform, gray with the letter *A*

in large dark-blue script on the left side of the shirt. The caps and socks were also in dark blue, and as Bill handed a box to each player, he said he hoped and prayed that he had measured everyone correctly.

I was loading bats and balls into the canvas bags when I sensed that Timothy was standing close by.

"Yes, Timothy?"

"Mr. Harding, thank you very much for all your help. My mother said to tell you thank you for her too. I know I'm a better player now." He grinned and then said, "Day by day . . . day by day. . . ."

I smiled and extended my hand. "Good luck, all season. You're going to do fine, trust me."

He nodded enthusiastically. I wanted to pick him up and hug him as I had always hugged Rick.

"Good night, Mr. Harding."

"God bless, Timothy. Don't forget. First game next Tuesday at five against the Yankees. Be here no later than four-fifteen."

I stood and watched until bike and rider turned the corner and were out of sight. Then I returned to the dugout and sat until long after darkness had fallen, praying to God for the strength to hold on. . . .

I X

J hadn't felt so nervous since that memorable day,
not very long ago, when I had stood to address the
board of directors of Millennium Unlimited for the first
time.

All the pregame activities had been completed and
the opening-day ceremonies were now drawing to a
close as everyone in Boland Little League Park rose to
the strains of our national anthem from the loudspeaker
system affixed to the top of the tall wire backstop.

It had been almost thirty years since I had played my
last Little League game, but the routine prior to the
game had not changed even a little in all that time. The
first-, second-, and third-base canvas bags had already
been anchored down at their proper spots on the diamond by the time Bill and I arrived at the park and un-

loaded our equipment. Since we were the designated home team for this opening game, our dugout was the one behind third base.

Bill broke out our ball bag, and our lads started throwing on the sidelines. Sid Marx, the Yankee manager, waved in our direction and then came across the diamond, shook hands, and we wished each other good luck. Each team took infield practice, Yankees first. When it was our turn, I hit three easy grounders to Paul Taylor at third, Ben Rogers at shortstop, Tony Zullo at second and Justin Nurnberg at first. Although they were all obviously tense, our infield handled all my batted balls flawlessly. Behind our dugout Todd Stevenson had already started his warm-up throws to Tank, while behind the Yankee dugout a very smooth left-hander named Glenn Gerston, who had impressed me at the league tryouts almost as much as Todd, was throwing hard. This opening game was probably going to be a low-scoring pitchers' battle.

Two umpires finally made their entrance through the opening in the fence that separated the field from the parking lot. Both were wearing light-blue shirts, open at the neck, dark-blue pants and baseball caps. One was carrying a chest protector and mask. When they arrived at home plate, they beckoned to Sid and me to join them, and after more hand shaking all around the umpire with the chest protector said that there was only one special ground rule for our field. Any batted ball that landed in the outfield in fair territory and then

bounced over the five-foot-high wooden fence that bordered the outfield, whether on the first bounce or the tenth, would be considered a double.

George McCord, a popular Boston morning-radio personality on WBZ and WBZA Radio for more than thirty years, before retiring to Boland, had been the League's public-address announcer for several years, the "best nonpaying gig I ever had," he kept telling everyone. I had heard nothing but praise for the old boy's ability to make every name in the lineup sound as if Ted Williams were coming to bat in the last half of the ninth with two out and the score tied.

After our meeting with the umpires, George's husky voice was heard, from his position at a bench and heavy oak table behind the home plate wire backstop, introducing Stewart Rand, who dramatically announced that the forty-fourth season of Boland Little League was about to commence. He instructed the Angel players, coach and manager to form a single file along the third-base foul line, from home plate, and the Yankees to do the same along the first-base line. Then he asked our Todd Stevenson if he would please walk out to the pitcher's mound and lead both teams in the Little League Pledge.

Todd turned to me in surprise, but when I patted him on the shoulder, he trotted out to mid-field, removed his cap with his left hand and placed his right hand over his heart. His voice quivered slightly as he began, but soon he was almost completely drowned out by twenty-three other eager and youthful voices.

"I trust in God. I love my country and will respect its laws. I will play fair and strive to win, but win or lose, I will always do my best."

All our players immediately turned, as they had been instructed to do, and ran back to the dugout as soon as the pledge had been completed. When they were all seated, I sat on the top dugout step facing them and said, "Well, guys, we've been working hard for several weeks to get to today. Just keep your mind on the game and keep doing the things you've been doing in practice and I know you will do well. We've got a good team. Now, let's go out there and start proving to everyone that we're the best team in the league!"

"We'll never give up!" little Timothy suddenly blurted out.

"Yeah," responded Todd. "We'll never give up!"

"Never give up, never give up, never give up!" the entire team was shouting when the plate umpire nodded toward us and pointed to the field.

"Okay, men," Bill barked, "let's go get them!"

As soon as the Angels had all taken their positions, accompanied by applause, cheers and whistles from the stands, the national anthem commenced, and every player on both teams faced the flagpole in deep center field, standing at attention with his cap clutched tightly to his chest until the music stopped.

Todd threw eight or nine final warm-up pitches to Tank before the home-plate umpire stepped in front of the plate and turned his back toward Todd as he leaned down to brush off the plate. Then he returned to his po-

sition behind Tank, put on his mask, adjusted his chest protector and yelled, "Play ball!"

I had decided to say nothing to Todd before he went out to the mound. No motivational pep talk. He had thrown well in warm-up and he looked to me as if he had things under control. Anything I said to him might do more harm than good if it affected his concentration. I went down into the dugout and sat next to Bill and our three nonstarters, Chris Lang, Dick Andros and Timothy.

"Bill," I said, "I just can't believe the size of this crowd. It's only five o'clock on a Tuesday afternoon, but this place is almost packed solid. Close to a thousand fans for a Little League game in a town of only five thousand or so people? Seems impossible."

"Not here in Boland, John. If you checked the stands, you'd find a lot of parents who care but also a large number of retired people who don't want to or can't afford to move to warmer climates. These games have become an important part of their lives. They will all select a favorite team as the season begins and cheer for that team all season. Gives a lot of them something to do, a place to visit and maybe a reason to wake up and get out of bed in the morning, something a lot of them need very much."

A reason to want to wake up and get out of bed in the morning? One never misses it until that desire isn't there anymore. Oh, how I knew! I turned toward Bill, but he was staring out toward home plate, and his face

showed no emotion. I patted him on the knee and said nothing.

Timothy Noble had moved to the top dugout step. His shrill voice suddenly resounded above the crowd noise, "Come on, guys, you can do it! Never give up, never give up . . . !"

Todd had a little trouble with the fresh sand around the pitching rubber and he walked the Yankee lead-off batter before settling down and retiring the next three batters in order on two grounders and a strikeout. As our team came in from the field, I called to Chris Lang, sitting on the bench, and asked if he would mind being our first-base coach. Without saying a word he jumped up and trotted across the diamond toward first. I would give the batters and base runners all the signals from my third-base coaching position, signals as to whether they should bunt, take the next pitch and also whether or not they should attempt a steal if they were on base. Bill West had agreed to monitor things from the dugout as well as keep our scorebook to be certain that every boy played the allotted number of innings.

Tony Zullo walked to lead off our half of the inning, and I decided to test the Yankee catcher's throwing arm immediately. The league rules declare that base runners shall not leave their bases until the ball has been delivered and has reached the batter, and when the first pitch to our second batter, Justin Nurnberg, was called a strike, I immediately touched my left elbow with my right hand, signaling that Tony was to break for second

base as soon as the next pitch crossed the plate. Standing at the plate, Justin also picked up my sign and swung well above the next pitch in order to distract the catcher as Tony broke for second. Zap! The ball was waiting for him when he hook-slid into the bag, and we knew in a hurry that the Yankees had an excellent catcher as well as a smooth pitcher. Then, as so often happens when a runner is thrown out stealing, Justin stroked a clean single to right field, but Paul Taylor, batting third, struck out on three pitches, bringing up Todd. The big guy hit the first pitch high to left field, and the scrambling young man out there, with more luck than skill it seemed, made a sensational catch over his right shoulder just before he ran into the outfield fence. Fortunately he was only shaken up, but he did hang on to the baseball and the crowd gave him a well-deserved standing ovation as he ran across the field into the Yankee dugout.

Both teams were scoreless in the second inning, although Bob Murphy stroked a beautiful double down the right field foul line before Jeff Gaston popped up to end our threat.

"Never give up, never give up!" Timothy Noble had become our self-appointed cheerleader. Stationing himself at the far end of the dugout, he repeated his favorite words again and again as he jumped up and down, both fists clenched tightly, while his teammates urged him on, often asking for more as they joined in: "Never give up, never give up!"

Both teams were scoreless after the third inning, and

as our guys were preparing to take the field to start the fourth inning, I substituted with my other three Angels, as we had planned. Chris Lang took over for Tony Zullo at second base, Dick Andros for Bob Murphy in left field and Timothy Noble for Jeff Gaston in right. Our subs would play the fourth and fifth innings. That way we would have all our regulars back in the lineup for the final inning.

Todd seemed to be getting stronger with every inning. He struck out all three Yankees who faced him in the fourth inning, and the Yankee ace, Gerston, almost matched him pitch for pitch, striking out two of our guys and allowing the third to hit a short pop fly to first base. Four innings of our six-inning game were now in the books. Still no blood. More and more it was beginning to look like one of those contests that is often decided by a single break.

The first Yankee batter in the fifth hit a hard drive to third that Paul Taylor did a great job of knocking down, but before he could pick up the ball and throw it to first, the batter had crossed the bag safely. The next batter struck out on three pitches, but the boy who followed hit a hard smash to deep shortstop. Ben Rogers dove for the ball, speared it in his mitt, leaped to his feet and fired the ball to Justin at first. Sensational! The batter was out by inches, but the runner who had been on first slid safely into second without a challenge. Now the Yankees had a man in scoring position, with two out, and their pitcher, Gerston, who batted as he threw, left-handed, was coming to the plate.

Bill leaned toward me and said softly, "If you know any prayers, John, now is the time to say them. I remember from last year that this kid pulls every ball he hits down the right-field line and he hits them hard!"

I immediately jumped up, called "time" and walked toward the third-base foul line, waving Timothy farther back toward the fence and closer to the line in right field. Finally I held up both hands, palms facing outward, and he stopped moving. Bill nodded as I climbed back down into the dugout.

Todd's first pitch to his mound opponent was a sizzling fast ball. Gerston wasn't waiting. He swung and smashed a high fly ball to deep right field.

"Oh, God," I heard Bill saying.

Timothy ran back several steps, staring up at the evening sky. Finally he turned and raised both his hands high above his head as the ball reached the top of its long arc and started its fall.

"He's right under it," yelled Bill as we both rose to our feet. "Come on, kid, grab that apple!"

The ball's descent was agonizingly slow. Timothy hesitated and then took another step backward, his glove held high, but the ball seemed to bounce off the tip of the glove's frayed fingers and landed on the grass behind him, rolling all the way to the fence. By the time Tim had retrieved the ball, one run had scored and Gerston was standing on third base, waving both hands high in the air while the crowd continued their applause. Todd struck out the next batter, but the Yankees now had a one-run lead.

As Timothy came down the dugout steps, I could see that his face was streaked with tears. I started to speak, but he just looked up at me, shook his head and hurried to the far end of the dugout. None of his teammates spoke to him or went near him, although there were a few angry glances. Sometimes kids can be so damn cruel. Bill rose and faced the bench after they had all taken their seats. He waved his scorebook and said, "Okay, men, our first three batters are Lang, Andros and Noble. We've got six more outs and we're only down by one. This is anybody's ball game, so let's get them!"

Chris Lang hit a feeble pop fly to the pitcher, Dick Andros went down swinging and then Timothy Noble approached the plate. His teammates, who had been shouting words of encouragement to both Chris and Dick, were suddenly silent. Standing in the batters' box, Timothy tugged at his pants, which seemed at least a size too large for his tiny frame. He dug in with his sneakers, assumed a slight crouch and waited. Gerston's first pitch was an inside fastball that almost hit Timothy, but he never backed away. He lunged at the next two curves and then stepped out of the batter's box, taking a deep breath and rubbing his hands in the dirt. Then he took another deep breath and stepped to the plate, his bat cocked as we had practiced. Gerston took a long and deliberate windup before he reared back and fired his fastball. Timothy's swing was smooth, but the ball made a loud sound as it plunked into the catcher's mitt. He walked slowly back to the dugout, placed his bat

carefully along the row of bats and returned to the far corner of the dugout, biting his lip.

The Yankees were retired in order again, in the sixth and final inning, but the Angels couldn't do much better. Tony Zullo did hit a line-drive single directly over second base, but Justin and Paul popped up to the infield, and Todd's long fly ball was the game's final out.

Todd had pitched a masterpiece, allowing one scratch hit, and yet he had only a loss to show for his magnificent effort.

"Okay, guys," Bill yelled as our team gathered in front of the dugout. "Let's get in a single file and congratulate the Yankees for a good game. Then will you all please come back here and have seats in the dugout for a couple of minutes. I know your folks are waiting, so we won't be very long."

Following the compulsory shaking of hands and "nice game" exchange from players of both sides, the Angels retreated to our dugout. I had never seen them more quiet or subdued as I stood to remind them that there was another game on Thursday and we would do a lot better. However, before I said anything, Todd jumped up, zipped his warm-up jacket, turned and walked down the dugout to where Timothy was sitting, his head in his hands. The dugout was suddenly very still. Todd leaned forward, placing his hands on his tiny teammate's shoulders and said loudly, "Hey, buddy, don't blame yourself. Even big-league superstars make errors. This just wasn't our day, okay? That doesn't mean we gave up. We never give up. Right? Never! You too! Okay?"

Timothy looked up at Todd, his eyes filled with tears. He nodded his head and replied softly, "Okay."

There wasn't much that needed to be said by me after that. "Our next game is with the Cubs, Thursday evening at five, boys. I'd like you all here by four, please. Paul Taylor is our scheduled pitcher. See you all on Thursday."

Driving home I replayed the game in my mind, agonizing along with Timothy as the ball bounced off the fingers of his glove and rolled to the wall. And then, suddenly, I was reliving another game, one I had played during my second year of Little League when I was only ten. I had made two errors, playing second base, and both errors had allowed a run to score. Final score had been a loss for my Angels of old, 3 to 1, because of me. Long after everyone had left the park, I walked out to the grass behind second base, slumped to the ground and bawled my eyes out. I don't remember how long I sat there, but I was too ashamed to go home and tell my dad what had happened. Finally, when it was almost dark, I saw the shadow of an old pickup drive into the parking lot, its headlights diffused by the wire fence. Soon I heard his familiar voice, filled with love and understanding, saying to me, "John, I think it's time to come home."

When I was finally on my feet, I hugged him ferociously, sobbing and crying. All he said was, "It's all right, it's all right. Hell, we all have bad days now and then. Ain't nobody perfect."

Suddenly I hit my brake pedal. I was almost home,

but I pulled over to the side of the road, made a U-turn and headed back to the ballpark. Twilight was giving way to darkness when I parked, walked through the fence opening and headed toward home plate. I could hear children shouting and laughing in the neighboring playground, but our playing field was empty—almost empty. He was sitting in the shadows on the grass in deep right field, his legs folded under him, elbows on knees, head bent forward. I walked slowly toward him and paused when I was about ten feet away.

"Timothy," I called.

His head jerked upward. "Yes?" he said, squinting in my direction.

"Are you okay?"

"Uh-huh."

"Don't you think its about time you headed home?"

He shrugged his shoulders.

"Why are you still here, Timothy?"

"I don't know. I guess I thought that if I just sat out here, where it happened, I'd be able to figure out how I messed up and lost us the game."

"And . . . have you come up with an answer?"

He shook his head, and I heard a muffled sob. Suddenly I had an idea.

"Could I please see your glove?"

He frowned, then reached under his right knee and tossed me an object, the most shredded and nonserviceable baseball glove I had ever seen in my life, its old leather dry, hard and cracked in thousands of places with virtually no padding remaining in its palm

or any of the fingers. Also, the webbing between thumb and forefinger was missing and someone had replaced it with strands of clothesline cord.

I flipped it back to him and said, "That thing should be in a baseball museum. It was probably used by Joe DiMaggio when he was a boy."

"No, it wasn't," Tim replied, a smile briefly flickering across his small face.

I leaned down toward him and extended my hand. He took it, and I pulled him to his feet, saying, "Don't you think it's about time you headed home?"

"I guess. . . ." He sighed.

I pointed to his old glove. "And I believe that's your problem—that glove. It's tough to do any job well without good tools."

The little boy stroked the top of the glove softly. He was obviously too embarrassed to tell me what I suspected, that his single-parent mother couldn't afford to buy him a new glove. I tugged at the visor of his new blue team baseball cap with the gold letter *A* and said, "Timothy, there's an almost brand-new Darryl Strawberry glove at home in a closet. It belonged . . . to . . . to . . . my little boy . . . but he didn't get many chances to use it. It's just hanging there now. I'll bring it for you on Thursday."

He stared up at me intensely. "Your little boy is dead, isn't he?"

"Yes . . . yes, he's dead."

"I'm sorry."

I just nodded. "Now, maybe you had better come a

little early on Thursday so that we can play catch for a while and start getting that glove broken in, okay?"

He nodded. "Thank you. I will. I'm sorry I lost the game. I hope the kids don't hate me too much. I feel awful, but I'll try harder, I promise."

"You'll never give up, will you?"

He shook his head and grinned. "Never!"

"Very good. Now, let's get home before it's dark. Do you have a light on that bike of yours?"

He nodded.

"Okay, see you Thursday, early."

"Good night, Mr. Harding."

Just as I was opening the door to my car, Timothy pulled alongside on his bike, the tiny headlight mounted on his handlebars shining brightly in my direction. "Mr. Harding, can I ask you a question?"

"Of course. Shoot."

"How did you know that you would still find me here at the park?"

I wasn't sure what to say to the little guy, but finally I replied, "I don't know, Timothy. I think maybe my dad told me you'd be here."

"Oh."

The bicycle turned, and its light beam began moving slowly out of the parking lot. Before it was out of sight, I heard a small voice shouting, "See you Thursday, Mr. Harding!"

X

$\it{W}$ednesday seemed to last for a week. After breakfast I tried all the time-passers I had been using lately. I jogged for perhaps an hour, worked on my pitching wedge in the backyard until I had hit at least two hundred golf balls back and forth, and tried reading, but my mind just kept wandering. I was constantly hearing voices in the other rooms. Sally? Rick? I even turned on the television set, late in the afternoon, but ten minutes with Oprah and then Phil had me diving for the "off" button. I didn't need any more pain.

I went to bed early, soon after the sun had set, and of course awoke before dawn on Thursday. With my eyes still closed and my head buried in my pillow, I reached across to touch Sally as I had done for so many years. Not feeling her soft body, I moved my hand gently and slowly across the width of the smooth, cool pillow be-

fore I sat upright in bed and pounded my forehead with the palm of my hand. What are you doing, dummy? Sally isn't lying next to you. Sally is dead. Dead. And so is your baby. So is Rick. Dead. Gone! Never to return!

I finally rose and showered. Didn't feel much like shaving, but then I remembered our game that evening. Couldn't let the parents of our Angels think their kids were being guided by a sloppy bum.

After an omelet, orange juice and coffee, I went into the studio, sat at my desk and stared at the page in our Little League scorebook that Bill had used to record our first game. We had only made three hits off Gerston, singles by Zullo and Nurnberg and a double by Murphy, so there didn't seem to be much I could do to improve the batting order based on game performance. Everyone had fielded amazingly well, except for Timothy's costly error, considering it was our first game. Unless Bill West had any suggestions otherwise, we would go with the same lineup and batting order this evening against the Cubs, except that Paul Taylor would pitch, Justin would move to third base and Todd would play first.

I closed the scorebook, again thinking about that terrible moment in bed when I had tried to touch my lady and there was no one to touch. I tugged at the bottom desk drawer, and it slid open easily. The ugly revolver was still resting on the glossy yellow cover of a NYNEX phone book that contained the listings for Concord residents and several neighboring towns including Boland. I reached inside the drawer but immediately withdrew

my hand before making contact with the dark-blue metal.

"Good morning, Mr. Harding."

I nudged the drawer closed with my right shin, acting like any kid who had been caught with his hand in the cookie jar. Some cookie jar!

"Rose. Good morning. I didn't hear you come in, and I guess I forgot it was your day to clean."

The old gal's smile immediately faded. "Is this a bad day, sir? I can come back some other time."

"No, no. Today is fine. It's just me. Too much on my mind, I guess."

Rose Kelley gripped the handle of our vacuum cleaner with both hands and tilted her head sympathetically. "I'm sorry. Is there anything special I can do for you?"

I shook my head.

"Mr. Harding, I hope you won't mind. I went to Maplewood Cemetery yesterday morning and said a few prayers at the grave, for Sally and Rick. It is a lovely spot on that small rise near the stone wall. Have you selected a gravestone for them as yet?"

"No, I haven't."

"Do you go there often, to be near them?"

I stared down at my hands.

"Mr. Harding . . . ?"

I shook my head again. "I haven't been there since the funeral, Rose. I've driven to the cemetery many times, but I've never parked the car and walked along that little

path to their graves. I can't . . . I just can't bring myself to get close enough . . . to look down at the grass . . . and . . ."

"Mr. Harding, please forgive me, for I am just an ignorant old cleaning woman, but you must go to the grave. You must. Not for them. For you! I remember my mother, God rest her soul, telling me an old Irish tale that she said had been passed on to her by her grandmother in County Galway. It seems that a young woman in a small village on the coast lost her only son in a fall from a cliff, and in the months that followed his burial she lived a life filled only with constant tears, anguish, heartbreak and mourning. When her dead son's next birthday arrived, she resolved to spend the entire day at his grave, and on the way to the cemetery she stopped to buy some flowers from an old man in the village square. After paying for her cemetery posies she started to leave, but paused to watch the old flower merchant who was carefully picking all the dried leaves and stems from the lower portion of a potted plant that seemed to have no life. 'Why are you wasting your time on that dead thing?' she asked and he replied, 'It is not dead. Oh, some of its leaves have finished with their lives, but see, up here, there is still some green showing in the stalk. I expect that with care and love this plant will live and produce flowers for many more years. Young lady,' he said, 'there are many people like plants. They suffer what is a terrible loss—perhaps a child or a wife or husband—and they allow what has happened to turn them into a shriveled stalk, empty of hope and life.

On the other hand, there are many, don't you know, who will suffer the dried-up parts to just drop off and then they go right on living and breathing and singing and smiling as they keep producing lovely flowers, year after year, just as long as God can use them.' "

"Mr. Harding," Rose continued, sounding more and more like a stern first-grade teacher as she lifted the vacuum cleaner off the rug. "We already have more than enough plants that have perished, back there in the woods. I don't want to see you shrivel up in sadness until you become one of them."

Some time in the afternoon I remembered that I had promised to bring Rick's almost-new baseball glove to Timothy. I went into my son's room, walked directly to the closet without looking left or right and pushed open the sliding doors. The glove was resting on a shelf I had built low enough so that Rick could store some of his more prized possessions at a level he could reach instead of stashing everything under his bed and dresser. Beneath the glove were boxes of Chinese checkers, dominoes, Trivial Pursuit Jr. Edition and Lego. Alongside were brightly colored Ninja Turtles and G.I. Joe action figures mingling with missile launchers, helicopters and Pizza Throwers, all surrounding a towering brown cylinder filled with Tinkertoy parts. Then there were the three cardboard shoe boxes filled with baseball cards. I lifted one off the shelf and held it lovingly in my hand. How many hours had Rick sat at our kitchen table, carefully transferring cards from one indexed box to another

as he continued to invest most of his allowance in his collection? I reached in and randomly pulled out a card: "NOLAN RYAN, Texas Rangers." One of Rick's favorite players. Mine too.

Timothy was waiting for me, pacing back and forth in the parking lot, when I arrived at exactly three-thirty as promised. He came racing over to my car, and as I stepped out, I flipped him the glove.

"Oh . . . wow . . . this is cool!" he exclaimed as he slid his tiny left hand into the leather finger slots. Then he pounded his clenched right fist, again and again, into the darker oiled palm of the glove as he flexed the heavy leather webbing that was between thumb and forefinger.

"Want to give it a tryout?" I asked.

"Okay!"

Bill West had all the team supplies and equipment in his car, but I had remembered to bring a baseball and my old glove. The two of us played catch in right field until the other players started to arrive. As Timothy and I strolled back in toward the infield, I asked him, "Does it feel comfortable on your hand?"

"Oh, yes. It's a very good glove, Mr. Harding. Thank you. Thank you. I'll do better now, you wait."

"Day by day . . . , Timothy?"

He grinned and nodded enthusiastically.

After a scoreless first inning our guys jumped on three Cub pitchers for eleven runs, and when I sent in my three substitutes in the fourth inning, the score was already 15 to 1, so I let Chris and Dick and Timothy play

the rest of the game without putting the regulars back in for the sixth inning. Final score was an embarrassing 19 to 2, and although we did get fifteen hits, the Cubs helped our cause by committing seven errors. I apologized to their manager, after the game, but Walt Hutchinson was a good sport about it all and said that the way his guys played, they deserved to get clobbered. We had two batting stars. Todd hit two home runs and a double, and Paul Taylor, besides pitching a four-hit game, striking out eight and walking only two, hit a home run and three singles. Timothy came to the plate twice during those final three innings. He struck out both times. No tears, no tantrums, no self-pity, no temperament. Instead by game's end the gutsy kid was hoarse from cheering for his teammates, and apparently they had all forgiven him for his error costing them the first game. "Day by day, in every way, we're getting better and better!" and "Never—never—never—never—never—never give up!" were chanted so frequently and loudly by our team, at Timothy's urging, that the spectators immediately behind our dugout picked up on it, and soon the entire grandstand crowd on our half of the field was repeating those valiant words, over and over, "Never give up!"

On Tuesday evening of the following week our opponents were the Pirates, managed by grandfather Tony Piso, who was also the town of Boland's treasurer. The Pirates had won their first two games, including a 9-to-8 slugfest against Sid Marx's Yankees, who had clipped us in the first game. We knew this was going to be a tough

one, and it was. We won, 2 to 0! Todd Stevenson allowed just one hit, a scratch single between short and third, and Tank Kimball singled to deep center in the fourth inning, driving in both Zullo and Nurnberg, who had walked and been advanced to second and third by a fine Paul Taylor bunt. We totaled only five hits, all singles. Timothy did finally make contact with two pitched balls, both of which he fouled over the backstop behind home plate before striking out, but he cleanly fielded a Pirate single, which had gone between first and second, and tossed it to second in time to prevent the runner from advancing. Day by day . . .

After the game I spent at least an hour shaking hands and talking to our kids' parents. What a great thrill to finally be accepted, but even more important than their kind words was hearing the unsolicited words of praise they were repeating that had come from the mouths of their youngsters about Mr. Harding and Mr. West.

On the following evening, Wednesday, we played Sid Marx and his Yankees for the second time. Our boys were out for revenge, and they got it. With Paul Taylor pitching another fine game, we won, 6 to 4, and this time our hitting star was Bob Murphy, who had a perfect night with two singles and a double. Two of our subs managed to get their first hits of the season. Chris Lang hit a short pop fly to right that dropped in for a single, and Dick Andros hit a hard line drive shot to left-center that went for two bases. It was a close and exciting game. Some of the parents afterward said that the difference between winning and losing had been our

little cheerleader, who never stopped urging his buddies on. Timothy, now the only player on our team without at least one hit, went down swinging, once again, in his only time at bat, but he hung in there on every pitch and never gave up on himself. As Timothy was running out to his right-field position for the fifth inning, patting his teammates on the back, Bill nodded in his direction and said, "John, that kid's heart must be so big, I'll never understand how the Lord got it inside such a tiny body."

Two weeks of the six-week season were now on the books, and to our great joy and surprise the Angels were leading the league with a 3 and 1 record while the Yankees and Pirates were close behind, at 2 and 2 for each of them. We still had four weeks and eight games to play. Anything could happen.

After that second Yankee game Sid Marx, their manager, and I had a rather long and friendly chat as we leaned against the wire backstop behind home plate. I liked Sid. We covered every possible subject, from the huge growth of the Little League program to how the kids of today compare with those of twenty and thirty years ago in ability and attitude. Sid finally said, "John, it's getting late, and I had better get rolling before Susie starts worrying about me. It was a good game, but we'll get you next time, I promise."

Driving home, I had passed through the old covered bridge and just turned right on Main Street when I saw the little guy, despite near darkness. He was moving along at a steady pace, but he stopped suddenly when I

pulled my car close to the narrow grass edging that separated the sidewalk from the street. I leaned over and pushed open the car door on the passenger's side.

"Timothy, you're walking home from our game?"

"Uh-huh."

"Why? Where's your bike?"

"The chain broke this morning. My mother took everything to the bike shop in Concord on her way to work today."

"Hop in and I'll take you home."

"I don't mind walking. And I don't want to bother you. I'll be okay. Don't worry."

I tried to replace the warmth in my voice with some authority. "Hop in!"

As soon as he was in the car and the door was closed, I said, "Now, show me the way." Following Timothy's instructions, we continued along Main Street through the center of town, turned right on Jefferson Avenue and after about two miles of bumpy asphalt we swung left on Route 67. We continued for about another two miles before I finally turned to Timothy and asked, "Did you walk all this distance to the ballpark today?"

Head bowed and clutching his new glove to his chest, he looked up at me through those long brown lashes and nodded, hesitatingly, as if he had been caught in some crime.

"Good Lord, how long did it take you to go from your house to the field?"

He shrugged his shoulders and sighed. "I don't know. I left the house around two o'clock, right after I made a

peanut butter sandwich for my lunch. My mom had to go to work early today."

Suddenly he sat upright and pointed. "See that mailbox, Mr. Harding? It's ours. Turn right, just after we pass it, on the dirt road. Our house is only a little ways in the woods there."

I did as I was told, driving along slowly and carefully on the narrow, rutted lane for perhaps a hundred yards before the beams of my headlights reflected off the front of a shabby wooden structure that looked like a storage area for wood or farm equipment. Many of the unpainted clapboards along the front of the shack were missing or cracked, and there was a large area, near one corner, where someone had nailed a large and unpainted square piece of plywood. A light shone from the uncurtained window to the left of the doorway, while more plywood was nailed across the window frame to the right. Off to the side, parked under several pine trees, was a rusting blue Renault sedan.

"That's my mom's car," Timothy explained. "She says it runs a lot better than it looks . . . and it does."

An uncovered, fly-specked light bulb shone above the front door, which opened slowly as a woman stepped out onto the landing, raising both her hands to cover her eyes. I immediately turned off my headlights. "That's my mom," Tim announced as we were both getting out of the car. I followed him to the steps, which were only cinder blocks piled loosely atop one another.

She was standing nervously and uncertainly just outside the door, grasping the doorknob with one hand and

her apron with the other. "Good evening, Mrs. Noble. I'm Timothy's Little League manager, John Harding. Saw him walking home tonight, so I thought I'd give him a lift."

Her voice sounded both youthful and weary, which was probably a good description of her appearance as well. "That is so nice of you, Mr. Harding. Won't you please come in?"

I hesitated, feeling more than a little uncomfortable, but a glimpse of Timothy nodding hopefully up at me was not to be ignored. The door opened directly into the kitchen, and as soon as we were inside, Timothy's mother extended her right hand to me tentatively and said, "I'm Peggy Noble, sir, and I'm so glad for this opportunity to thank you in person for all that you have done for my son."

She wore little makeup, her blond hair needed brushing and combing and her face was slightly flushed. Two pans were on the stove emitting steam. Mrs. Noble was obviously preparing supper, but she said, "Please, Mr. Harding, have a seat," as she pulled a plastic-covered chair out from behind a small table that was already set for two. Beyond an old refrigerator, at the other side of the kitchen and close to the ceiling, I could see what looked like a piece of clothesline stretched across the room. Bedsheets hung from it as a sort of curtain, but they didn't quite conceal the two unmade beds, barely visible in the shadows beyond. Timothy and his mother, I immediately realized, were living in a one-room camp

that probably, in bygone years, had been used only by hunters each fall.

"Have a seat, Mr. Harding," she repeated.

"No, thank you, Mrs. Noble. I've got to be going. Now, how about next week? Our first game is on Tuesday. Will Timothy have his bike back by then, or should I come by and pick him up?"

Her gray eyes filled with tears. "You are so kind, sir. So kind. No, they told me that I could pick up the bike this Saturday, so Timothy will be okay next week."

"Great! Then I'll be on my way. Didn't mean to disturb your supper, but it was still nice to meet you. This is a lucky boy to have you."

"I'm afraid I don't do so very much for him. It's hard, and I try because I love him so. But, Mr. Harding, most of all, he is lucky to have you in his life . . . at this time. So lucky. Thanks be to God you selected him."

She moved closer to me, stood on her toes and kissed my cheek.

I drove home very slowly.

XI

*L*ate Saturday afternoon, after stocking up on milk, bread, soda pop and frozen dinners at the local convenience store, I walked around the backyard that Bobby Compton and his crew had mowed and trimmed so neatly on Friday. Along both sides of the deck, pink Simplicity roses that Sally had planted so carefully, back in March when I thought it was still too early in the season, were now covered with blossoms. I snapped one off, inhaled its faint fragrance and pushed its thorny stem carefully into my shirt pocket. Then I strolled out into the meadow beyond our lawn to check on the wild-blueberry bushes. The clusters of berries were still pale green except for an occasional dab of pink. They were at least two or three weeks from picking, but even when ripe none of them would ever find their way into a Sally Harding pie or muffin or one of her giant blueberry

turnovers that I remember holding in both hands, while still warm, before taking that first bite. Memories! Here I go again. All our lives, it seems, someone is trying to teach us how to remember better. There are even scores of memory courses and lectures on the subject, but I've never heard of a course on how to forget, and I'm certain that for some it would be a very popular seminar. Many of those who are so proud of their great ability to recall people and dates and events may well admit, someday, that their blessing has become a curse.

On Tuesday evening we gave Chuck Barrio the starting assignment against the Cubs, and the classy left-hander was almost perfect for four innings. We were leading 8 to 1 when the Cubs came to bat in the fifth inning and exploded for twelve runs. They scored seven runs off Chuck before I relieved him with Paul Taylor, since Todd was scheduled for the Thursday game against the Pirates. Paul didn't have it, either, walking the first three batters he faced before allowing two singles and a double. I blame myself for his poor performance, since I didn't insist that he warm up longer after we sent him to the mound, even though the umpire was willing. In any event, we let a game that was won get away from us. The final score was 15 to 9, Cubs. Ben Rogers, our silent man at shortstop, was our batting star with two doubles and a single, and Todd hit another home run. Since all the Angels were now well aware that Timothy was the only one on the team without a hit, they all agonized on every pitch when he went to bat in the fifth, but the

little guy went down swinging, once again, to end the inning.

On Thursday, against Anthony Piso's Pirates, we had a field day. Todd pitched shutout ball, and we unloaded on four Pirate pitchers for fourteen runs, never scoring less than two in any inning. Although our guys made twenty hits, according to Bill West and his scorebook, they all seemed more concerned about Timothy getting his first one. All the time he was at the plate, in the fourth inning, our dugout sounded more like a huge concrete high-fidelity speaker blaring, "Never give up, never give up, Timothy, Timothy, never give up!" until the home-plate umpire finally called time, came over to our bench and asked the boys if they would all kindly lower their voices to no more than a loud roar so that his calls could be heard. Our Angels stood and applauded as he walked back to the plate before renewing their cheers for Timothy. He did get his bat on one pitch and hit a fairly hard line drive down the right-field line that was foul, but then he missed the next two pitches. When he tossed his bat toward our dugout and ran out to his position in right, Bill beckoned to me to sit next to him.

"What's up?" I asked.

"Timothy. Does he seem okay to you?"

"Yeah, why?"

"I don't know. He looks even more pale than usual, and when he ran in from the outfield, after the last inning, he acted as if he was having a tough time just

keeping his balance. I asked him if he felt okay, and he just nodded his head."

When the game ended, after we had exchanged congratulations with the Pirates at home plate, I made it a point to talk with him. "Timothy, how's the new bike chain?"

He nodded vigorously. "Great. It's like I have new wheels."

The words were spoken as individual utterances, with long pauses between each, not as a single, total sentence. Strange.

"Are you feeling okay?"

He nodded again. "I'm a little tired. My mom had to go to work early today and I heard her making breakfast, so I woke up."

I patted him softly on the head. "Get a good night's sleep tonight, you hear?"

He nodded and forced a half smile. "Good night, Mr. Harding."

Bill's car was parked next to mine in the parking lot. He was leaning against his vehicle, waiting for me, a concerned look on his face. "What did you find out, John . . . about Timothy?"

I shrugged my shoulders. "He said he was tired because he was accidentally awakened early by his mother, but, I don't know, his voice pattern sounds a little weird, like someone speaking while they are under hypnosis."

Bill sighed. "The most amazing thing to me, John, is that the kid is still playing at all. I've coached a lot of Little League kids through the years, and when they

keep striking out and do little or nothing very good in the field, they will usually quit, after a few games, rather than continue to be embarrassed by their lack of ability or coordination. Not this boy! He comes to play every day, hustles all the time, tries his very best, asks for no sympathy and instead of moping at his own failures he cheers loudest of all for every one of his teammates. That is one brave little Angel. We can all learn a hell of a lot from him."

We can all learn a hell of a lot from him. I kept hearing Bill's words, over and over, long after I had put out the light and crawled into bed.

The mid-July afternoon was hot and muggy, and huge waves of cumulus clouds were gathering overhead when I pulled into the Little League parking lot for our important Monday game against Sid Marx and his Yankees. After having completed half of our twelve-game schedule, we now shared the league lead with the Yankees, having both won four and lost two, while the Pirates and Cubs had each won two and lost four.

In the lot, parked next to Bill's car was a white panel truck with red lettering on both sides and the rear doors: NEW HAMPSHIRE'S LEADING TELEVISION STATION— CHANNEL 9—WMUR-TV—MANCHESTER, N.H. I didn't give it another thought until I stepped through the opening in the fence and onto the grass and saw two young men in blue jeans and T-shirts fussing over a tripod and television camera that was facing toward the first-base dugout, our dugout for the game, as we were the designated

visiting team. Another young man, in a dark business suit, who had been standing behind the camera, looked up as I approached and said, "Here he is now, guys. Perfect timing."

"Mr. Harding," he said as he extended his hand and smiled, "I'm Tom Land, one of the sportscasters at Channel Nine in Manchester. We'd like to interview you for our *Eleven O'Clock News* this evening, if you don't mind. Our station has already cleared it with your league president, Mr. Rand."

"Why in the world would you want to interview me? There are hundreds of Little League managers in New Hampshire, and if you want to talk with a real good one, he's probably already in that other dugout. His name is Sid Marx. Great coach, and the kids love him."

"Well, sir," he said, nodding his head, "there may be hundreds of other Little League managers and coaches in this state, but I promise you that none is as well known in New Hampshire, and the nation, as John Harding. I doubt there are many of our viewers who are not familiar with how you rose to become president and chief executive officer of Millennium Unlimited at such an early age before . . . before . . ."

He stared at the ground, finally forced a smile and said, "And now, to see such a celebrated American example of success coaching a small-town Little League team instead of running that Fortune 500 corporation, gosh it's an unbelievable story. I'm glad we found you before the networks!"

"Well, now, whom do you want to interview, John

Harding, manager of the Angels or . . . or John Harding, former and very brief chief executive officer of mighty Millennium?"

Deep furrows suddenly appeared in his wide forehead. "Why . . . why . . . both!" he stammered.

"I'm sorry, but I'm going to pass."

He acted as if he hadn't heard me. "Mr. Harding, it won't take us very long. Perhaps ten minutes. I have just a few questions I want to ask you, questions that I'm certain our audience would like to hear you answer, such as how you have handled the past few months, since the terrible tragedy, and then perhaps some questions comparing the old days of Little League when you were an all-star right here, on this very field, with the conditions and players of today."

"Mr. Land, we're trying to get ourselves ready to play a ball game. I thank you and your fine television station for this honor, but my answer is no, and I'm afraid you and your people will have to move that camera and pretty damn quickly. As you can see, my kids are starting to arrive, and that thing is exactly the kind of distraction they don't need. Now, if you care to shoot some of the game, be my guest. Back there, behind the home-plate wire backstop, you will find a handsome old boy named George McCord. He's our public-address announcer, and I'm sure he'll be glad to show you where you can best set up your camera." I extended my hand. "Nice to meet you, Mr. Land."

He stared at me in disbelief, his mouth partially open. "You mean you won't do the interview?"

I patted his shoulder. "Correct! Now, kindly move your camera so that these kids can get themselves ready to play ball."

It was a tough game. With Channel 9's camera stationed in the stands behind third base, the Angels and Yankees both played as if their very lives hung in the balance. Our guys took an early 2-to-0 lead in the second inning when Bob Murphy tripled to deep center, scoring Zullo and Nurnberg, but the Yankees came back in the fourth with four straight hits after Paul Taylor had some control trouble, and we were down 4 to 2. We managed to score one more in the sixth, but the losing final score was a bitter pill to swallow, 4 to 3. Tank Kimball finally found his batting eye, collecting two singles and a double, and Timothy came to bat with two men on in the fifth and a chance to be a hero. I found myself saying silent prayers, asking God to please let him get a hit, just a single, as if God had nothing more to worry about than a small-town Little League game. Later in the evening, recalling that moment, I would realize that it was the first prayer of any kind I had said since the funeral.

After swinging wildly at the first two pitches, Tim refused to bite at the next two, which were both over his head, before he dug in with both feet, swung and connected. It was only an infield pop fly to the third-baseman, but he had finally hit a ball in fair territory during a game, and our entire team leaped to their feet, applauding and shouting as Timothy stepped on first base before he turned to jog back to the dugout. He

paused, halfway back, doffed his cap and waved it toward the television camera behind third base before taking his seat on the bench. I was watching him carefully. When he came down the dugout steps, he seemed to be swaying from side to side and he was breathing hard. Then, when he went to sit, he first reached toward the bench with both hands before he lowered himself onto the wood.

We bounced back on Wednesday evening against the lowly Cubs. Everyone in our lineup—that is, everyone except Timothy—managed to get at least one hit, and three of our guys had perfect nights, three for three! Final score was 13 to 4. Todd experimented with a few new pitches, including a knuckleball his older brother was using successfully in high school, or I'm certain he would have had another shutout. Timothy took some good cuts, but went down swinging on four pitches. He did, however, finally catch his first fly ball of the year, a fairly well hit ball that went right at him. He just held up his new glove and caught it as any major-leaguer would. Of course that produced another chorus of cheers from all the Angels, whether they were in the field or on the bench, and gave him another chance to doff his cap. What a little ham! And when he arrived in the dugout, he shouted, "Day by day, in every way, I'm really and truly getting better and better!"

Now, with only four games remaining, the Yankees had a record of six wins and two losses, and we were second with five wins and three losses. Since the top

two teams would play a single game at the conclusion of the season, for the league championship, I would have been satisfied if the regular season had ended right then. But we still had four more to play, and both the Pirates, with three wins and five losses, and even the Cubs, with two wins and six losses, could possibly catch us. We couldn't relax yet.

. . . And Timothy Noble, still without a base hit, was running out of games.

XII

❧❀❧

$\mathcal{M}$ost New England towns fire off as large a display of fireworks as they can afford, usually on their most spacious athletic field, in celebration of Independence Day. Not the township of Boland. Of course most of its citizens drive to nearby Concord to enjoy fireworks displays on July Fourth, but then they have their own special celebration. Since town hall records show that Boland's first settler, Isaac Thomas Boland, arrived among unfriendly animals and natives on July 17, 1735, that was the day when most of the townspeople always gathered in the grandstand and parking lot of Boland Little League Park. When darkness fell, rockets, Roman candles and a varied assortment of aerial bombshells were launched from the outfield area, exploding high above in a noisy and brilliant spectrum of blazing colors while the crowd "oohed" and screamed and applauded.

Since July 17th fell on a Monday, our scheduled games, normally played Monday through Thursday each week, were all moved ahead a day, and our game against the Pirates was listed for Tuesday evening. Bill had phoned, sometime in mid-afternoon on Monday, asking if I wanted to go to the fireworks with him and Edy. I thanked him but declined. After some pastrami on rye with a glass of skim milk for supper, I went out on the deck, settled into my favorite chaise lounge and had almost dozed off when the first aerial bombshell exploded, almost directly over the house. Startled, I looked up just in time to see scores of flaming stars of all colors falling lazily out of a swirling pillar of white smoke. I sat up and watched as glowing rockets and bright balls of light climbed, one after the other, high into the heavens, arching up from the playing field a half mile or so away, which was hidden from view by tall pines and oaks.

After several minutes it became very difficult for me to watch. Almost from Rick's infancy, fireworks had fascinated him. From the time he was only three, back in Santa Clara, and then for the two years in Denver, Sally and I had always taken him to see "the works!" on each Fourth of July. I remember holding him on my knees for the first couple of years. He would bounce up and down constantly while the rockets soared higher and higher, his big blue eyes opened so wide that there were deep furrows in his forehead as he pointed upward with the forefingers of both hands and shrieked his appreciation of each swishing rocket when it exploded to discharge

multicolored stars and glowing balls of magnesium while the odor of burning sulphur and charcoal filled the summer air.

I watched the Boland township's celebration of lights in the sky for perhaps twenty minutes. It was probably the loneliest twenty minutes of my life. Then I went into the house and climbed into bed, hoping that I would never awake.

Our kids were obviously getting a little cockier with each game and there was already talk of the big championship game against the Yankees, even though Bill and I kept reminding them that they hadn't clinched anything yet. On Tuesday evening the whole team seemed higher than a kite at batting practice, and they were teasing Timothy because he had arrived wearing a brand-new pair of white Nike baseball shoes with molded cleats of black and red. When he saw me, he came running over and said, "See my new shoes, Mr. Harding."

"They look great! How do you like them?"

He nodded eagerly. "They're nice. Doc Messenger took me to Concord this morning and bought them for me. He said my old sneakers were no good to play ball in!"

With that he turned and ran to the outfield, arms pumping furiously, straining to land on his toes with each step like the most graceful of runners.

Our game against the Pirates began as a real pitchers' duel. For the first two innings neither team was able to

get the ball out of the infield, and Paul Taylor was throwing harder than I had ever seen him throw. Then, as swiftly as the wind can change directions here in New England, the game turned into a wild slugfest after both Todd and Tank hit home runs, back to back, in the third inning and our guys followed by scoring seven more. Tony Piso and his boys came right back with six of their own when Paul lost his control in the fourth inning, although I did let him stay in the game and he finally got the side out.

In the fifth inning, as Timothy was walking to the plate, his teammates commenced their chanting, "Timothy, Timothy, never give up, never give up!" Then they began clapping their hands in rhythm, and soon the crowd directly behind our dugout started to clap until the entire grandstand had joined in. Everyone was rooting for the little guy to get his first hit. He tried. Oh, how he tried! Looked good at the plate, took smooth cuts at the ball, but . . . he struck out on three pitches as the crowd groaned their disappointment.

We did finally win the game, sloppy as it was, 14 to 9.

He was leaning against the trunk of an old Jaguar sedan, parked next to my car in the parking lot, and although he didn't need to introduce himself because I recognized him, he did anyway.

"Mr. Harding," he said, smiling and extending a large hand, "I'm Doc Messenger. When someone told me that I was parked next to your buggy, I couldn't pass up the

opportunity to hang around long enough to tell you how much I admire you, your courage and the great way you handle your team. Kids always see right through phony adults, and it's obvious that the Angels respect you and enjoy playing for you."

"Thank you, sir. Much appreciated. I'm so glad to finally meet the legendary Doc Messenger after all I've heard about you. Timothy Noble talks about you often. He's a lucky kid to have you keeping an eye on him."

The old man folded his arms, smiled, and replied in a deep baritone voice, "Well, I don't know about that. What I do know, for sure, is how fortunate he is to be playing for a man like you."

"Doc, is Timothy okay? Sometimes he seems to lose his balance, and other times he looks as if he's in pain when he runs, but he says he isn't."

He stroked his long white beard several times before replying, "He's okay. Just a few childhood problems, but I'm keeping an eye on him. I've even come to all your games."

"Day by day, in every way . . ."

He smiled. "The little fellow has really taken to those old self-motivators, hasn't he? I only taught him two, but they seem to keep him positive and with a good outlook on life, even if they haven't produced a hit as yet. Amazing and powerful tools, self-motivators. They could be a miracle treatment for so many if only we could get more people to believe in that mysterious power contained in simple words. All we have to do is program our subconscious mind with positive thoughts

and words, and when we do, we can work wonders in our lives. So many of us, perhaps all of us, talk to ourselves throughout the day anyway, so why not feed ourselves positive words and ideas that are beneficial. 'I can win, I can get the job done, I can make the sale' are just as easy to say as 'I can't win, I can't complete the job, I'll never make the sale.' Norman Vincent Peale, W. Clement Stone, Napoleon Hill, Maxwell Maltz and so many other great minds have tried to teach us this simple technique to change our lives for the better. Self-affirmations, employed by man or woman to improve production, behavior and even thinking have been used successfully for thousands of years. Did you know that Epictetus, the old Roman philosopher, even offered us special words to help us deal with the terrible loss of a loved one? He said, 'Never say about anything, I have lost it, but only I have given it back. Is your child dead? He has been given back. Is your wife dead? She has been returned.' " He leaned over and patted my shoulder. "Keep up the good work, Mr. Harding. I'm so glad we had this chat." Then he turned and unlocked the door of his car, and I turned toward mine, unable to say anything.

Thursday's game against Sid Marx and his Yankees turned out to be another nail biter, with Todd Stevenson pitching against their best, Glenn Gerston. No one reached third base, on either side, until Justin Nurnberg cracked a double between left and center field that rolled all the way to the fence, and then he advanced on

Paul Taylor's infield grounder to second. However, we couldn't bring our man home, so we had a scoreless tie on our hands as we began the fourth inning with the top of the Yankee batting order coming to the plate. Todd struck out the first two, but then he walked the next, and Sid's cleanup batter followed with a line drive down the left-field line that kept rising and rising until it disappeared over the fence, and we were suddenly trailing by two. The next batter, after fouling several pitches, hit a high fly to right field, and Bill West, sitting next to me, buried his head in his hands and groaned until the crowd roared and nearly everyone rose to their feet as Timothy, after making a fine two-handed catch as I had taught him, came jogging into the bench while the crowd applauded. Then he glanced over toward me and shouted, "Nothing to it!"

At the plate things were not so productive for Timothy. After fouling off several pitches, he finally went down swinging. Actually none of our bats were very potent against Gerston, and we suffered our third defeat against only one victory for the year against the Yankees.

On the following Monday, with Chuck Barrio on the mound for us, we handled the Cubs easily, 17 to 5, and that win clinched second place in the league, which meant that a week from Saturday we would tangle once more with the Yankees, this time for the league championship. Ben Rogers and Bob Murphy both had three hits, and Tank poked another home run in our lopsided

victory. I let Andros, Lang and Noble play the entire final four innings, and Timothy got to bat twice since all our guys were really pounding the ball. He struck out both times, but both times he came back to the bench with head still held high. What a special kid!

While our team was running out onto the field for the sixth inning, Bill West came over to where I was standing and asked softly, "Have you heard about Timothy?"

"No. What's wrong?"

"Well, the kids were telling me that his bike is out of commission again. Apparently the new chain his mother bought snapped on the way here today, so I guess he just left the old thing by the side of the road and ran the last couple of miles to be here on time. How's that for desire?"

After the game, as we were loading the equipment into the trunk of Bill's car, I called to Timothy as he trotted by.

"Yes, sir?"

"How about a ride home?"

He sighed, and dragged his new shoes in the sand. "Someone told you about my stupid bike?"

"Yup."

We had been riding for perhaps ten minutes before the little guy exclaimed, "This isn't the way home."

"It is for me."

"We're going to your house? Why?"

"Wait and see. We'll be there in a couple of minutes."

I finally turned into my driveway, drove up the grade, pushed the button on my garage-door opener and

waited until the door was all the way up and the lights had turned on.

"Timothy, jump out for a minute. There's something I want to show you."

He followed me uncertainly into the garage. I walked over to where Rick's new red Huffy "Street Rocker" bicycle was hanging on one of the walls, suspended by two large metal brackets. Holding my breath, I reached up to feel both tires and was relieved when they felt hard. Then I grasped the frame in both hands and lifted Rick's last birthday present from its place on the wall. I lowered it to the concrete floor, in front of Timothy, and said, "This is yours. It's not giving enjoyment to anyone, just hanging there, and I'm sure Rick would want you to have it if he knew you."

Timothy's two tiny hands moved slowly across the chrome handle bars and down the dusty but bright frame. "It's brand-new, Mr. Harding!"

"Yes, just about."

"Is it really mine, forever, or just until baseball is over?"

"It's yours forever and ever."

"Wow!" he exclaimed, "I'll take good care of it, honest I will."

"I know you will. Now it's almost dark, so let's put the bike in my trunk and I'll drive you home. Then tomorrow you can start riding it, okay?"

He nodded eagerly. "It's the first new bike I've ever owned, Mr. Harding!"

When we pulled up close to Timothy's home, the outside light did not go on.

"I don't think my mom is home from work yet. Her car isn't here."

I removed the bike from the trunk and leaned it against the side of the house where clapboards were missing.

"Will you be okay?" I asked.

"Oh, yes, my mom will be home soon. Do you know what she promised, Mr. Harding?"

"No, what?"

"She said that if we got to play in the championship game next Saturday, she would take the day off, even if her boss got mad at her, and come to see me play. Won't that be neat?"

"It certainly will be."

"She's never seen me play. Did you know that? Maybe I'll get a hit in that game, while she's watching."

"I sure do hope so, Timothy. Now, don't forget Wednesday night's game, the last one before the big one. We're playing the Pirates, and we can all start getting ourselves ready, in that game, for the championship tussle. Okay? See you Wednesday."

"Yes, sir. Thank you, Mr. Harding. Thank you."

I guess our kids were already looking ahead to the championship game against the Yankees, a week from Saturday, because they were terrible in their final game against the Pirates. I pitched Todd for three innings and

Paul Taylor for three so that my two aces would have some work in preparation for the big one, but the team as a whole played a sloppy game, and I think we managed to squeak out an 11-to-10 victory because the Pirates, certain to finish third in the league standings no matter what the outcome of our game, played as if they didn't care.

Since we had clinched our spot in the championship game, I let Timothy play the entire six innings, hoping he would get that base hit he wanted so badly. He did hit a hard grounder to the pitcher in the second inning, but then he went down swinging the other two times he batted.

The ballpark and parking lot were nearly empty by the time Bill and I had gathered all the baseball gear and piled it into the trunk of his car. In the twilight I moved close to my old friend, extended my hand and said softly, "I'll never be able to repay you for what you have done for me."

Bill cocked his head and frowned. "What are you saying, John?"

"You came back into my life at just the right time. You gave me something to worry about, to think about, to live for—the Angels. You and those great kids actually returned my life to me when I didn't want one anymore. God bless you."

We embraced and said good night. However, when I was perhaps twenty feet away, walking toward my car, Bill called after me. I turned.

"Maybe we all contributed a little bit, John," he called

out, "but you had better not forget to thank our smallest Angel. He's taught all of us how to deal with life, day by day."

I don't remember how long I sat in my car before I turned the key in the ignition.

XIII

❧

$\mathcal{D}$uring what seemed like an agonizingly long week leading up to the championship game on Saturday afternoon, we held two practice sessions for our Angels on Monday and Wednesday afternoons, while Sid Marx put his Yankees through their paces on Tuesday and Thursday. We concentrated on basics, especially batting, and although the kids were in great spirits, I couldn't say the same for Bill and myself. Following the final game of the regular season we had learned from Paul Taylor's mother that he would not be available for the championship game. Plans had been made and hotel rooms reserved by the Taylors almost a year ago to take Paul to Bermuda for two weeks of golf and scuba diving, and unfortunately their scheduled departure was just a day before the big game. As Paul's mother said, "Who knew, ten months ago, that our son would be needed to

help win a ball game—the championship game?" However, before Monday's practice, Paul's smiling dad came over to Bill and me with the joyful news that he had managed to postpone his vacation for a week as well as change the family's reservation dates at the exclusive Sonesta Beach Hotel. A miracle! Neither Bill nor I could believe our good luck.

The big game was scheduled to begin at two P.M. on Saturday, but when I arrived, slightly before one P.M., the stands were almost filled to capacity and people had already started to open their folding chairs in both the left- and right-field foul territory, a custom that had apparently been initiated many years ago for the annual championship tussle. In the grandstands, to add to the special flavor and ambience of baseball on a warm summer afternoon, two vendors dressed in white were already busy selling ice-cream bars and boxes of popcorn. Behind home plate George McCord was doing his best to get the crowd into the spirit of the day by playing college marching songs over the loudspeakers, with the volume turned up a little bit louder than usual.

Bill saw me as soon as I came through the fence opening onto the field, and he immediately came jogging over. "Couple of things, John," he said as he wiped the perspiration from his forehead. "Over there, behind home plate," he said without looking in that direction, "are some reporters—from the *Concord Monitor* and the *Manchester Union Leader*."

"For a Little League game? This isn't for the state championship, for God's sake!"

"No. They said they were here to observe how a billion-dollar executive manages a bunch of kids under thirteen."

"Great! Just what I need."

"They're nice guys. Not to worry."

I glanced around the playing field. Four Angels had already arrived. Tony Zullo was playing catch with Timothy, and Paul Taylor was fielding grounders that Justin was rolling to him from his first-base position. "Bill, what else did you want to tell me?

"Well, I thought you'd like to know that Timothy's mother did come. She's sitting in the first row of seats behind the third-base dugout, with Doc Messenger. Wearing a white T-shirt and a pink hat."

"I see her. Thanks, Bill."

I walked over to the stands, removed my Angel baseball cap and extended my right hand. "Mrs. Noble . . . Doc . . . I'm glad you are both here. I know this means a lot to Timothy."

Mrs. Noble smiled and nodded. "Nothing could have kept me away today, Mr. Harding. Nothing. I hope you win."

"Thank you. Doc, it's good to see you again."

The old man nodded as he shook my hand. "It's mutual, sir. Mr. Harding, if you would, please refresh my fading memory for me. Am I correct that Timothy has yet to achieve his first hit of the season?"

"Yes, I'm sorry to say it's true."

The old man removed his battered cowboy hat

and stared at it. "This game, then, is his last opportunity."

"Yes, I'm afraid so, for this year anyway, and it won't be easy. The Yankees are throwing their ace pitcher at us, and he's very tough for anyone to hit."

"Well," he said softly, "I wish you the very best for your team, and I guess we'll just have to pray extra hard when our young man comes to the plate."

"Thank you," I said, turning back toward the field as the familiar strains of the "Notre Dame Marching Song" echoed through the ballpark.

On a folding bridge table, behind home plate's heavy wire backstop, Stewart Rand and Nancy McLaren had placed twenty-four trophies that sparkled in the bright sun, each a golden life-size baseball mounted on a square wooden base that held a small metal plaque already engraved with each player's name, team, and the words BOLAND LITTLE LEAGUE CHAMPIONSHIP GAME. There were no losers in our league.

Finally two umpires approached home plate and beckoned to Sid and me. The tall one, Jake Laughlin, would be umpiring at home, and the other blue shirt, on the bases, was Tim Spelling.

"Gentlemen," Laughlin said hoarsely, "this is the only Little League game played here, all season, where the home team is not designated by the league schedule. Mr. Marx, I'm going to flip this quarter. While it's in the air, will you kindly call heads or tails? In this toss there are no options. The winner of the toss will be consid-

ered the home team, bat last, and have the third-base dugout, understood?"

We both nodded, and while the coin was still above our heads, Sid yelled, "Tails!"

Another stroke of good luck. The familiar profile of George Washington stared up at us. My Angels would bat last. Fortunately our guys had already dropped most of their equipment and gloves in the third-base dugout as if they were unafraid to tempt fate, so they all cheered lustily when I told them they could stay and that we had last "ups" at bat. After they were all seated, except Todd, who was warming up behind our dugout, I walked slowly from one end of our bench to the other, my hands in my back pockets, leaning slightly so that I could look into the eyes of each boy. Finally I said, "Well, you made it to the big game, and each of you should be proud of the important part you played in the success of the Angels. Now, I have just one thing to say to all of you. Yes, this is the big one, but I want everyone to have fun today. That's what this is all about. Being here today is your reward for your efforts all season, but rewards aren't much good if you can't laugh and smile and enjoy them. Remember, the sun will still rise tomorrow, whether you win or lose, and your best years are still ahead of you. Sure, it would be nice to win, but this is not life or death. It's just a ball game, so stay loose, enjoy the day and remember what Timothy Noble has been telling us all season." I pointed toward the little guy. "Remind them once more, Tim."

He stood, raised his small arms above his head,

clenched those tiny fists and yelled, "Never give up, never give up, never give up!" Immediately the entire team joined in, "Never give up, never give up, never give up!"

The tall ump was waving at both dugouts and pointing toward the foul lines running from home plate. The Angels raced out onto the field and took their single-file positions down the third-base foul line, while the Yankees did the same down the first-base line, both teams close to home plate. Following an upbeat rendition of the national anthem that George McCord played over the loudspeakers, Todd walked out to the pitching mound, but this time, as previously arranged, he was joined by Yankee ace, Glenn Gerston, and together the two of them led the others in reciting the Little League Pledge. Then the home-plate umpire raised his mask high above his head, and our Angels leaped from the dugout shouting, "Never give up, never, never, never!" as they ran to their positions on the field.

The forty-fourth annual Boland Little League Championship game was about to begin.

Following Bill West's suggestion, I had asked Todd Stevenson to warm up for at least ten minutes more than he usually did to prepare for a game, and the tall blond was faster than I had ever seen him. He opened the game by striking out the first two Yankees to face him. Then he walked the third batter before the Yankees cleanup slugger smashed a double to deep left-center and the Yankees suddenly had runners on second and third, bringing up their pitcher, Gerston. Todd worked

very carefully on his opposite number until the count was three balls and two strikes before Gerston swung at a fast inside pitch and cracked a hard shot between first and second and we were suddenly behind by two runs before we nailed down the final out of the inning.

In our half of the first, although Tony Zullo walked to lead things off, Justin and Paul hit easy grounders to the infield and Todd went down swinging after hitting two balls over the left-field fence—both foul.

We managed to retire the Yankees in order in the second inning but they did the same to us after both Tank and Charles Barrio walked. Opportunity wasted. Then, as Bill and I had planned, we inserted our other three Angels into the lineup at the top of the third inning. Chris Lang went in for Tony Zullo at second, Dick Andros went to left, replacing Bob Murphy, and Timothy Noble jogged out to right, replacing Jeff Gaston.

Sid Marx also made several changes. His scorekeeper and Bill exchanged the names of each team's substitute, near home plate, after they had both notified the game's official scorekeeper, who was seated at another folding table next to Nancy and the trophies, behind the wire backstop.

The first Yankee batter in the third inning smashed one of Todd's fastballs down the third-base line, just inside the bag. I still don't know how our Paul Taylor managed to get to the ball, but he did, making a sensational diving backhand catch before falling to the ground. The crowd leaped to its feet, applauding and

cheering for at least five minutes before both umpires went to the pitching mound and raised their arms, until the appreciative fans reluctantly settled back in their seats. It had been one of the finest baseball plays I had ever seen. Todd then struck out the next batter, and the side was retired when their lanky catcher hit a towering fly to center field, which Charles Barrio handled easily. Both teams, so far, had played errorless ball despite the pressure of the championship, but the Yankees had a two-run lead as we came to bat in the bottom of the third inning.

Standing behind third, in the coach's box, I was beginning to feel a little desperate. Gerston was pitching a great game, and he showed no sign of weakening. We needed to force a break of some kind. As our lead-off batter, Chris Lang, walked toward the plate, I flashed him the bunt sign when he looked my way. He let the first pitch go, for a called strike, then dropped a near-perfect bunt down the third-base line, but it wasn't good enough. He was out—by just a half step. Justin Nurnberg was our next batter. I was tempted to flash another bunt sign but didn't. He hit a slow dribbler to the pitcher's right which Gerston fielded smoothly in time to catch Justin, again by no more than a half step. Paul Taylor glanced in my direction anxiously as he stepped into the batter's box. I flashed him no signs. Good thing. He caught Gerston's second pitch, an inside fastball, and drilled it high over the left-field fence for a home run! Now we were only down by one run. Todd

was the next batter, and he hit a drive to center, but it wasn't long enough, and the inning was over with the Yankees still leading us, two to one.

In the fourth inning Todd seemed to be throwing even harder than in the early innings. No Yankee hitter got the ball out of the infield. Three up, three down.

"Kimball, Barrio and Andros," Bill said loudly, announcing our first three scheduled batters as the Angels came into the dugout. "Let's get 'em guys! Now! Big inning!" he shouted as he walked up and down the dugout floor, tapping each Angel lightly on top of his cap.

"Never give up!" shouted Timothy, and the others immediately joined in. "Never give up, never give up!"

Tank led off by drawing a walk. If it had been anyone but Tank, I would have tried to move him along with a sacrifice bunt, but the big guy was just too slow, so I had Charles Barrio hit away. He hit a hard grounder to the shortstop, who fielded it cleanly, flipped the ball to the second-baseman, who then turned and threw to first. Double play! Dick Andros followed with a swinging strikeout, and we were still trailing by a single run going into the fifth inning.

As the first Yankee scheduled to bat, in the fifth, was selecting his bat from the rack, Sid jogged by, close to our dugout, on his way to the third-base coaching box.

"Hey, John!" he yelled.

"Yes, Sid?"

"It doesn't get much better than this, does it? Great kids! Both teams!"

I smiled and nodded.

The first Yankee batter attempted a bunt, but he popped the ball into the air, and Todd caught it easily. The next batter, a short and very muscular left-hander who played first base for Sid's team, took two called strikes before he swung at an inside pitch and smashed a hard line·drive to right field, directly at Timothy.

"Oh, no!" I heard Bill cry, but Timothy raised his glove above his head, turned his feet slightly so that his right foot was a brace for his small frame, and the sound of the ball popping into his new glove could be heard throughout the entire park, which had momentarily grown very quiet. When the crowd realized that Timothy had caught the ball, they rose to their feet, cheering. Timothy just smiled and nodded as he flipped the ball back in to Justin at first base. The next Yankee struck out, and now the Angels were coming to bat. The first three batters, according to Bill's announcement, would be Rogers, Noble and Lang.

Glenn Gerston showed no signs of tiring, and he was still throwing strikes for the Yankees. But our Ben Rogers surprised us. He managed to work the count to two balls and two strikes before he caught a waist-high fastball and hit a smash into left-center between outfielders. Although I knew the play would be close, since the centerfielder had already retrieved the ball, I waved Ben toward me as he raced around second, and held my breath as both runner and ball converged at third base. Ben made a perfect hook slide, and the sweep of the third-baseman's glove, holding the ball, just missed his right foot. "Safe!" yelled the umpire, and the stands

erupted in a crescendo of noise and whistles as Timothy
Noble walked slowly to the plate with the tying run
only sixty feet away!

The little guy paused, perhaps ten feet from the batter's box, scooped up a handful of dirt and rubbed his
hands in it. He turned and looked toward me. I flashed
the "hit away" sign. He nodded. Then he stepped into
the box very slowly, pulled up his pants, tugged on the
visor of his cap and assumed his batting stance. It was
then that both Bill West and I witnessed something we
had never seen before, even back in our own playing
days. All the Angels were now standing and leaning forward, their elbows on top of the dugout wall, staring intently out at Timothy. In silence! In complete silence,
almost as if they were all praying! Suddenly the entire
grandstand also grew very still, so still that one could
even hear a train whistle in distant Concord.

Timothy cocked his bat several times, waiting.
Gerston glanced over at Ben, standing on third base, before he went into an elaborate windup and tossed a slow
ball to Timothy that almost floated on its way to the
catcher. Timothy grinned and stepped out of the batter's
box. Ball one!

Back in the box Timothy cocked his bat, crouched
and waited. Gerston's next pitch was a fastball, right
down the middle. Timothy let it go. Strike one! The
next pitch was another fastball. Strike two! I turned and
stole a glance at Mrs. Noble and Doc. Both were staring
down at their hands as if they were unable to bring
themselves to watch the action at home plate. The next

pitch was another slow ball that Timothy ignored. He stepped out of the batter's box. Ball two. Now the count was two and two! Timothy moved slowly back into the box, tapped his bat on the plate, cocked it behind his shoulder and waited. Gerston's pitch, after another long windup, was belt-high and across the center of the plate. Timothy swung. His bat made solid contact! The ball bounced on the grass once, to Gerston's left, then it dribbled across the unseeded surface between first and second, barely eluding the first-baseman's sweeping glove as it rolled slower and slower toward the right-fielder, who was racing in to field the ball. Ben Rogers scored the tying run easily, from third, and Timothy was standing proudly with both his feet on first base! There was a look on his face that I shall never forget as he flashed a wide smile and raised his cap triumphantly above his head. He looked over at me and waved, then he turned and waved toward his mother and Doc, who were both standing and applauding along with everyone else in the park.

Now the top of our batting order was coming up, the score was tied and there were no outs! Sid Marx called time and walked slowly out to the pitcher's mound to talk with Glenn and his infield. While waiting, I walked back to our dugout from my coaching spot at third. Our next batter, Chris Lang, was waiting to move into the batter's box, but he ran back to join Nurnberg, Taylor and Stevenson as they gathered around me.

"Guys," I said, "I think this is it. Swing those bats nice and loose, just as you've been doing all year, and some-

thing tells me you'll win yourself a championship. Then you can have the rest of the summer off, okay? No lawn mowing. No weeding the family garden. No chores. How's that?"

They all grinned and nodded as the tall home-plate umpire exclaimed, "Let's play ball, gentlemen, what do you say?"

Sid patted his pitcher on the shoulder and jogged back to the dugout.

Chris Lang took his place in the batter's box as the umpire pulled on his face mask and yelled, "Play ball!"

Lang swung at the first pitch, hitting a high fly ball to left field that was caught on the run. One out. Timothy Noble, our go-ahead run, was still standing on first base.

Justin Nurnberg appeared overeager. He swung at the first two pitches even though they were well below his knees, but the third pitch was up around his chin, and he punched it into right field for a single, advancing Timothy to second base. The next batter, Paul Taylor, worked the count to a full three balls and two strikes before hitting a hard grounder to second base, but the only play was to first, so Timothy advanced to third, and Justin slid into second, bringing Todd Stevenson to the plate with two out.

Todd took hard rips at the first two pitches and missed both. Then he stepped out of the batter's box, inhaled deeply several times, stepped back in and stroked Gerston's next pitch over second base for a single, scoring Timothy with the go-ahead run and advanc-

ing Justin to third. Unfortunately Tank flied out to right to end the fifth inning, but now we were ahead for the first time, we were just three outs away from winning the league championship, and Timothy Noble had driven in the tying run plus scored the go-ahead run!

As our team took the field, I accompanied Todd out to the pitcher's mound. "How's the arm, big guy?" I asked, trying not to sound concerned.

He nodded, and wiped the perspiration from his brow. "It's okay. Okay."

I rubbed his right shoulder gently. "Does it have three more outs in there?"

He nodded again, unsmiling. "It's okay. Honest."

The first Yankee batter worked the count to three and two before hitting a high fly ball to left field. One out! Todd then walked the following batter on four pitches. The next went down swinging. We needed only one more out—but the top of the Yankee lineup was coming up. Their leadoff man stroked four line-drive foul balls down the left-field line before finally working Todd for a base on balls. Now the Yankees had the tying run on second and the winning run on first!

Bill West, sitting at my right, said quietly, "Boss, I think you ought to go out there and have a little chat with our man, right now."

I jumped to my feet, called "time" and walked slowly out to the mound. Todd, with his back to the plate, was staring down at the ground, pounding his glove incessantly against his right thigh.

"How are you feeling, buddy?" I asked.

"Fine. Fine."

"A little weary, maybe?"

"Nope. I'm okay. Honest."

"This guy coming up is pretty good with the stick. Can you get him?"

He just nodded. I patted him on the shoulder and jogged back to the dugout.

Todd stepped to the rubber, turned, took a fleeting look at the runner on second and quickly threw a belt-high fastball across the center of the plate.

"Strike one!"

Tank plucked the ball from his catcher's mitt, waved it above his head and tossed it back to Todd. With no windup, Todd immediately planted his left foot and fired the second pitch to a very surprised batter and catcher.

"Strike two!"

Bill turned to me, smiling. "See what Todd is doing, John? He's afraid you might take him out of the game, so he's working as fast as he can to get the Yankees out before you can get your duff off this bench and replace him."

Tank, now also sensing what his battery mate was up to, this time settled down into his catching position before flipping the ball back to Todd. Again Todd quickly reared back, with no windup, and fired his fastball across the heart of the plate.

"Strike three!"

We win!

Whistling and screaming, our kids dashed for the

pitcher's mound, where Todd was raised on small shoulders and proudly paraded around the bases as the Angels chanted, "We never gave up, we never gave up!" The entire crowd was now on its feet and applauding. Then, as the team approached third base, another figure was suddenly lifted on high to join Todd—Timothy! With both fists clenched, he pumped his small arms up and down while his teammates raised his small body as high as they could.

When the Angels finally arrived at home plate, they returned their two game heroes to earth while the standing crowd continued to cheer and whistle and clap their hands for what seemed like forever.

Eventually both teams lined up to receive their trophies. First the Yankees, then the Angels, as the loudspeakers delivered "The Impossible Dream." Standing at the end of the Angel line to receive the obligatory handshake of congratulations from Stewart Rand, I suddenly remembered where and when I had last heard that song: while facing the microphone on the bandstand of the Boland town common, waiting to address the huge crowd that had gathered to welcome Sally and Rick and me.

Later, as the shadows were lengthening and I was preparing to leave the field, Timothy came racing over to me, still carrying his trophy. "Mr. Harding, thank you again for everything. My bike. My glove. All your help. I really mean it."

I reached down and picked him up, burying my head in his tiny chest. Shouldn't have done it because I began

to sob. "You don't have to thank me, Timothy. I thank you. You've done so much more for me than I've done for you."

"I have?" he asked, obviously puzzled.

"Yes, you have, and I love you."

"I love you, too, Mr. Harding." He held up his trophy. "Thanks to you, I'm now a real champion."

I kissed his cheek and lowered him to the ground. "You've always been a champion, Timothy. Always."

XIV

❧

Although I was still on a high from our victory, I had no difficulty falling asleep once my head hit the pillow on Saturday night. Certainly I had no plans at all for Sunday, yet on the following morning I awoke shortly after sunrise, showered, shaved, dressed, had a light breakfast and then drove to Maplewood Cemetery, parking the car on a narrow hardtop road just a short walk to Sally and Rick's grave. Fresh grass, recently mowed, already covered their resting-place, but only a short distance away, as a stabbing reminder, was a narrow rectangle of loose gray soil on a fresh gravesite, covered with several faded floral wreaths and baskets containing withered flowers.

I slipped slowly to my knees and then sat back on the grass, hands folded in my lap, as if I were relaxing in a park and waiting for someone to open a picnic basket

and begin passing out soft drinks and sandwiches. It was still early, so I was probably the sole human visitor in the cemetery. The only sounds came from several chickadees in a nearby old maple. I closed my eyes, trying to remember prayer words that my mother had taught me long ago. As I said them, haltingly and silently, a blissful peace swept over me, reminiscent of that wonderful feeling of relaxation I would always enjoy whenever I came home late from the office, strung out from pressure until my nerves were at their breaking point, and Sally would insist that I lie on the living-room couch with my head in her lap so that she could caress my temples and forehead with her soft, gentle hands.

With my eyes still closed, I heard myself saying, "Hon, I'm sorry for not coming before now, but I know that you and Rick understand. I just couldn't bring myself to accept the truth—that both your bodies were here, in the ground. But I'm beginning to feel, now, that nearly all my self-pity has just about drained away, that I'm ready to face the world again . . . even . . . even including that job in Concord that was going to mean so much to the three of us and our future. Most of all I think I owe it to the memory of both of you to get on with my life, so will you two please pray for Dad? I'm going to need all the support I can get in the days and weeks ahead."

I rose to my feet and started to walk away before turning to say, softly, "Oh, by the way, I'm sorry there's still no headstone here. No excuse for that. I'll do something about that tomorrow, I promise."

On Monday morning I made two phone calls, which both produced appointments. After spending almost two hours with a patient saleswoman at the Concord Monument Company and finally selecting a very simple red-granite headstone, I had lunch at Millennium Unlimited, in the executive dining room with my good friend, Ralph Manson, who had been functioning in my place as Millennium's acting president. Three other company executives, including Larry Stephenson, chief financial officer, also joined us at my invitation, and everyone seemed actually pleased—shocked and pleased, I guess—to hear my announcement that I was returning to the company.

On the day after Labor Day, thanks to Ralph's tireless cooperation and long hours of meetings, I was back at the helm. Millennium was just about ready to introduce a powerful new word processor software package, called Concord 2000, that our brightest people had been working on long before I had originally joined the company, so the timing of my return was not the best for corporate good. However, everyone just kept smiling as they worked a little harder and a little later each day. Ralph, bless him, was even willing to part with Bette Anton, who had been my secretary and right arm when I joined the company, and she had functioned in that same capacity for Ralph. With Bette's help I managed to survive my first few weeks back on the job, and the long hours didn't bother me at all because now there was nothing to go home for. I probably averaged fifteen-hour days, including Saturdays, until we finally intro-

duced Concord 2000 at a software show in Las Vegas, early in November. It got rave reviews, and I made certain that those who had done so much work on the project were rewarded with promotions and raises, especially Ralph, whom I named my chief operating officer.

One night, following the same routine I had for many weeks, I arrived home shortly after nine, removed the mail from the mailbox, drove up the incline into my garage, made a cup of tea in the kitchen and then walked with teacup, mail and attaché case down the hall into the den, where I would open envelopes, review whatever I had brought home from the office that needed to be read and check my phone messages, if any. This particular night I took a long sip of tea and then tapped the Play button below the slowly blinking red light on my answering machine. The familiar voice of Doc Messenger was saying, "Mr. Harding, sir, you are indeed a difficult man to corral. I've been phoning you for about a week now, and I confess I've been hanging up when your machine comes on. That's no reflection on your message, but my own temerity in dealing with these modern contraptions. However, I have finally decided that what I have to say is important enough for me to risk making a fool of myself with this . . . recording. Sir, it is just a little past seven in the evening as I speak these words, and I beg a favor of you, if you will. Please, no matter what time you return to your home this evening, will you kindly give me a phone call? It is extremely important, or I assure you that I would not be

bothering you. My telephone number is 223-4575. I thank you."

"No matter what time you return to your home". . . ? That was enough for me. I dialed his number, and he answered on the first ring.

"Doc, this is John Harding. Just walked in the door and got your message."

"I thank you so very much for returning my call. Now, may I ask another favor of you?"

"Of course."

"I'm certain you have already had a long and grueling day, but how close are you to retiring for the night?"

"Oh, I guess I'm good for about another hour or so."

"Sir, I live just ten minutes away. May I impose on our friendship by asking if I might come visit you to share a matter that I believe you will agree is of great importance? I promise you that I will not take very much of your time."

I stared at the telephone receiver for perhaps ten seconds before replying, "Of course, Doc, come on ahead. I'll put the outside lights on for you."

The line clicked dead. He hadn't even waited to thank me.

Since the front door bell was still out of action, I kept watch out one of the living-room windows until I saw car lights coming up the driveway. Before the old boy could reach for the bell button, I opened the front door and extended my right hand, "Welcome, Doc, come on in."

"Mr. Harding, it's good to see you again."

"Please call me John, Doc."

He smiled and nodded. "I hope all is well at Millennium."

"Well, most of the time I'm not sure. The giant is so huge that keeping all its parts functioning in good health is almost an impossible task, as General Motors and IBM and many others are finally discovering. I guess that nature has been trying to tell us that for centuries. A human who is six feet tall can perform in record fashion in all sorts of endeavors. And yet a human unfortunate enough to be eight feet tall can barely dress and feed himself. Size, in the long run, has very little to do with competency or success."

Doc kept nodding as he walked at my side down the hall to the den. When he entered the room, he looked around admiringly, started to speak and then wisely remained silent. I guess he realized that I needed no more compliments on what a wonderful decorating job my Sally had done. He shook his head when I offered him a drink, and we both sat on the couch that faced out into the now dark backyard. There was no small talk, no talk at all for several minutes while Doc rolled his old hat nervously around in his hands. I thought the smartest thing for me to do was just to sit and remain quiet. I did.

Doc finally leaned forward, his elbows on his knees, frowning as he stared down into the crown of his old headgear. His voice sounded much huskier than usual when he finally began to speak without even glancing in my direction.

"John, I'm afraid I am the bearer of sad news, as if you haven't had enough already to last a lifetime or two. In any event, as you know, little Timothy Noble and his mom have been under my care as a physician ever since they moved here to Boland and Timothy's father departed for warmer climates. Timothy was first brought to me when, according to his mother, he had developed problems with maintaining his balance and occasionally complained of seeing two of everything—double vision. After examining the young man twice I decided, with his mother's approval, that a few of my colleagues at the Dartmouth-Hitchcock Medical Center should take a look at him. They put Timothy through a long series of tests."

Doc suddenly stood, facing away from me. I had a sudden urge to jump up and run out of the room. I didn't want to hear anymore!

"John, they discovered that Timothy has a brain tumor, and because of its unusual position it is inoperable. *Medulla blastoma* is one of the more exotic medical names for the damn thing. We considered chemotherapy for a while, but smarter heads than mine finally convinced us that, because of the tumor's location, we had little or no chance of inducing any sort of remission for any worthwhile length of time. So the decision was made by his mother, after several very difficult discussions with me, to allow Timothy to continue his normal day-to-day schedule like any other child his age as long as he could. That pleased Timothy very much, of course, except that the young man hung a condition on things.

He made both of us promise that we would tell no one about his problem. He said he didn't want anyone, especially his school friends, feeling sorry for him and giving him special breaks because they knew he was soon going to die. He wanted to be treated just like every other eleven-year-old."

I had heard Doc's words clearly. I had understood exactly what Doc had said. And yet . . . and yet, I found myself saying, "Doc, are you telling me that Timothy knew that his life was doomed, that he was going to die? He knew it?"

"He did. His mother, Peggy, is a special and tough little lady. As I said, the two of us had several talks before she made the decision that Timothy deserved to know. I distinctly remember the evening when, with tears running down her cheeks, she said that if God had decided that she could only have her baby for eleven or maybe twelve years, then the very least she could do was to tell the boy the truth so that he would be able to at least try to handle the gift of each new day as he wanted to handle it."

I caught myself raising my voice. I apologized. Then I said, "Doc, this whole baseball season. You saw it. That kid never stopped hustling. He never stopped trying and he was always cheering for his teammates. Remember 'Day by day, in every way' and 'Never, never, never give up'? God only knows how much he meant to the Angels. Are you telling me that little boy played and acted the way he did, with enthusiasm, hustle, drive, cheers and smiles, always encouraging the other kids, even

though he knew . . . even though he knew he was soon going to die?"

Doc stared down at the floor and slowly nodded his head.

"And it was okay for him to play?"

"I thought it would be good for him, when he asked me in the presence of his mother, since no possible additional harm could come from playing and it would help keep his mind on other things. Playing, if anything, I believed, might help lengthen his term of mobility."

"I haven't seen him for more than three months, Doc. How is he?"

"Well, these days he has to work a lot harder to keep a smile on his face, since he's now in constant pain, has a hell of a time keeping his balance and about the only way he can get around is in his wheelchair. However, there isn't very much area to cover in that little home of theirs, so he manages okay."

"What about his mother?"

"Well, she quit her job and stays close by his side. His school sent home books and stuff for a while, but she couldn't handle that, so she feeds him and keeps him clean and just tries to be a companion. She told me this morning that he's sleeping a lot of the time now, and when he isn't, he tries to read and watches a little television."

"If she's not working, Doc, how are they getting by? Is there any money?"

He shook his head, still avoiding my eyes. "There's

none. I'm helping out some. At my age I don't have anyone else to worry about or spend it on anyway."

Doc finally sat down again, now closer to me. I
reached out and placed my hand on his shoulder. "How
about a hospital? Would Timothy be better off there?"

"I don't believe so. Not yet, anyway. Be it ever so
humble, I think he's better off in his own home and his
own bed. Special hospital facilities and equipment can
do very little to relieve his condition, and Peggy has no
group hospital insurance. We've just got to keep him
comfortable as long as possible."

"Doc, what can I do?"

The old man smiled faintly and said, "I was hoping
that you would ask. The best thing you can do, John, is
pay the little guy a visit. He's still constantly talking
about his base hit and how Mr. Harding taught him the
right way to hold a bat and swing. Do you know what
he sleeps with?"

"What?"

"The baseball glove you gave him."

On the following morning I phoned Bette at the office,
telling her I'd be two or three hours late. She reminded
me that I was having lunch with a couple of editors
from the magazine *Macworld* at noon, and said she'd
hold down the fort until I got there. I drove down to
the bank and withdrew a thousand dollars in twenties,
waved to Stewart Rand in his office and got out of the
building before he could corner me in a long and mean-

ingless conversation. Then I went into Jerry's Bike and Toy Shop, next to the bank, and bought the complete boxed set of Topps Major League baseball cards for the two previous years. Jerry's wife was nice enough to gift wrap them for me.

A light rain was falling when I finally arrived at the gray mailbox with NOBLE painted on the side in uneven streaks. I turned on the muddy road, just beyond, and drove up close to the front door. Peggy Noble must have seen or heard my car approaching, because the door opened before I had a chance to knock. She was standing in the doorway, in an old green warm-up suit, touching her protruding right forefinger again and again against her pursed lips in a signal for me not to speak. Slowly she closed the door behind me and whispered, "I'm so glad you came. Timothy dozed off a little while ago while watching some cartoons on television."

I turned toward the old black-and-white television set. Not far away from it was a wheelchair, and in it was Timothy, his head tilted back, mouth partially open, sound asleep. I moved closer to the chair and knelt down so that I could get a better look at him. While I was staring at his small handsome face, his eyes suddenly opened wide. He immediately leaned forward with both arms reaching toward me.

"Mr. Harding, you came to see me! Wow! Mom, look, Mr. Harding is here!"

"Yes, I know. Isn't that nice, dear?"

I couldn't help myself. I leaned forward, wrapped my

arms around him and kissed his cheek, then his forehead. He returned my kisses with both his arms around
my neck.

"I knew you would come. I knew it! I knew it!"

I wiped at my face with the palms of my hands and
handed him the two gift-wrapped boxes, which he immediately opened. "Oh, wow! Mom, look! Baseball
cards! Hundreds of them! Neat! Here's Bobby Bonds and
here is . . . Wade Boggs! Wow! Thank you, Mr. Harding.
Thank you."

"Timothy, I would have come to see you before, but
I didn't even know you were sick. Honest. I've been
working in Concord . . . long days . . . so I never knew
until Doc Messenger told me."

"Did he tell you that I was going to die?"

I didn't know how to respond. Finally I just nodded.

He ran his tiny fingers through his blond hair and
grinned. "But I got my wish, Mr. Harding. I prayed to
God, you know. I asked God to let me play the whole
schedule of games and get a hit, and I did . . . I did,
thanks to you . . . and . . . and God."

He reached under the blanket that covered the lower
part of his body and held up his baseball glove. Then,
as suddenly as he had awakened, his energy seemed to
drain away and his eyes began to close. Within minutes
he was sound asleep. I patted his arm, turned, and went
over to his mother, who had been patiently sitting at
the kitchen table, having left Timothy and I to our
"men" talk.

"Would you like a cup of coffee, Mr. Harding? I just made a pot."

"I'd love a cup. Thanks."

Sitting next to her, in that tiny kitchen, I felt so helpless. Then I remembered, reached into my inside jacket pocket and removed the brown envelope with the money. I slid it across the table toward Mrs. Noble, reached out for her hand, grasped it and placed it on top of the envelope.

"What's this?" she asked.

I held her hand. "Just call it a little unemployment compensation, okay? Now, don't say anything, please."

I then reached back inside my jacket, removed my personal checkbook and ballpoint pen and wrote out a check to her. "And I would like you to use this, as you wish, so that you and Timothy can get whatever you need. Also," I said, removing one of my business cards from my wallet and scribbling on the back, "here is my home phone number. You need anything, you call me, promise? The office number is on the front, and I'll make arrangements so that if you phone me there, the call will get right through to me."

She just sat and stared at me, shaking her head, looking completely confused. "Why are you doing all this for us? You hardly know us, Mr. Harding."

"Mrs. Noble . . ."

"Peggy, please."

"Peggy, when that little boy of yours came into my life, early this summer, I was about ready to end it.

Without my wife and son I had absolutely no desire to go on living. My life had no value at all to me, but Timothy's courage and soaring spirit penetrated my blackest moments of despair, picked me up, brushed me off, taught me how to smile again, reminded me to count my blessings and encouraged me to deal with each day, one at a time. Timothy's struggle on the diamond reminded me of the miracles any of us can accomplish when we refuse to give up. That little boy taught me how to live again. What's my life worth? How can I put a price on Timothy's salvage work? How could I possibly repay him for the candle he lit in my life? What price?"

I buried my head in my hands.

"Mr. Harding, sir . . . ?"

Timothy had awakened. I rose, walked over to him and sat on the floor, next to the wheelchair. "Yes, Timothy?"

"Do you pray for your little boy?"

"I sure do."

"Will you pray for me, too, when I'm dead?"

"Every time I pray for Rick, I'll pray for you too."

He nodded and smiled. "And as long as I'm here, will you still come to see me?"

"I promise."

And I kept my promise, several times each week, even including Thanksgiving . . . and Christmas . . . and New Year's . . . and Valentine's Day. . . .

X V

imothy Noble died on April 7th.

He was buried in a plot not far from Sally and Rick.

As I had promised, one day I drove Peggy Noble to consult with the helpful saleslady at the monument company. Although I had told her that she was free to pick out any stone and size she wanted for Timothy, she finally selected a piece of dark-gray granite in the shape of a small obelisk, on which she had engraved:

TIMOTHY NOBLE

March 12, 1979   April 7, 1991

I never, never, never gave up!

On Memorial Day, early in the afternoon, I visited Maplewood Cemetery and lovingly placed a wicker basket of pink Simplicity roses close to the red stone mark-

ing Sally and Rick's resting-place. After several prayers I remained on my knees for I don't know how long before I finally rose and walked slowly to Timothy Noble's grave. I knelt near the side of his gray stone, close enough to touch it, and removed from a paper bag the baseball glove I had given Timothy. At my request his mother had returned it to me, a few hours ago, without any questions. Now I placed it at the front of the stone with the base of the glove spread widely so that it stood balanced on the grass with its leather fingers pointed upward as if they were reaching for heaven with a small hand still inside.

"Thank you, little guy, for being *my* angel of hope and courage. I'll always love you, and every time I take a breath, I owe you a little more."

Sometime during the warm days of summer baseball, three years hence, the township of Boland will celebrate their opening of a new public library. All the arrangements have been finalized for it to be erected on the site of the old one that was destroyed by fire. I have already taken care of all the financial details.

The library will be called the Harding-Noble Public Library—and in its carpeted foyer will hang separate oil paintings . . .

. . . paintings of two little boys.

OG MANDINO is the most widely read inspirational and self-help author in the world today. His eighteen books include *The Spellbinder's Gift* and *Secrets for Success and Happiness.* He and his wife, Bette, live in New Hampshire.